"Don't patronize me!"
Cynthia snapped

"I'm not—" J.T. started, only to be interrupted by her again.

"Oh, yes you are," she said, her fury on the rise once more. "According to everyone on this damned ranch, I can't hold a candle to the incomparable Pauline. Hell's bells," she went on, "even *I* think I'm a terrible wife and mother."

"You're not a terrible wife and mother," J.T. said. "You just have a lot to learn."

"Let me tell you something. We all can't be Paulines, and I'm sick to death of hearing about her."

The frown puckering J.T.'s forehead smoothed with dawning comprehension. "You're jealous of Pauline."

Cynthia snapped her fingers. "Bingo," she said. "Give the man a prize."

J.T. still didn't quite get it. "I love you, Cynthia. Why would you be jealous of Pauline? She's dead."

Cynthia shook her head. "Is she? Sometimes I'm not so sure."

When J.T. only stared at her, she t̶̶̶ ̶̶̶ ted for the bedroom ̶̶̶ ̶̶̶ ̶̶̶ t enough. As she ̶̶̶ ̶̶̶ caught her uppe ̶̶̶

"Let me go, J.T.," ̶̶̶ ̶̶̶ swear I'll scream ̶̶̶

Penny Richards is acknowledged as the author of this work.

Special thanks and acknowledgment to Sutton Press Inc. for its contribution to the concept for the Crystal Creek series.

ISBN 0-373-82526-9

PASSIONATE KISSES

Penny Richards

PASSIONATE KISSES

Harlequin Books

TORONTO • NEW YORK • LONDON
AMSTERDAM • PARIS • SYDNEY • HAMBURG
STOCKHOLM • ATHENS • TOKYO • MILAN
MADRID • WARSAW • BUDAPEST • AUCKLAND

Dear Reader,

Here's what the critics have had to say about some of the Crystal Creek books so far:

DEEP IN THE HEART by Barbara Kaye
"Harlequin's new special series called Crystal Creek wonderfully evokes the hot days and steamy nights of a small Texas community... impossible to put down until the last page is turned."

—*Romantic Times*

COWBOYS AND CABERNET by Margot Dalton
"... You'll never know what will happen next, and the combination of romance and suspense is a real winner..."

—*Affaire de Coeur*

THE THUNDER ROLLS by Bethany Campbell
"... Campbell, one of the instigators of this fine series, takes the reader into the minds of her characters so surely... one of the best so far... it will be hard to top...."

—*Rendezvous*

With reviews like these, the writing was on the wall! Our readers were thirsting for more Crystal Creek stories, and we're delighted our romance with Crystal Creek continues! Margot Dalton and Bethany Campbell will be contributing several more books to the series, and they'll be joined by Barbara Kaye, Penny Richards and Sandy Steen, who've already planned lots of surprises for you—including a touching and funny glimpse at J. T. McKinney's first marriage, right here in *Passionate Kisses*, as well as the scandal-packed past of the Reverend and Mrs. Blake, and some insights into the life and times of the irrepressible Hank Travis.

And you'll love Bethany Campbell's *Rhinestone Cowboy* next month, a thoroughly romantic and emotional reunion between a bad-boy country singer who rose to fame and Liz Babcock, the local music teacher, who believed in him against all the odds.

So stick around in Crystal Creek—home of sultry Texas drawls, smooth Texas charm and tall, sexy Texans!

Marsha Zinberg
Coordinator, Crystal Creek

A Note from the Author

Envisioning the small-town setting of Crystal Creek was no problem for me, since I grew up in a town of fifteen hundred, but coming in on an established series with established characters was downright scary. Fortunately, the Crystal Creek authors I met in Austin were generous and gracious with their input as well as their insight into the characters. They made this newcomer feel right at home.

At first, I was skeptical about going back into the past and writing about J.T. and his first wife, Pauline. But when I looked over the characters and time frame I'd be dealing with, I started seeing the possibilities. A lot of questions came up:

- Why was an upstanding guy like J.T. such a good friend to someone like Bubba? (Once a scoundrel, always a scoundrel?)
- Why had Lettie Mae never married? (The truth, and that's no jazz.)
- Why was almost everyone in Crystal Creek an only child? (Something in the Claro River?)
- How did the Baptist preacher come to marry an *actress?* (Check book #21 to find out more.)

Inquiring minds wanted to know. Did I dare answer these questions? And . . . (gasp!) did I dare give these people siblings?

How could I resist? Playing God is always such a heady experience!

I drew a lot on my own teenage memories to write *Passionate Kisses.* I remembered how grown-up I thought I was at eighteen (the way Pauline did) and how silly I must have really been. I recalled the highs and lows of those first tempestuous romances, the ups and downs of peer pressure and parent problems. I thought a lot about the changes in our society and found myself wishing my grandchildren could grow up in a time as relatively innocent as the fifties. Writing this story was, in many ways, a nostalgic visit to a place and a way of life that is gone forever.

I enjoyed "filling in the blanks" in the characters' backgrounds and helping mold J.T. and Pauline into the people we've all come to know and love. Telling the parallel stories of J.T. and Pauline and J.T. and Cynthia was the most fun I've had with the creative process in a long time. It is my sincere hope that you enjoy reading about it as much as I enjoyed writing it.

Happy trails!

Penny Richards

Who's Who in Crystal Creek

Have you missed the story of one of your favorite Crystal Creek characters? Here's a quick guide to help you locate it easily:

Available at your local bookseller, or see the Crystal Creek back-page ad for reorder information.

CHAPTER ONE

"MAYBE SHE HAS COLIC," J. T. McKinney said over the sound of his five-month-old daughter's ear-splitting wail. "Whenever the older kids had colic, Pauline put them on their stomachs and rubbed their backs."

Using her bare foot to give a hard shove to the rocking chair that J.T.'s first wife had used with their three children, Cynthia Page McKinney gritted her teeth and regarded her husband of sixteen months with a combination of irritation and weariness. She'd been up with Jennifer the better part of the night, trying by trial and error to calm her fretful daughter.

Nothing had worked. Not the changing of wet diapers, or the administering of the colic medicine Dr. Nate Purdy had prescribed, or the rocking and singing of lullabies in a faltering, off-key voice.

Cynthia was worn-out physically, wrung out emotionally. She was sick to death of the sound of her own voice and the rhythmic *squeak, squeak* of the ancient rocking chair. And she was heartily weary of having Pauline thrown in her face. If she heard one more time how Pauline "did it" or what a wonderful mother—not to mention loving wife, dutiful daughter and model citizen—J.T.'s first wife had been, she would scream. She was mighty close to screaming anyway.

"She doesn't have colic."

J.T. leaned over her shoulder and peered into Jennifer's anguished, red face. "It must be colic. She's damn sure hurting somewhere."

"I have a college degree, J.T.," Cynthia said, striving to maintain a calm she was far from feeling. "After being up with her most of the night, I think I'm smart enough to figure out that something's wrong. I just don't know what it is."

The not-so-subtle sarcasm lacing her voice was impossible to miss. J.T.—no dummy himself—gave her shoulder an awkward pat.

"Well, of course you are, sweetheart." He stood there uncertain for a moment, then asked, "Do you want me to rock her a while?"

"No!" Cynthia said, her voice sharp. Seeing the look of hurt that leaped into his eyes, a feeling of remorse swept through her. It wasn't his fault she was so inept as a mother. It wasn't his fault she couldn't figure out what to do about Jennifer's crying. Cynthia swallowed back the sob of weariness and frustration climbing up the back of her throat. "Just go back to bed."

J.T. looked as if he wanted to say something, but glanced out the window instead. The eastern sky was tinted with mother-of-pearl hues of pink and gold. "It's almost time to get up. How about I make us a pot of coffee, then?"

Cynthia was too tired to reply. Zombielike, she lifted Jennifer to her shoulder and began to rock harder. Jennifer gave a deep, shuddering sob and scrubbed at her eyes with chubby fists. Was she starting to wear down? *Please, God, let her go to sleep.* The thought of finally getting some rest brought a quick rush of self-pitying tears to Cynthia's eyes. She murmured to the baby in a low, loving tone, cuddled her closer and pressed a kiss to her soft forehead. Poor little thing. She must be exhausted, too.

Cynthia glanced across the room. J.T. was pulling on a clean pair of Wranglers. She watched as he donned a crisp, short-sleeved plaid shirt. It came to her with a bit of surprise that the sight of his still-firm buns and broad chest didn't move her in the least. She closed her eyes. If she hadn't been so tired, the realization might have been more than a little disturbing.

She heard the bedroom door close and felt something akin to relief. The old adage was wrong. Misery didn't love company. At least hers didn't. She didn't like J.T. seeing her this way... tired, unkempt, her nerves as frayed as the cutoff shorts she hadn't had a chance to change out of the night before. No doubt the perfect Pauline had produced perfect children who never got sick or wailed all night or...

Dear God, what was happening to her? She'd never been a jealous, spiteful person before. But the past few months, she'd gone from being a confident, self-assured woman who knew who and what she wanted from life, to a person who was groping her way through each day, trying to figure out how to cope with each new crisis. So much for the happily-ever-after she expected when she and J.T. had said their "I do's."

It had taken her more than a year, but she felt that if she hadn't earned the friendship of his family and friends, she'd at least earned their respect.

Cynthia rubbed her lips against the baby's downy head, thankful that she'd dropped off to sleep at last. In spite of everything, she loved her daughter dearly. She should put Jennifer down, but she was afraid to move. She was almost afraid to breathe.

She gave the rocker another gentle push, wondering how she and J.T. had come to this...how the entrance of Jennifer into their lives could have changed so many things between them. Initially, the knowledge that they were going to have a baby had gone a long way toward restoring J.T.'s masculinity and helping motivate him to stick to the doctor's orders after his heart attack. *That* scare had reminded them that life made no promises, that happiness could be fleeting at best. Discounting the usual adjustments necessary in a new marriage and a few minor altercations, the past eighteen months had been some of the best of her life.

Until Jennifer came along.

Knowing this would be her one and only shot at motherhood, Cynthia had wanted to participate in the experience to the fullest. She had wanted to breast-feed, but it wasn't the breeze she'd thought it would be, and Jennifer, difficult from the moment she'd drawn her first breath, had been hungry and fretful all the time. Then, Jennifer had developed colic, and Cynthia and J.T. had spent many sleepless nights walking the floor.

It had come as something of a shock to Cynthia to realize that the thing she'd longed for, the very thing she'd thought she couldn't live without, had wreaked such havoc in her life. She'd mistakenly assumed that if she was organized, the arrival of a baby would make minimal impact on her life. After all, she was used to juggling a dozen things at once at the bank while dealing with irate people and stressful, impossible situations. But it hadn't taken long to learn that babies defied organization and that organizing a life around the demands of a fussy infant was another impossibility.

They were just getting a handle on the colic when the precocious Jennifer had cut her first two teeth at four months. The discomfort meant even less sleep. And now something else was wrong.

As she had often during the past five months, Cynthia wondered if she'd made the right decision in marrying J.T. and having his child. Maybe she wasn't cut out for marriage and motherhood. Maybe her ineptitude was a genetic flaw, like her inability to produce enough milk to satisfy Jennifer's hunger.

Though he hadn't said a word, she knew she was failing J.T., too. Making love was something she and her husband seldom indulged in anymore. Initially, her looks were what had attracted him to her, but she still hadn't lost all the weight she'd gained during her pregnancy, and she doubted that her stomach would ever regain its former flatness. She hated J.T. to see her so out of shape.

She had intended to exercise daily, but that was before she'd realized how much time it took to care for a baby. She seldom found a few minutes to put on her makeup in the mornings, much less exercise, and her classic, chin-length hair had grown down to her shoulders. No matter how hard she tried, there never seemed to be enough hours in the day to accomplish everything, and her inability to be as efficient in her home as she had been at her job was making serious inroads on her self-esteem.

But instead of sharing her doubts and fears with J.T., she did her utmost to be the best darn wife she could in every other way. No matter how tired she was, she made time to do his computer work, and insisted on doing at least part of the cooking and taking care of all of the baby's needs.

Though Lettie Mae and Virginia often offered to help, Cynthia felt she had to prove herself, had to do something to redeem herself in J.T.'s eyes. As it was, she felt fat and frumpy, a failure, both as a mother and as a wife. Maybe she should have stayed in Boston, doing what she did best. Just because a person wanted something didn't mean that something was the best thing for them.

My, aren't you just chock-full of self-pity this morning? She was; she knew it, and intellectually, Cynthia realized that all the things she was going through would pass, that someday she would be rested again, someday she would enjoy making love with the husband she adored again, but . . .

So why are you letting this get you down? Why are you so miserable?

She gave a mighty sniff and a wide yawn. She wasn't. Not really. She was just tired to the bone, as Lettie Mae would say. And she *had* learned a thing or two since Jennifer's arrival—enough to know that this new bout of sleeplessness wasn't colic or teething. It was something else, something she hadn't dealt with yet, and she intended to be on Nate Purdy's doorstep as soon as the physician opened his office doors. Maybe, she thought, stifling another yawn, he could prescribe something to calm her nerves while she was there.

She wasn't sure how much time passed before she felt the touch of lips against her forehead, rousing her from a light sleep. The scent of some rugged, masculine after-shave told her that J.T. was nearby.

She lifted her lashes and saw him smiling down at her. Despite her weariness, despite her misgivings, her heart turned over at the tenderness she saw reflected in his dark eyes.

"Coffee's ready." His voice was a soft rumble.

"Good," she said, smiling at him. "I could use some."

"Want me to take her?" J.T. asked, as she attempted to get to her feet without waking the baby.

She shook her head and whispered, "I don't want to wake her if I can help it."

As carefully as if she carried an armful of nitro-glycerine, Cynthia rose and carried Jennifer to her crib, easing her down onto the pale yellow sheet. There was a tense second when she gave a fretful wail, but thankfully, she took a few hard sucks on her pacifier and went back to sleep. Cynthia heaved a sigh of relief.

J.T. slid his arm around her waist and drew her to his side. "Do you want me to stay with her?"

She shook her head. "Believe me, we'll hear her if she wakes up."

"True," J.T. said with a wry smile. "Lettie Mae is up. How about some breakfast?"

Cynthia nodded and let him lead her from the room.

"Whoee!" Lettie Mae said, when Cynthia and J.T. entered the spacious kitchen. "You look plum tuckered out."

"I am," Cynthia admitted.

"What's wrong with that child, anyway? I heard her cryin' most of the night." Lettie Mae's forehead was puckered in a frown of concern.

"I don't have a clue, Lettie Mae," Cynthia said, seating herself at the table and wrapping her hands around a steaming mug of coffee, "but I intend to find out as soon as Nate Purdy's office opens."

Lettie Mae set a stack of golden pancakes in front of J.T. and looked at Cynthia. "How about some breakfast?"

"No pancakes, thanks," Cynthia said. "They look wonderful, but I still need to lose about ten pounds. I'll just have some fruit."

"You may never lose all that weight, honey," Lettie Mae said. "Some don't." Her eyes held a faraway look, and a fond smile claimed her wide mouth. "If I recollect right, Miz Pauline never had a bit of trouble getting back to fighting weight."

Of course she didn't. Cynthia pretended that the death grip she had on her mug was around the divine Pauline's throat.

"I don't suppose she gained more than ten or twelve pounds with any of the kids." Like Lettie Mae's, J.T.'s tone was thoughtful, reminiscent.

"Well, I suppose some people just have better metabolisms than others," Cynthia said, injecting a light note into her voice, while struggling to keep a tight rein on her temper.

J.T. patted her hand. "You look great, to me, sweetheart. I like you with a little more meat on your bones."

Cynthia knew he was trying to be sweet, to tell her it didn't matter, but darn it, it did matter! Once again, she swallowed back her tears and anger and forced a false smile to her lips. "Well, *I* don't like me this way. Besides, I've got to do something if I want to wear that gorgeous new dress you bought me for Beverly and Jeff's wedding."

"Don't worry your pretty head about that, sweetheart," J.T. said in an offhand manner. "I can take it back and get a bigger size."

Cynthia's tenuous control over her temper and emotions snapped like a rubber band stretched to the limit. She saw red—literally. Without stopping to consider what she should do or say to keep the peace and make sure she was seen in a positive light—God forbid she show any emotions that might be construed as less than civilized and perfect—she shoved back from the table so quickly that her chair crashed to the floor.

At the sink, Lettie Mae whirled around, wide-eyed. J.T. leaped to his feet, obviously afraid that something was wrong with her. Something *was* wrong. *Everything* was wrong.

"Sweetheart? What's the matter?"

"What's the matter?" Cynthia shrieked. "Everything's the matter." She held out her arms. "Look at me. I'm fat."

A knowing smile curved J.T.'s mouth. "Is that what this is all about?"

"Yes!" Cynthia cried. Then, "No! Not just that." She held out her hand; it trembled like a leaf in a breeze. "Look at me. I'm a wreck—physically and emotionally." The tears started then, chasing each other down her cheeks unchecked. "I'm tired, J.T.," she said in a quaking voice. "I'm tired to my very soul."

J.T. rounded the table. "I know you are, sweetheart," he said in a soothing tone as he tried to draw her into his arms. "And you're not a wreck—or fat."

"Don't patronize me!" she snapped, pushing at him and backing away.

"I'm not—" J.T. started, only to be interrupted by her again.

"Oh, yes, you are," she said, her fury on the rise once more. She clenched her fists to her heaving breasts. "According to everyone on this damned ranch, I can't hold a candle to the incomparable Pauline. Hell's bells," she went on, using one of Grandpa Hank's favorite phrases, "even *I* think I'm a terrible wife and mother."

"You're not a terrible wife and mother," J.T. said. "You just have a lot to learn."

"I realize that! But does everyone have to rub in how great Pauline was at handling everything?" she railed. "To listen to all of you, Pauline was born knowing how to please her man, how not to make waves, how to stay up all night with sick babies and still look like a million dollars the next morning."

She held up her hands, palms out. "Oh, wait! Excuse me. I'm sure Pauline wouldn't have been so inconsiderate and uncouth as to give birth to anything less than perfectly healthy babies. Well, let me tell you something. We can't all be Paulines, and I'm sick to death of hearing about her."

The frown puckering J.T.'s forehead smoothed with dawning comprehension. "You're jealous of Pauline." It was a statement, not a question.

Cynthia snapped her fingers. There was a mocking smile on her lips and a look of disgust in her eyes. "Bingo," she said. "Give the man a prize."

If the expression on his face was any indication, J.T. still didn't get it. "I love you, Cynthia. Why would you be jealous of Pauline? She's dead."

Cynthia shook her head. "Is she? Sometimes I'm not so sure."

When J.T. only stared at her, she turned and started for the bedroom. She couldn't get out of there fast enough. As she passed J.T., he reached out and caught her upper arm in a loose grip.

"Let me go, J.T.," she said with quiet menace, "or I swear I'll scream this house down."

Without a word, he did as she said.

CYNTHIA ESCAPED to the bedroom, leaving both J.T. and the cook standing in the kitchen. The stunned surprise on his handsome face and the stark disbelief on Lettie Mae's would haunt her for a long time. She was already starting to regret her outburst. Lettie Mae was probably fearing that J.T.'s Yankee bride had lost it . . . flipped, gone over the edge. At the moment, she was just too tired to care.

Cynthia threw herself onto the bed her husband had vacated earlier, the bed she had had only a nodding acquaintance with of late. Throwing an arm over her eyes, she gave in to the scalding tears that trickled down her temples and into her hair.

In a matter of minutes, she heard J.T. start his pickup. He was probably going out to check the vineyards with Tyler. Good. She needed a little space.

Three hours later, Cynthia buckled Jennifer into her car seat and climbed behind the wheel of her new

Lexus. After a long soak in the bathtub—the first she could remember taking in ages—and a short nap, she'd awakened Jennifer and readied her for the trip to Nate Purdy's office.

How long had it been since she'd been out of the house, off the ranch? she wondered as she drove through the gates. She wasn't sure, but however long it had been was too long.

With great sympathy for her and the baby, Nate checked Jennifer over carefully and announced that she had an ear infection.

That nagging feeling of failure reared its ugly head. Surely she'd know if Jennifer was *sick*—wouldn't she? "But she didn't have any fever."

"A little fever is good—both for a warning that something's wrong and to fight infection—but I've seen many a young'un with ear and sinus infections who wouldn't have a smidgen," he told her as he scribbled a prescription on a pad. "I don't know why, but some kids just don't run fever."

"So I'm not a terrible mother for not knowing what was wrong?" Cynthia asked, needing his reassurance like the Hill Country needed rain in the summer.

"A terrible mother?" Nate said with a slow smile. "Now where'd you get that idea?"

Cynthia gave an embarrassed shrug. Fighting her feelings of inadequacy, she succumbed to the overwhelming need to confess her fears to an impartial observer. "All I've heard for five months is what a wonderful wife and mother Pauline was—from everyone who knew her. She was such a saint, I'm surprised they haven't canonized the woman."

Nate Purdy offered her an understanding smile. Rising, he handed her the prescription slip with one hand while he gripped her shoulder with the other. "I know you've had a hard row to hoe since you and J.T. got married, what with his kids and his illness and jumping right into the thick of things with a baby and all, but you're a strong woman, Cynthia. You can handle J.T. and his family and anything they throw at you."

As Cynthia soaked up his praise, she felt her eyes tearing up again.

"As for Pauline... I think it's only natural for everyone who knew her to compare the two of you in every way."

"Oh, Dr. Nate," Cynthia said on a sigh, "I don't think they're saying those things deliberately to hurt me, but it's hard on a person's self-esteem to be compared to someone day after day, especially when that person doesn't seem to have possessed even the tiniest flaw."

"Now, Cynthia, everyone has flaws. Why even I have a few, according to my wife," Dr. Purdy said, tongue-in-cheek.

The smile he hoped for materialized on Cynthia's tired face. "I'll never believe that," she said.

Nate smiled back. "Why, thank you, Cynthia," he said with false modesty. "I'll tell her you said so." His smile faded. "What you've got to remember is that just because you don't do things the way Pauline did, doesn't necessarily mean you're doing anything wrong.

"Pauline McKinney was a good woman," he went on, corroborating everyone else's opinion. "She was a wonderful wife and an excellent mother, but from what I've observed, so are you, and don't you forget it."

AFTER GIVING Cynthia what he considered adequate time to cool off, J.T. drove back to the house to have it out with her. His reaction to her outburst fluctuated between sorrow at what was happening to him and his wife and guilt for not recognizing his part in it sooner. He'd been insensitive, selfish... a jerk. She'd been rude, cruel... a bitch.

He burst into the kitchen, bellowing her name.

"She's not here," Lettie Mae said, without bothering to look up from the lettuce she was cleaning.

J.T. pushed his Stetson to the back of his head with a lean forefinger. "Where is she?"

Lettie Mae looked askance at him. "She was going to take Jennifer to the doctor, remember?"

He'd forgotten. "Well, I'm going to get cleaned up and go look for her."

"What for? Lunch'll be ready soon, and I ain't never seen an argument that couldn't be put off for a while. Besides, she's probably on her way home by now."

J.T. considered that possibility. Lettie Mae was right. No sense going off half-cocked. He nodded. "You've got a point. I'm going out to the barn and check on that filly of Lynn's. Call me when lunch is ready."

"You be back in ten minutes," Lettie Mae said. "It'll be waitin' on you."

THE THINGS Nate Purdy told her were the very things Cynthia wanted, needed to hear. Thanking him, she left the office and strapped Jennifer into her car seat. She knew she would carry Doc Purdy's words of wisdom and praise with her to the grave.

Feeling as if a giant load had been lifted from her, she glanced back at Jennifer, who was about to drift off to sleep. *What now?* she thought, glancing down the street at the people coming and going, taking care of life's necessities.

She wasn't ready to go home yet. *Admit it, Cynthia, you aren't ready to face the music after your little temper tantrum this morning.* Physically, she was feeling better. Emotionally, she was ashamed of her outburst.

She passed the Curl Up and Dye, a beauty shop whose sign depicted a woman with masses of curls tumbling over her forehead and shoulders. The gorgeous hairdo reminded Cynthia that her own hair was in dire need of help. Without stopping to fully consider what she was about to do, she pulled into the asphalt parking lot, grabbed her sleeping infant and went inside.

The beauty shop smelled of perm solution, mousse and hair spray, and was filled with the sounds of half a dozen different conversations. On a television in the waiting area, a country music channel was about to play three videos in a row by Lorrie Morgan.

Suzi Hamilton, who'd trimmed Cynthia's hair several times in the past, was surprised to see her. After cooing at Jennifer, Paula said she could take Cynthia right then, because she'd had a cancellation.

While Cynthia had her hair shampooed, Lorrie sang about a woman trying to keep her husband's interest after they'd had a baby, by "Looking for Something in Red." Paula combed out the wet tangles and Cynthia watched the video reflected in the mirror.

"Just a trim?" Paula said.

"No. I want something different."

"Have you got anything in mind?"

Cynthia pointed to the television and the short jagged locks of Lorrie Morgan's sexy, head-hugging hairdo. "Cut it like hers."

Thirty minutes later, feeling naked but curiously sexy herself, Cynthia left the beauty shop. Still with no clear idea in mind of where she was headed, she started the car.

As she drove past the Longhorn Coffee Shop, she thought about stopping for a cup of coffee and a piece of their famous chocolate pie. After all, Cynthia thought, it was ages since she'd been anywhere just for the sake of going. Besides, she could show off Jennifer.

As usual, the café was busy, but Nora Jones was nowhere to be seen. Kasey Bradley, a young, single mother who was supplementing her child support payments by working part-time at both the Longhorn and the Claro County Library, approached the booth, a menu in her hand, a friendly smile on her face.

"Hi, Mrs. McKinney. I almost didn't recognize you with your new haircut."

"Hi, Kasey. How are you and Josh getting along?"

"Pretty good. How've you been? We haven't seen much of you around here lately."

Cynthia, the proud mother now that her daughter was sleeping peacefully in her car seat, bestowed a loving glance on Jennifer. "I've been sticking pretty close to home. Jennifer and I got off to a pretty rocky start."

"Colic, huh?" Kasey said in that intuitive way of mothers.

Cynthia nodded.

"It'll go away sooner or later."

"Sooner would be better," Cynthia said, and Kasey laughed.

"Would you like to see a menu?" the waitress asked.

"No thanks," Cynthia replied, as a picture of chocolate pie and mile-high meringue danced through her mind. She'd opened her mouth to place her order when the tempting image was displaced by a vision of the dress J.T. had bought her. It was a gorgeous creation, slim and formfitting. Immediate desire was weighed against her self-esteem. Pride won. Darn it, she would wear that dress to Beverly and Jeff's wedding if she had to starve to get into it.

She sighed in regret. The Longhorn's pie was the best in Claro County, if not the whole state. Cynthia glanced up at Kasey. "Just coffee, please. Black."

"Sure thing." Kasey wrote down the order on her pad and disappeared.

For the next thirty minutes, Cynthia drank her coffee, watched the residents of Crystal Creek stroll up and down the streets and relaxed, something she'd had little time for lately. She found herself wondering if Nora, who had inherited the Longhorn when Dottie died, and Ken Slattery, J.T.'s foreman and right-hand man, had set a wedding date yet. She hadn't heard J.T. say...but then, she and J.T. hadn't had been indulging in many pillow talks lately. Come to think of it, she hadn't had a good talk with *anyone* lately. Every waking hour seemed to be filled with taking care of Jennifer.

Cynthia had decided to ask Kasey about Nora and Ken when she paid for her coffee, but by the time she was ready to go, Jennifer was awake and being her most charming self. The question slipped her mind.

"Are you going to be in town a while?" Kasey asked as she rang up Cynthia's coffee.

Cynthia hadn't given it much thought, but going back to the ranch and facing J.T. and Lettie held little appeal. "I don't know. Why?"

"Aunt Eva hasn't been feeling well," Kasey said, referring to Eva Blake, the local Baptist preacher's wife. "Something about her heart. She could use some cheering up."

Though Cynthia didn't know the Baptist preacher or his wife that well, they had visited her in the hospital when Jennifer was born and had sent both flowers and a baby gift. Kasey was right; it would be a nice gesture to stop by and say hello while Jennifer was on her best behavior. Besides, it would postpone the inevitable confrontation with J.T.

"I'd be glad to stop by," Cynthia said with a smile. "See you later."

She carried Jennifer out into the bright, early May sunshine and got into the car. It was a short trip to the Blakes' house, but when she got to the parsonage, it was Millie Daniels, the part-time housekeeper, not Eva Blake, who answered the doorbell's summons.

"I'm sorry, but Mrs. Blake isn't here," Millie said. "She went in to Austin to visit her sister."

"Oh," Cynthia said, trying to hide her disappointment. "I'm glad she's feeling better. Will you tell her that Cynthia McKinney stopped by?"

"Sure will," Millie promised.

As Cynthia started down the sidewalk, she glanced at the church. "Is Reverend Blake in his office?"

"I don't rightly know, ma'am."

Cynthia smiled. "I think I'll stop by and see while I'm here." She bade the housekeeper goodbye and followed the brick path around the First Baptist Church to the back, where Howard Blake's office was located.

Lola Driggers, Howard's secretary, gave her a warm welcome and informed her that Reverend Blake wasn't in. He was at the hospital sitting with one of the deacons, whose wife was undergoing surgery.

Well, Cynthia thought as she retraced her footsteps to the car, it wasn't a very good morning for visiting. There was nothing else to do but go home and face the music, she thought as she settled Jennifer into the plush interior of the Lexus.

She started the car and headed for the ranch, feeling more than a little sorry for herself. How the mighty had fallen! Once popular, socially active Cynthia Page McKinney so desperate for companionship that she was willing to visit people she hardly knew!

It occurred to her with something of a shock that she had no real friends in Crystal Creek. No woman friend. She'd been so caught up in adapting to her new husband and her new life that she hadn't had the time or inclination to cultivate any of those friendships that are so vital to women.

She couldn't confide in Lettie Mae or Virginia. The age difference and the employer-employee relationship created a distance between her and the cook and housekeeper. And, while she'd grown closer to J.T.'s daughter, Lynn didn't have the experience or maturity to appreciate the complexities of what she was going through. Beverly, J.T.'s niece, was too young, too self-absorbed. . . .

There wasn't a single person her age she could confide in, which was a sobering thought. The closest to a friend she had was Pauline's sister, Carolyn, who'd been one of the few people who had readily accepted her when she first started seeing J.T. For that, Cynthia would always be grateful.

TWENTY MINUTES LATER, Cynthia and Jennifer headed up the drive to the Circle T Ranch. Carolyn must have heard the car, because she met Cynthia at the back door of the stone house, a smile on her pretty face.

Forcing a smile herself, Cynthia got out of the car and was enfolded in a warm embrace. "My goodness, Cynthia, what brings you this way? I was beginning to think you were mad at us or something."

Cynthia found herself returning Carolyn's hug. "Why would I be mad at you? I just thought you and Vern might like some time alone. Aaand—" she drew out the word and cocked a thumb at the baby, who'd fallen asleep again during the drive "—I've been slightly busy with the kid here."

Carolyn peeked into the car and turned to Cynthia with misty eyes. "Oh, Cynthia, she's so beautiful...just like her mother."

A short, humorless laugh burst from Cynthia's lips. "I might have been attractive once, but not these days."

Carolyn's surprise showed. "Do I detect a hint of low self-esteem, here, hmm?"

"As Lettie Mae would say, 'Just a tad.'"

"What you need is a good cup of coffee and a friendly ear. Maybe even a shoulder to cry on."

It was Cynthia's turn to look surprised. "How did you know?"

"I remember how I was after Beverly was born. C'mon, now. You get the baby out, and I'll make the coffee."

Ten minutes later, Cynthia was sitting at the long oak table that dominated Carolyn's cheerful blue-and-white kitchen. A cup of coffee rested on a blue gingham place mat before her.

"So," she said when Carolyn had seated herself across from her, "what's happening with everyone? I feel as if I've been in hibernation. How are Beverly's wedding plans coming along?"

At mention of her daughter's wedding, Carolyn's forehead furrowed. "At the moment, the wedding's off. Of course, that doesn't mean anything. Beverly's called it off twice before and changed her mind again in less than a day."

"Cold feet?"

"Not exactly," Carolyn said. "Since Nate got her involved with those kids at the hospital, she's got this crazy notion she should go to medical school. She can't decide what she wants more—Jeff or a degree in medicine."

"Well, from what I hear, she's certainly smart enough to handle either option," Cynthia said.

"She's not cut out for medicine," Carolyn said. "She's my daughter, but believe me, she's not the stuff doctors are made of."

Cynthia had to agree. Beverly was extremely bright, but it was next to impossible to picture the former Miss Texas cutting into a cadaver.

"Well, whatever she decides, I'm sure she'll make the right decision," Cynthia replied.

"I hope so."

"I stopped by the Longhorn before I drove out, but I didn't see Nora anywhere."

"Of course you didn't. She's on her honeymoon."

"Her honeymoon?" Cynthia couldn't hide her surprise. Had she been so preoccupied that she'd missed news of Ken's wedding?

Frowning, Carolyn nodded. "Nora and Ken eloped a couple of days ago. Didn't J.T. tell you?"

"No." Cynthia concentrated on stirring some creamer she didn't want into her coffee. "Is Nora going to keep the café?" she asked, hoping to sidestep the issue of her and J.T.'s lack of communication.

"No," Carolyn said. "Vernon says she's looking for a buyer."

"Well, it should certainly make a good investment for someone."

"Yes, it should." Silence reigned at the table for a long moment. "Okay," Carolyn said at last, determination shining in her eyes, "let's have it. What's going on with you and my brother-in-law?"

That brought Cynthia's head up. "What do you mean?"

"I mean that when a man doesn't tell his wife that their foreman has gone off to get married, there's a serious communication problem."

Cynthia wanted to deny that anything was wrong, but the urge to share her misery was greater than her need to maintain what was left of her battered pride.

She picked up her coffee and took a fortifying sip. "J.T. and I don't talk much anymore."

"Oh? And why not?"

"There's a lot going on," Cynthia said with a nonchalant lift of her shoulders.

"So?"

Cynthia looked up. "Well, we're both awfully busy. He's helping Tyler and Ruth with the vineyard, and I have the baby, and—"

"Bull."

At Carolyn's blunt comment, Cynthia's facade of composure crumbled. She drew in a shaky breath. "Oh, Carolyn, I swore I wasn't going to dump on you."

Carolyn reached across the table and patted Cynthia's hand. "Dump, honey. That's what friends are for."

Cynthia stared down into the murky depths of her coffee, as if it were a crystal ball and she might find the answers to her problems there. "J.T. and I aren't getting along the way I'd like."

"Is J.T. jealous of the time you spend with the baby?"

Cynthia's eyes widened. "It's nothing like that. He's crazy about Jennifer. It's just that she's been such a fretful baby, and I'm so tired that all I want to do when I'm not taking care of her is have some time to myself."

"Ah, I recall those days well." Carolyn's smile was reminiscent. "And if I remember correctly, you're worried sick about getting your figure back, and embarrassed that you haven't, and when you do get the baby down at a decent hour and can go to bed yourself, you'd much rather sleep than make love."

The shock on Cynthia's face would have been comical if it hadn't been so heartbreaking. "How did you know?"

"I was a new mother once, too. The problems of adjusting to a baby are universal. A period of orientation is just part and parcel of the whole motherhood experience. Every woman goes through it."

"Not everyone," Cynthia said, compressing her lips into a hard line to stop their trembling.

"Oh?" Carolyn queried with a lift of her fair eyebrows. "Do you mean to tell me there's some paragon out there who hasn't gone through what I did? Tell me who she is, and I'll scratch out her eyes."

Cynthia couldn't help smiling at Carolyn's pretended indignation.

"Come on. Tell me who it is."

"Your sister," Cynthia said, meeting Carolyn's twinkling blue gaze.

The spark of humor in Carolyn's eyes changed to puzzlement. "Pauline?"

Cynthia nodded. "I don't mean to speak ill of the dead, and your sister at that, but the more I hear about what a perfect wife and mother Pauline was, the more I wonder why J.T. married me."

"Pauline?" Carolyn repeated, as if she was having trouble absorbing the whole concept.

Cynthia nodded again. "If Lettie Mae is to be believed, the perfect Pauline got her figure back in record time."

It was Carolyn's turn to nod. "Pauline always could eat J.T. under the table and never gain an ounce. I doubt she gained fifteen pounds during any of her pregnancies."

Cynthia's heart plummeted. So Pauline was everything her family claimed. But Cynthia was on a roll and intended to get all her feelings off her chest while she had a willing audience.

"According to J.T., his and Pauline's children were exemplary babies, and she knew exactly what to do and how to do it." Cynthia gave a hopeless shrug. "Everywhere I go I feel as if my performance as a wife and a mother is being measured against Pauline, and I'm coming up short."

She shot Carolyn an apologetic look. "Don't get me wrong. I'm glad J.T. and Pauline were so happy and that they had such an ideal marriage. It's just that I'm so darn sick of competing with a ghost . . . and such a perfect ghost at that."

Carolyn's smile held a wealth of understanding. "I see where you're coming from, but are you sure you're talking about my sister Pauline when you're talking about perfection?"

"Of course I am. Why?

"The Pauline I grew up with, the same Pauline who was once married to your husband, was far from flawless. She was my sister, and I loved her dearly, and she did grow up to be one of the finest women I've ever had the pleasure of knowing, but she wasn't always that way."

Cynthia listened in disbelief as Carolyn continued.

"Believe me, being a good wife and mother wasn't programmed into Pauline's genes or learned overnight. As a matter of fact, when she and J.T. got married, I'd have taken bets that my big sister was the most spoiled girl in the county."

"Pauline?" Cynthia said, her incredulity mirroring Carolyn's of a few seconds before.

"Pauline," Carolyn said with a nod. She rose. "I'm going to start us some lunch—with lots of calories."

"Oh, I can't—"

"Sure, you can. The endorphins will do you good," Carolyn said with another smile. "And while I cook and we eat, I'm going to tell you about my sister and her marriage to J.T. It didn't start out a match made in heaven, let me tell you."

"It didn't?"

Carolyn shook her head. "Nope. Over the course of the years I heard both sides." There was a reminiscent gleam in Carolyn's eyes. She flicked a glance at Cynthia. "You do know she tricked him into marrying her, don't you?"

"Pauline?" The idea was preposterous. Unbelievable.

"Well, actually, I guess it was a toss-up as to who tried to trick whom." Carolyn looked at Cynthia with raised eyebrows. "Oh, my sister was a piece of work in those days, let me tell you...."

CHAPTER TWO

May 26, 1958

Buttery moonlight poured through the open windows of Emily McKinney's pale yellow Edsel, which she'd graciously lent her son in honor of his escorting Pauline Randolph to her big postgraduation party. The problem was that Pauline was unable to show off either her date or his car, for once they'd escaped her tearful parents and family of well-wishers, they'd made it no farther than their favorite parking place, a secluded spot on the banks of the Claro River.

Though he was otherwise engaged, a part of J.T. McKinney's mind registered the sound of croaking frogs, the occasional call of a nightbird and the rustle of wind through the post oak trees that shielded the car from vehicles cruising the nearby farm-to-market highway.

J.T. was in the driver's seat and Pauline was facing him, her petite body wedged between his chest and the steering wheel. He'd unfastened the row of pearl buttons securing the back of her white sundress, and had pushed the crisp piqué down to her waist. Her small breasts were covered with a lace-trimmed, slightly padded bra and his eager, caressing hands. The feel of her breasts thrusting against his palms, the taste of her mouth and the heady aroma of her perfume— something light and flowery that wafted up from her warm skin—made him drunk with need, made him forget all about his promise to himself that he would break off with her...tonight.

Instead of pulling away from her as his common sense warned, he was drawing her closer, plundering her willing lips as if he would drain her mouth of every drop of sweetness it held. Hell, he should never have allowed things to go this far, but he didn't seem to be able to help himself. Whenever he kissed Pauline Randolph the way he was right now, he felt as if he was getting a fix for his particular addiction—his addiction to her mouth, her kisses. Lord, but he was drowning in desire, being towed under by an escalating passion that was carrying them closer and closer to a never-before-reached destination.

Trembling, Pauline ended the kiss and pressed the hand covering her breast even tighter against her. He could feel the bud of her hardening nipple beneath the fabric of her bra. Wanting her so much he hurt, he gave a soft groan.

"I love you, J.T." The declaration was a breathless whisper against his lips.

A sobering wave of reality washed over him, dousing his desire and making him gravely aware that his inability to control himself with Pauline wasn't helping his case any.

He jerked his hand away as if her flesh had suddenly grown hot to the touch. What was he doing, making out with a girl who'd made it crystal clear that what she wanted more than anything was to trade in her graduation diploma for a marriage license?

Pauline drew back against the steering wheel. The question in her eyes was reflected by the moonlight that gilded her ivory flesh and glinted off the senior class ring hanging from a gold chain around her neck. His ring. The same ring he'd vowed to have on his finger when he delivered her to her front door at midnight.

"Is something wrong?" she asked.

J.T. took her bare shoulders in his hands—Lord, but her skin was soft!—and set her away from him. He crossed his forearms over the top of the steering wheel. Resting his chin on his hands, he stared out the windshield. In direct contrast to the emotions roiling inside him, the waters of the Claro slid past, flowing like molten silver in the luminescence of the moon. "This is crazy," he said at last.

"What?"

"All this kissing and stuff."

"Why?"

His dark eyebrows snapped together and he shot her a sharp, sideways look. "You know why."

"But I thought you loved me." Pauline's voice trembled. "I thought we were going to get married."

"I never said that!" J.T.'s voice was as cutting as his gaze.

Her gasp echoed throughout the silence of the car, and J.T. felt a stab of pain in the region of his heart. He wasn't sure when he'd felt more like a heel, but what he'd said was true. He'd never led Pauline on...not with words, anyway. He sneaked another look at her. Her bottom lip quivered. Aw hell, was she going to cry?

"Look," he began, intent on soothing her bruised feelings. "It's nothing personal. You're a nice girl, and I like you. I like you a lot."

A solitary tear tracked a silvery trail down her cheek. She brushed it away with the knuckle of one finger, smearing the moisture across the crest of her delicate cheekbone. *Damn!*

"I'm just not ready to settle down," he told her. "And whether or not you realize it, you aren't, either."

Though J.T. had an easygoing personality, and a live-and-let-live attitude, he was a dutiful son, the kind who did what was expected of him. To his parents' delight, his above-average intelligence had enabled him to skip a grade. He'd graduated from Crystal Creek High at seventeen and had just finished his junior year of college.

Lately, it had occurred to him that he'd spent so much time with his nose stuck in a book—to please his parents—that life was passing him by. He knew that when he graduated the following year, his dad would expect him to take his place on the ranch, and he'd never get to have any fun.

After having had his nose to the grindstone for so long, J.T. was ready to live it up, to experience his youth before life encroached and took it away. Not only was he not ready to settle down, he was pretty sure he didn't want to settle down with Pauline Randolph, even though she was probably the most popular girl in the 1958 senior class and undoubtedly the prettiest, with her blond hair, delft-blue eyes and petite figure. Pauline was nice enough, but in J.T.'s estimation, she was a tad immature and more than a tad spoiled.

When it came to land, no one in the county owned more than the McKinneys, but when it came to money, the Randolphs won hands down. Pauline and her sister had the most and the best of everything a young girl's heart could desire. Why just tonight, Pauline had bragged that as soon as the '59 cars came out in the fall, her daddy was buying her whatever one she wanted. J.T. often wondered if anyone ever told her "no."

"I'm old enough to know what I want," she said.

"Look, Paulie, you're barely eighteen, and I just turned twenty. We're too young to get married."

He fastened his serious gaze on her while he waited for her to respond to what he considered his sound reasoning. There was no denying she looked real pretty sitting there in the moonlight, her bare shoulders glowing like alabaster, a pout on her full lips. He wanted to kiss her; he wanted to shake her. In spite of his determination to put an end to her not-so-subtle suggestions that they get married, her near-nakedness caused his heart to race. It was a crying shame he couldn't get his hormones to agree with his mind.

J.T. sighed. Pauline was okay—more than okay, he supposed—but he, John Travis McKinney, didn't want to hitch his star to hers—at least not any time soon. And if he kept on messing around with her, that was just what he ran the risk of doing.

He watched with a bit of regret as she drew up the fitted bodice of her dress and slid her arms through the narrow straps. He could almost see her gathering her dignity around her. He felt like a dog. Like the lowest form of life. Pond scum, maybe.

She reached up and clasped her fingers around the senior ring she'd had for five months...ever since his best friend Bubba Gibson's New Year's Eve party.

J.T. had made one trip too many to the punch bowl that night, and had awakened the next morning to find that his ring was missing. When he pieced together the events of the evening before, he realized that after a couple of hours of passionate kissing and heavy-duty petting, he'd given the ring to Pauline.

He'd spent the past five months alternately congratulating himself for having the most gorgeous girlfriend in the county and trying to figure out how to get out of the predicament gracefully. He'd finally come to the realization that there was just no way to call any relationship quits without someone getting hurt.

And here he was. Smack-dab in the middle of one of those real-life situations, as Bubba would say.

"I guess you want your ring back?"

"Well...yeah," J.T. said, unable to meet her tortured gaze. He cleared his throat. "I'm sorry if I hurt you, but I'm trying to be honest about how I feel."

Pauline looked as if she might burst into tears any second.

"I don't want to get serious with any girl right now," J.T. explained. "I want to go out messin' around with the guys, float down the Guadalupe, maybe do some bareback riding. I want to play this year, before my dad makes me knuckle down and start working on the ranch."

"I understand," she said, turning her head away, but he knew she didn't.

He reached out and took her chin in a light grip, raising it until she was forced to meet his gaze. "Hell, sweetheart, I just think we're playing with fire... coming out here, parking like this every time we have a date. All it'll do is get us in a heap of trouble. A guy can just take so much of that sort of stuff."

She caught her bottom lip with her teeth and sniffed. "I never meant to be a tease."

"I never thought you were," he told her gallantly. "So... this is it?"

He moved his broad shoulders in a careless shrug. "I guess so."

She nodded. "Will you take me home now, J.T.?" she asked, her voice trembling.

"Sure."

She swiveled in the seat, turning her back to him. "Will you do up my buttons, please? I can't reach them. You can unhook the chain and get your ring, too."

J.T. had no choice but to comply. Starting at the fitted waist, he began fastening the tiny buttons.

Funny. He didn't remember being so clumsy when he'd undone them. He was trying to undo the catch to the gold chain that held his ring, when she leaned back against him with a soft incoherent noise that sounded like a sob.

When he leaned forward, she tilted her head back and, reaching up, slid her hand around his neck, forcing his head down until his mouth met hers. J.T. was stunned by the action...and his reaction. He could taste the salt of her tears, and his heart ached with the knowledge that he was the cause of them. But even more devastating than his feeling of empathy was the sudden scorching passion that blazed between them.

His mouth opened over hers; her tongue made a darting foray between his parted lips. His hands slid around her narrow rib cage to capture her breasts once more. She sighed in satisfaction, moaned in need. She sipped at his lips with hers...nipped, teased, rubbed...driving him crazy. All thoughts of breaking up with her fled. They kissed and touched until she called a breathless halt and said it was time for her to be getting home.

In a daze of desire and the accompanying agony of frustration, J.T. drove her to the front door of the Rocking R ranch house and deposited her on the front steps with another lingering kiss. He was all the way to the entrance of the Double C before he realized that Pauline still had his ring.

THE NEXT DAY, the United States government intervened in his behalf. He was coming in from repairing a bad section of fence when his mother met him at the back door, her face white, her eyes red and swollen from crying.

"What's the matter, Mom?" he asked, frowning at her obvious distress.

"Your dad talked to Cale Hardisty today." Emily's teeth sank into her bottom lip so hard J.T. was afraid it would bleed. Something about her attitude filled him with a sense of doom.

"So?" he asked in a wary tone.

"You know Cale is on the draft board."

The feeling of doom began to take on a vague shape and substance. "Yeah."

"He said he knew he shouldn't say anything, but he thought your dad might want to know. Your number is coming up."

"My number?" he questioned. But he knew what she meant, even though his mind was still trying to absorb the shock.

"You're going to be drafted. The letter should be here any day."

Feeling as if he'd been poleaxed, J.T. staggered to the kitchen table, where he sat down like an old man who'd stood on his feet too long. He sucked in deep lungfuls of air and propped his elbows on the table, covering his face with his hands.

Where did the friggin' government get off drafting him when he'd finally decided to enjoy life? Dammit, how could they do this to him? He wanted to have some fun, act his age. He was tired of people telling him what to do, sick of rules. Where was his freedom? Wasn't this America?

"J.T.?"

He raised his head and looked into his mother's troubled countenance. Her eyes held a strange combination of sorrow and fear and dread, those feelings mothers have when they come face-to-face with the fact that the sons they carried in their wombs for nine months might be snatched from them by some cruel, unseen hand.

"Yeah?"

"Maybe your dad can get you out of it. He knows some pretty powerful people around here, and you are our only son."

For an instant, J.T. shared the hope reflected in his mother's eyes, but deep down, he knew he was only fooling himself. Oh, he'd go all right. He'd go because it was expected of him. McKinneys were upstanding, hardworking citizens. They didn't run from duty; they embraced it. And he was a McKinney through and through.

"There's no war going on right now, Mom," he reminded her.

Emily looked crestfallen. "I know, but there's no telling what might happen next week...next month...."

Wearing his much practiced, signature to-hell-with-it smile, which was meant to show her that everything was okay, J.T. rose and took his mother in a close embrace. "I have to go, Mom. You know that. But I'll be damned if I'll go to the Army."

"What are you going to do?"

"I'm going to drive into Austin to the nearest Air Force recruiter and tell him I want to learn to fly airplanes, that's what I'm going to do."

Emily drew away and looked up at her son with tears in her eyes. "Why the Air Force?"

He took a step back. "Now don't have a coronary or anything, but I've gone up with Bud Adams a time or two."

Bud Adams was the local crop duster. He'd taken J.T. up in his biplane on several occasions, at J.T.'s insistence. J.T. had discovered that he loved the feeling of freedom he experienced as he soared through the heavens. Looking down on the smallness of the world made his problems seem far away, insignificant. With that in mind, joining the Air Force seemed like a logical move.

"Bud Adams!" Emily cried. "He took you up in that little bitty plane of his without our permission?"

"Yeah," J.T. said with a nod and an unrepentant grin.

Emily searched his face. Attempting a smile herself, she laid her palm against his cheek. "All right, son. You join the Air Force and you be the best darned recruit they've ever seen."

"I will," he promised. And he would. But he didn't have to like it.

"YOU JOINED the Air Force? Why?" The shock on Pauline's face was comical.

It was the evening of the day he'd heard about his imminent call to duty. Less than twenty minutes after his mother had broken the news to him, J.T. was in his pickup and on his way to Austin, where the Air Force recruiter had been only too happy to sign him up.

He'd been impressed with J.T.'s academic record and, on learning that he wanted to fly, he'd scheduled a battery of tests to see if J.T. fit the criteria for that type of training. Then he'd told him he'd leave in three weeks for Lackland Air Force Base for six weeks of basic training. If things turned out as J.T. hoped, basic training would be followed by ninety days of officers' training school at Randolph Air Base in San Antonio and then a year's pilot training, also at Randolph.

Feeling as if he'd signed over control of his life, J.T. had left the recruiter and driven straight to Pauline's to break the news to her. Pauline might argue with him; she might make him feel guilty for breaking up with her; she might be able to win him over with tragic looks and tender kisses, but she couldn't evoke any of those emotions from the United States government. Though he wasn't crazy about going into the service, he had to admit that joining the Air Force gave him a perfect reason to break off with Pauline, one that even she couldn't argue with.

"I didn't have any choice," he said. "Cale Hardisty told my dad they were fixin' to draft me. It was either join the Air Force or be drafted into the Army. And if I have to go, I want to fly."

"Where will you be stationed?"

"Randolph Air Force Base in San Antonio." He grinned. "Is that name a coincidence or what?" Pauline didn't answer. "Hey, none of your relatives own it, do they?" he asked, in a feeble attempt to lighten the situation.

She didn't fall for it. "Won't you be scared being so high, going so fast?"

J.T. shook his head. "I've been up with Bud. I love the way I feel up there."

She swallowed. "When do you leave?"

No tears. No arguments. Just resignation. Good. *Great!*

"In three weeks."

"Three weeks!" Giving in to her grief, Pauline threw herself into his arms and pressed her mouth to his. J.T.'s first reaction was to slide his arms around her, which he did, but reason followed closely on the heels of temptation. He couldn't do this. With extreme reluctance, he clamped his hands on her narrow hips and set her away from him.

"Stop it, Paulie. This isn't going to change things."

Tears filled her blue eyes, trembled on her lashes and trickled down her cheeks. "I can't stand it if you go."

"You've got to stand it. I don't have any choice, and I think it's best if we break up. It's not fair for me to expect you to give up your fun this summer, or for however long I'm in the Air Force."

Pauline raised her chin and regarded him through her tears. "You can't fool me, J. T. McKinney. You're not worried about messing up my summer." Her lips puckered into a pretty pout that both irritated and enticed him. "You're just worried about not getting the most out of what's left of yours."

J.T. felt his temper flare. It was time to stop pussyfooting around. Time to make a stand. No spoiled piece of fluff was going to twine him around her little finger, just because she had a mouth that could drive a saint to sin.

"Look, I haven't made any secret about how I feel. Regardless of what I said last night, this changes things. Even if we were serious—which we aren't—" he was quick to add "—I'd want to break up with you. It isn't fair to keep you dangling. It isn't like when I was at college and could come home every couple of weeks."

Recognizing a temporary defeat, Pauline retreated. "Okay, J.T." she said with a sigh. "You win. You can have back your ring." She turned her back to him. "Unhook the chain, will you?"

For a split second, J.T. was caught in a feeling of déjà vu. "No funny stuff like last night, okay?"

Pauline glanced at him over her shoulder and shook her head. "No, J.T. No funny stuff."

THESE HAD BEEN the most miserable two days of her life, Pauline thought, jabbing her pillow with a small fist and succumbing to a fresh bout of tears and self-pity. She wasn't sure she would ever live down J.T.'s rejection. She'd stayed close to home, pretending to be sick and refusing to see or take calls from any of her friends. She knew she'd have to come out and face the world soon, but what would she tell everyone? What would they think? How could the no-account, sorry sidewinder do this to her?

"What's the matter, Paulie? Did J.T. finally get tired of your tricks and dump you?"

Carolyn entered Pauline's pink and white bedroom with a smug look on her lightly freckled face.

"Who told you that?" Pauline asked, sniffing and grabbing a handful of tissues from the box near her bed.

Carolyn shrugged. "I was at the Trents' drugstore having a cherry Coke with Vernon when Peggy Gibson came in and told us she'd heard Martin Avery and Bubba talking to J.T."

Peggy Gibson! Rats! Bubba's little sister was an obnoxious little brat at best. No telling who all she'd told—or what she'd told them. "Well, Bubba ought to blister his nosy little sister's behind for eavesdropping—not to mention spreading lies," Pauline said with convincing indignation, hoping to nip the tale in the bud. "For your information, J.T. didn't break up with me," she lied. "I broke up with him."

Carolyn hooted with laughter and flopped down on the bed, smearing a smudge of dirt on the white chenille bedspread that was spattered with pale pink roses. "When pigs fly! You're crazy about J.T. Why would you break up with him?"

Pauline sat up, squared her shoulders and brushed a heavy swath of blond hair away from her flushed face. "Yes, I am crazy about him," she said, doing her best to act cool, adult and collected. "But J.T. found out he was going to be drafted, so he went and joined the Air Force. When he told me what he'd done, I let him know in no uncertain terms that it just wasn't fair for him to expect me to sit around and wait for him."

"Drafted? What's that?"

"Don't you ever listen in your civics class?" Pauline asked. "He was going to be called to serve his country, and there's no getting out of it. He'd have to go, so he decided to sign up with the Air Force."

Carolyn turned to Pauline, concern replacing the glee in her eyes. "Do you mean J.T. has to go to war?"

"We aren't involved in any wars right now, silly," Pauline said in a superior tone.

"Then why does the government want him?"

"Because they do, and that's that. What else did Peggy say?"

Carolyn thought about that for a moment. "Nothing important. Just that J.T. is taking Dottie Little to the Lions Club dance this Friday night, but I don't guess that matters since you broke up with him."

"Dottie Little!" Pauline cried. J.T. and the buxom Dottie? The thought of his comparing Dottie's generous bosom to her own modest endowments was not to be borne. How could he rob the cradle like that? Dottie was only a sophomore—well, since the school year was over, she was technically a junior, and she was supposed to be crazy about Duff Jones. Did they break up, too?

"How come you look so mad, Paulie?" Carolyn asked.

"I'm not mad," Pauline said, plastering a fake smile on her lips. "Why don't you go on outside and play, Caro? I have a bad headache, and I think I'll take a nap."

"Sure." Carolyn hopped up from the bed and half ran, half skipped from the room. At the door, she whirled, a wicked smile on her dirt-smudged face. "If I hear any more gossip about J.T. I'll let you know, okay?"

"I'm not really interested in what John Travis McKinney is doing," Pauline said, but both she and Carolyn knew she was lying.

"Whatever you say, sister dear," Carolyn quipped before disappearing through the door.

Pauline sank back against the pillows and flung her forearm over her burning eyes. Darn that little snot, anyway! How could she be so astute at her age? Though Carolyn gave every appearance of being a normal ten-year-old, she was wise beyond her years in a lot of ways—like insisting that their dad was unhappy. He seemed fine to Pauline. He kept busy, and he was always there for dinner, and he went to see all their plays and dance recitals. He was just . . . Daddy, the same daddy she'd always had. How could Carolyn imagine there was anything wrong?

How could Carolyn know about the tricks she'd played on J.T.? Well, not tricks, not really, but she did know just how to get him—and everyone else in her life—to do almost anything for her. And how did her sister know she was so crazy about J.T.? The child was a witch, Pauline decided, and that was a fact.

Pauline blew her nose. She'd lied to Carolyn about being mad. She wasn't mad; she was furious. But worse than being mad, she was sad... and depressed. She felt as if she'd been betrayed. She wanted to die! J.T. and Dottie Little, for crying out loud! She'd *kill* J.T. for embarrassing her this way. Pauline chewed on her lip in contemplation. How could she ever face her friends again? But more important, how could she get J.T. back?

SHE CALLED HIM the next morning. His mother said he wasn't at home. He'd gone to Bubba's house. Mrs. Gibson said that Bubba and J.T. had driven to Crystal Creek with Martin Avery for something or other... she wasn't sure what. Pauline hung up, wondering what she should do.

Bubba was older than J.T. by a couple of years, and they'd known each other all their lives. The fact that they were such good friends was a constant source of amazement to Pauline. She knew it had something to do with an overnight camping trip down along the river when they were about twelve. Some kid had pushed J.T. in...just for kicks. Taken off guard, he'd hit his head on a rock and been knocked unconscious. Everyone present said he'd have drowned if Bubba hadn't jumped in and towed him back to shore. They'd been best buddies ever since.

Childhood hero or not, she didn't much like Bubba, and she had an idea that the feeling was mutual. Bubba, who hadn't had a steady girlfriend in a long time, liked nothing more than to go out with his friends and have a good time. If you looked up "fun" in Webster's Bubba's name was probably listed in the definition. Pauline was sure he wielded a lot of influence with J.T. Why, it was probably all Bubba's idea for J.T. to break up with her so he could "hang out with the guys," she thought with sudden inspiration. The more she thought about it, the more convinced she became that it was all Bubba's fault, and the angrier she got.

PAULINE WAS still seething when she saw J.T.'s pickup sitting outside of Goodman's Pool Hall an hour later. She jumped out of the open Jeep she was driving, stepped onto the sidewalk and let her anger carry her through the doorway of the male-dominated establishment.

For a moment she couldn't see a thing. The sudden change from the bright sunshine to the dimly lighted, smoky interior blinded her to the room's occupants. Even though Chuck Berry blared from the jukebox, she had the sudden sensation of the room going quiet. Why else could she hear the sound of her own heart beating? Someone cut loose with a loud wolf whistle. Whirling, Pauline saw three figures standing across the room to her left. It took her only a second to realize that one of them was J.T.

He stood there, staring at her in disbelief, as handsome as the late James Dean in his starched white shirt and creased jeans, a lock of hair from his carefully combed Elvis-like pompadour falling over his forehead. Her breath caught on a surge of love. She couldn't bear to think of him going away, couldn't stand the thought of him being with Dottie Little...or anyone else, for that matter. He was hers, and someday, some way, he would realize it.

"Looks like you got yourself a visitor, John Travis."

Only when she heard Bubba's slowly drawled words did she realize that he and Martin were looking at her, too—and so were the dozen or so other guys who'd stopped by for an afternoon of fun. Bubba's blue eyes, squinting against the smoke of the cigarette dangling from his mouth, held an unholy glee.

The tender feeling of love faded in the face of reality. Furious at herself for being such a fool as to come looking for J.T., and at him and the entire United States government for putting her in the position she was in, Pauline couldn't even speak. Instead, she bent her index finger and motioned for him to come to her, turned around and marched from the room. Even as she left, she could hear the catcalls and the taunts that told her he was obeying her silent command.

She was halfway to the Jeep when his hand curled painfully around her upper arm and he jerked her around to face him. "What in the hell do you mean following me here, and crooking your little finger like you own me?"

Pauline lifted her chin to a haughty angle. "I meant for you to come, and you did, didn't you?" she taunted with a sarcastic lift of her lips.

Looking at her with so much fury she thought she couldn't stand it, J.T. released his hold on her and shoved his hands into his back pockets. "What do you want, Pauline?"

"I want to know if Bubba put you up to breaking up with me."

J.T.'s surprise couldn't have been more obvious. "Are you back on that? Of course he didn't. I don't need anyone telling me what to do with my life. Believe me, I've got enough of that already."

Her anger softened the slightest bit, but there was still the matter of Dottie to settle. Before she could take J.T. to task for taking out the younger girl, he broadsided her with a salvo of his own.

"What do you mean, telling everyone in town that you broke up with me?"

"A girl has to take care of herself and her reputation the best way she can. I'd have been the talk of Crystal Creek if everyone thought you'd done the breaking up."

"But I did break up with you."

Pauline placed her hands on her hips. "Well, since you're so interested in the truth, J.T., tell me—are you taking Dottie Little to the dance this weekend?"

"And if I am?" he challenged.

"Then you lied to me!"

J.T. put his hands on his hips in a similar gesture, and they faced off angrily. "How do you figure that?"

"You said you wanted to break up with me because you wanted to spend time with the boys...not because you wanted to date some...some...junior with big boobs."

J.T. flinched at Pauline's choice of words. His face flamed with color. "The size of Dottie's breasts has nothing to do with anything."

"No?"

"No!"

"Maybe she's the kind of girl who doesn't stop a guy the way I do. Maybe she—"

Before she could gather any more steam, J.T. grabbed her shoulders, yanked her against him and crushed her mouth beneath his. Pauline's anger dissipated like the fog over the Claro beneath the rays of the early-morning sun. Her spirits soared. Her breasts tingled and her mouth clung to his in unabashed hunger.

Then, before she realized what he was doing, he released her so quickly that she staggered and almost fell. One look at his face told her that he was as affected by the kiss as she. She took one step toward him; he backed up a step.

"No," he said, giving his head a slow shake.

Without thinking of her actions, she reached up to brush back the errant lock of dark hair that fell over his forehead and contributed to his appealing bad-boy look.

He grabbed her wrist before she could touch him and forced her back a step. There was a wistful note in her voice as she asked, "Is that it, J.T.? Are you looking for someone who'll go all the way?"

J.T.'s jaw knotted, and fresh anger sprang up in his dark eyes. "No, I'm not. But if I was, it would be no business of yours. And I'd better not hear that you've said one word about Dottie Little.''

"Oh, so now you're protecting her name.''

"She's a nice girl, Pauline. Not that it's any of your damn business, but Dottie and I are going to the dance together as friends because she and Duff just broke up, and neither of us has a date. But that's a concept your tiny little mind probably can't comprehend.''

Pauline gasped. In all the years she'd known J.T., in all the months she'd dated him, she'd never seen this hard, harsh side of him.

J.T. reached into his back pocket and pulled out a small pocket comb. With a few deft strokes, he'd restored the strand of hair to its proper place and swept the hair at the back of his head into its customary DA. He pinned her with a furious look and pointed the comb at her. "Not one word,'' he said. Then he turned and disappeared through the doorway of the pool hall, where the sound of Elvis crooning "Don't Be Cruel'' spilled out into the street.

CYNTHIA, who was peeling cucumbers for a salad, looked up at Carolyn, shock on her face. "He just left her there, in the middle of the sidewalk?''

"You betcha,'' Carolyn said with a wink. "Served her right, I say.''

"Carolyn! I'd have been mortified.''

"I like to think of it as a character building experience,'' Carolyn said dryly. "Lord knows she needed it.''

Cynthia smiled. "And was this Dottie you were talking about Dottie Jones who owned the Longhorn?"

"The same."

"Did J.T. start dating her?"

"Just as friends," Carolyn said. "You know how Dottie was. She had a heart of gold even back then. J.T. said she was easy to talk to, a good listener. I think they just liked each other's company. Dottie was nursing a broken heart over Duff's defection. He'd broken up with her to go with Billie Jo's mom, Laura Cassidy. Of course, Billie Jo was still playing with the angels back then, or maybe that was the imps," Carolyn said, an oblique reference to the recent, flagrant affair between Billy Jo and Bubba Gibson.

Even though Bubba and Mary Gibson's marriage seemed to be on the road to a solid recovery, it would be a long time before the residents of Crystal Creek forgot the indiscretion.

"Be nice, Carolyn," Cynthia said with a smile. "By all accounts, Billie Jo is a new woman."

"When pigs fly!" Carolyn said. "The little twit," she added under her breath.

"Carolyn!" Cynthia warned, but she was smiling. "I've never known you to be anything but the perfect lady. I didn't think there was a mean bone in your body."

"Hey," Carolyn said, brandishing the knife she was using to slice the chicken breasts on the chopping board in front of her, "a person ought to be able to fall off her pedestal every now and then."

WHILE CAROLYN REGALED Cynthia with tales of J.T.'s and Pauline's past, J.T got out of the shower and dressed, only to find that his wife and daughter still weren't home. Lettie Mae put lunch on the table, and J.T. ate the chicken and rice casserole and salad without really tasting it. He kept one eye glued to his watch. Where on earth could Cynthia be? he wondered. What could she be doing?

Meanwhile, back at the ranch...

FINISHED MAKING the salad, Cynthia scrubbed the cutting board. Carolyn had just told her about a time she'd taken a piece of Pauline's crewelwork and entered it in the county fair under her own name. "When I won first place, my scout leader was so proud of me. Of course Pauline was furious and Mama and Daddy gave me a lecture on honesty and a paddling—in that order. I was a mess back then," she confessed with a laugh. "Thank God, we grow up. Most of us, anyway."

"What about your family? Were you right? Was your dad unhappy?"

The tender light of reminiscence filled Carolyn's eyes. "Yeah," she said with a sigh. "I was always closer to Daddy than Pauline. I'd follow him around the ranch. It was called the Rocking R back then— Frank and I changed it to the Circle T after Mama died. Anyway, sometimes I'd catch him sitting on his horse or resting his arms on the fence, just staring out across the ranch with this *hunger* in his eyes, like he wanted to go out there and taste everything the world had to offer.''

''What happened?''

''One day, Mom, Pauline and I went in to Austin to do some shopping. When we got home, we found a note. He just packed up and left.''

''You're kidding!''

Carolyn shook her head.

''How old were you?''

''Almost twenty. Frank and I had been married about a year. I wasn't a kid, but it still hurt.''

''I'm sure it did.''

Wanting to erase the sorrow in Carolyn's eyes, Cynthia said, ''Let's get back to Pauline and J.T. Did she give up after the pool hall episode?''

''Give up? Pauline?'' Carolyn shook off her mood with a laugh. ''Honey, Pauline was like the Mounties. She *always* got her man.''

Cynthia smiled and popped a bite of cucumber into her mouth. ''Did J.T. go on to basic training then?''

Carolyn nodded. ''He left in three weeks, just like he was supposed to. There wasn't much Pauline could do about that.'' Her eyes clouded with memory. ''You'd have thought he was going into the thick of battle the way the people in Crystal Creek carried on. Everyone has always loved J.T.''

''That's understandable. He's a wonderful man,'' Cynthia said.

Carolyn pointed the knife at Cynthia. ''Just don't forget that during all this, and you'll be okay,'' she said.

"I won't."

"Anyway, the McKinneys threw a big going-away party with fireworks and bunting draped over a pavilion they had built especially for dancing, and American flags waving everywhere."

She chuckled. "Calvin McKinney must have barbecued four or five yearlings, and I'll bet Emily made a hundred pounds of potato salad and slaw. Old Hank even came in from the oil fields to give 'the boy' as he called him, a proper send-off. It was some picnic, I'll tell you."

"You still remember it?"

"Honey, I'll never forget it."

"Did Pauline go?" Cynthia asked.

Carolyn shook her head. "She wanted to, but she wouldn't give J.T. the satisfaction. Besides, staying at home by herself gave her plenty of time to map out her strategy...."

CHAPTER THREE

May 1958

COMPARED TO THE MISERY she felt after their argument outside the pool hall, the days following Pauline's breakup with J.T. were nothing. She spent days, weeks, agonizing over her confrontation with him. Had anyone seen them arguing? How many people had witnessed him kiss her so...so humiliatingly? The questions rolled around in her head like stones tumbling along a creekbed. But she didn't come up with any answers.

According to Carolyn, who'd found out from her buddy Vernon Trent, who'd overheard Martin Avery and Bubba Gibson talking, J.T. had indeed taken Dottie Little to the Lions Club Memorial Day dance.

Unable to bear the thought of everyone knowing she was sitting at home dateless, Pauline had concocted a story about going to her cousin's in Fort Worth for the weekend, instructed her mother to relate the tale to anyone who might call and shut herself up in her bedroom.

She spent the weekend writing poems and listening to Little Richard and Eddie Cochran and the Coasters, while doodling hearts pierced with cupid's arrows and roses dripping dew—or tears. And she covered pages scribbling Mr. and Mrs. John Travis McKinney, Pauline McKinney, Paulie and Johnny and other combinations of what she and J.T. might be called if they were married.

It was a miserable weekend. A lonely weekend.

By the day of J.T.'s going-away party, she'd worked her way past her hurt and arrived at full-fledged anger. Who cared what people thought? Since she could hardly use the same story for the barbecue J.T.'s parents were hosting as she had for the dance, she'd gathered her courage and simply told her mom she didn't want to go with them to the Double C.

After her parents left for the McKinney ranch, Pauline had packed her swimming things and taken the Jeep to the Crystal Creek Country Club, where she spent the afternoon drinking cola and flirting with Rose Purdy's younger brother, who was spending the summer with his sister and her husband, Nate, an intern at the local hospital.

They had a good time; Lyle Paxton was handsome, flirty and fun—just what the doctor ordered. But when he called the following day and wanted to take Pauline to the movies, her reaction was lukewarm at best. She went, and she had a nice time, but when he kissed her good-night, all she could think of was J.T. She went to bed and cried herself to sleep, a ritual that was fast becoming a habit.

The day J.T. climbed onto the big Greyhound bus that would take him to Lackland Air Force Base, she watched his send-off from behind dark sunglasses and the revolving paperback book rack in the window of the A&P, while pretending to be interested in the latest Georgette Heyer romance. When he waved goodbye, she pressed her palm to her breast, as if the gesture might stop the increasingly unbearable pain in her heart.

She had no way of knowing that, when J.T. climbed aboard the bus and waved goodbye to the cluster of family and friends who had come to see him off, his gaze roamed the crowd in a restless search. If anyone had asked him, he couldn't have said who it was he was looking for.

WHEN J.T. RETURNED home six weeks later, on August first, the United States exploded an atomic bomb in the South Pacific to demonstrate its new ICBM technology. The minute J.T. stepped off the bus, Bubba Gibson exploded another bomb.

"I hate to break it to you, buddy," Bubba said with a consoling grip on J.T.'s shoulder, "but Matt Jeffries is telling everyone that Pauline went all the way with him while he and some of the gang were in old Mexico. I thought you ought to know."

The news was staggering. J.T. felt as if he'd been kicked in the gut. He shrugged, making a conscious effort to hide his pain. "It's nothing to me."

Bubba didn't look convinced. "If you say so."

"Hey, I was the one who wanted my freedom. I broke up with Pauline. What she chooses to do with Matt or anyone else isn't any of my business."

Even as he was trying to convince his best friend, J.T. was trying to figure out why Bubba's announcement hurt so much. Maybe, he thought, it was because he had butted heads with Matt on and off the football field throughout their growing-up years, and his old rival had scored with Pauline and he hadn't. Whatever his reasons, he could hardly enjoy his reunion with his buddies for wondering what he was going to do.

During the past six weeks J.T. had undergone radical changes. The first thing the Air Force had done was give him a shower, a thorough physical and a bunch of shots. Then they'd shaved off his hair, his pride and joy. His only consolation was that Elvis had been forced to undergo the same humiliation.

The first couple of weeks had flown by on wings of misery. He was homesick. He missed his mom's cooking. He missed the ranch, his friends, the freedom he felt that was so important to him. He hated to admit it, but he missed Pauline.

Pauline believed that life should be grabbed with both hands and squeezed of every drop of excitement it held. With some time and distance between them, he could see that, being a serious, play-by-the-book kind of guy himself, her zest for living was one of the things that had drawn him to her, still drew him. The truth was, that even though he knew she was a conniver and a spoiled brat, he missed her quick smile and her ready laughter.

While he was still in Crystal Creek, it had been okay to think of her hiding out in her room at home, too embarrassed about their breakup to face the world. It was an altogether different matter to lie awake in the barracks in his bunk at night alone and lonely, and come to the realization that he was suffering through many of the same emotions she had endured.

And lying in his solitary bed with nothing but his memories to keep him company, he realized that he didn't only miss her laughter, he missed her kisses. Just thinking about the whimpers of pleasure she made whenever they kissed, recalling the tentative yet exciting way her tongue delved between his lips, and the way she swallowed her soft moans when his tongue filled the honeyed void of her mouth made for many a miserable night.

The memory of how she'd let him kiss and caress her—only above the waist—of the way her small breasts fit into his hands, the way she parted her legs the slightest bit and ground her lower body against his when they stood kissing outside her back door, was enough to make him instantly, uncomfortably aware that he was probably the only twenty-year-old guy in Crystal Creek who was still a virgin, a state of affairs he intended to remedy at his first opportunity. To heck with Pauline. He didn't need her teasing when there were plenty of girls out there who would be glad to give him what he wanted.

The weeks passed with a slowness that he was certain would drive him insane. He longed for the day he could go home, longed for something intangible, something that was missing from his life. In the Air

Force, because he had little choice, he convinced himself that something was his freedom.

Basic training had been tougher than tough—his drill instructor was a refugee from hell who seemed determined to take back as many recruits as possible, and the Air Force imposed more rules than any mortal could imagine.

His recruiter had told him that basic training was tough so the Air Force could get the civilian ways out of the recruits. Knowing that the light at the end of his particular tunnel was the opportunity to fly an airplane, J.T. had swallowed his impatience, his pride and his anger and given it his all. His parents were proud to brag that he'd finished tops in his squadron, and J.T. could honestly say that he was looking forward to learning to fly. But he was looking forward to some fun first.

He'd thought that coming home would be his chance to unwind, a chance to let himself go for a while, a chance to impress the chicks with his new uniform, but when Bubba announced the news about Pauline, J.T.'s bubble of euphoria popped like the proverbial balloon. Considering how the news affected him, he spent long agonizing hours toying with the ridiculous possibility that his feelings for Pauline went deeper than he thought....

ACUTELY AWARE that J.T. was home on leave, but blissfully unaware of the ugly rumor Matt had started about her, Pauline had made up her mind that she was going to get J.T. back while he was at home. She'd be sweet; she'd be nice; she'd be sexy. She'd seduce him if she had to, and she'd probably have to.

She knew J.T. cared for her. No one could kiss another person the way he kissed her and not be in love. Oh, she'd heard all the lectures from her mother about confusing love with passion—Lord knew she and J.T. shared plenty of that, too—but the deepest part of her heart told her he loved her. Besides, in a rare burst of sisterly affection, Carolyn had said that J.T. really did love her, which was sanction enough for Pauline.

She wanted J.T. to admit his feelings, and if she had to go all the way with him to get that commitment, she would. Recalling how hard it was to stop him, and the delicious way his kisses and caresses made her feel, she didn't think that giving in to what they both wanted would be a hardship. She loved J.T. It wasn't as if she was easy or anything. The hardest part would be convincing J.T. to take her out.

When Bubba had called to invite her to the welcome-back party he was throwing for J.T., she decided to go alone. She didn't want a date around while she was busy beguiling him into seeing her again.

In honor of the occasion, she wore a sleeveless black-and-white-polka-dot sundress with a fitted bodice and a skirt so full she wore two starched and ruffled crinolines underneath. The white of the dress was a wonderful contrast to the tan she'd been working on. She only hoped J.T. appreciated the hours she'd spent sweating beneath the sweltering July sun, her body dripping a loathsome mixture of baby oil and iodine.

She took extra pains with her makeup and hair, painting her pouty lips with a bright coral Tangee lipstick, sweeping her cheekbones with a hint of creme rouge and her eyelashes with two coats of cake mascara that she painted on with a little brush, powdering them carefully between layers to gain extra length and fullness.

She wound her long blond hair into pin curls so that her ponytail bounced with every step she took in her pointed-toe, high-heeled shoes. Having made sure the seams of her nylons were straight, she splashed generous doses of Tabu perfume to her neck, her wrists and the backs of her knees and decided she was as ready for J.T. as she'd ever be. She only hoped he was ready for her.

The party was in full swing when she arrived at the Gibson ranch late that afternoon and headed around the house toward the sounds of merrymaking. Bubba's new stereo system—the first stereo anyone in the crowd had bought—was blaring out "Whispering Bells," one of her favorite songs. Several couples were trying to do the hop to the impossibly fast tune. Pauline found herself smiling at their efforts. The aroma of mesquite wafted through the air. She made her way through the crowd, smiling at those people she knew and feeling a little uncomfortable, since she'd spent the better part of the summer at home instead of mingling with her former classmates.

Her only excursion had been a trip to Mexico with Patty Helms and Lola Massie. The weekend had been ruined for her when she realized that Patty and Lola had schemed so that their boyfriends, both guys from nearby Hillsboro, would be in Mexico at the same time. It was one thing for her friends to conspire to spend an illicit weekend with their boyfriends, but another for them to invite Matt Jeffries along for her.

It wasn't that Matt wasn't good-looking—in fact, a lot of girls thought he was better looking than J.T. Pauline wasn't one of them. Matt was as good scholastically as J.T., and like J.T. he was an excellent sportsman. The problem was that he might be as good as J.T., he might be a lot like J.T., but he wasn't J.T.

Unlike J.T., Matt wasn't one to take no for an answer. She'd spent the entire weekend fighting off his advances—literally. When she'd slapped him for grabbing her breast, he'd shocked her by pinning her against an adobe wall with his muscular body and kissing her until she could hardly breathe, his hands moving over her in rough caresses while he raped her mouth with his tongue.

"Who do you think you're fooling?" he'd asked when he came up for air. His blue eyes were filled with anger, and something else she couldn't define. He moved away from her a step and cupped her breasts in his palms. "Everyone knows you and J.T. were messing around. I'm a lot better than he is, I promise. Hell, I'm better than he is at almost everything. I've proved it a hundred times."

Pauline stared up at him with utter loathing. "You aren't good enough to lick J.T.'s shoes, Matt Jeffries," she'd said in a low, deadly voice. "Now let me go."

Instead of doing her bidding, Matt dipped his head toward hers again. In an action she would hardly recall later, Pauline had rammed her knee into his crotch with as much force as she could, and left him writhing in the hard-packed dirt, clutching the family jewels and cursing her with every breath he took. His screamed threats followed her for a block.

When she got to her room, she'd told Patty and Lola that she was ready to go home. There was such anger and determination in her eyes that they'd complied without even asking why. As the three girls had parted from their male companions a couple of hours later, Matt had leaned over into Patty's convertible and whispered, "You're gonna pay for what you did, Pauline. You're gonna pay dearly."

The threat hadn't bothered her. His pride was hurt, that's all.

Now, as she watched the fun everyone was having—the dancing and flirting, she realized with a sudden rush of sadness that this summer's self-induced exile had caused her to miss a lot of good times, just as she'd missed her friends. She'd be going to college in a month, leaving her family and all that was dear and familiar behind. Life as she'd known it the past four years would be gone forever.

The only people she would know at school were Patty and Lola, and she'd cut herself off from them for daring to interfere in her life. It was a sobering, terrifying thought to realize that she'd have no one when she went away. She made herself a promise to call and apologize to them first thing the next morning.

She was lost in her troubled thoughts when she bumped into someone and found herself looking up into Bubba's wicked blue eyes.

"'Lo, Paulie," he said, giving her a perfunctory hug. "How've you been?"

"Just great, Bubba—and you?" she asked, forcing a wide smile to her lips.

"I'm just wonderful, sweet thing." He draped his brawny arm over her shoulders. "Where've you been keeping yourself?" he asked in a concerned tone. "No one's seen much of you this summer."

Pauline didn't trust the consideration in Bubba's eyes. There was no way she'd let him know she'd cried over J.T. every night since he'd climbed onto that big Greyhound bus six weeks ago. "I've been staying pretty close to home," she said.

"Been dating anyone since you and J.T. split up?"

She shook her head, and her long ponytail brushed her bare back. "No one special."

"What about Matt Jeffries? I got the impression you two were pretty thick."

"From whom?" she asked indignantly, not liking the speculative gleam she saw in Bubba's eyes.

"From Matt. He made me think you two were an item."

"He wishes! Actually, I've dated Rose Purdy's brother more than anyone this summer, but we're not serious."

"Been getting around a lot with those out-of-town guys, haven't you?"

"What are you getting at, Bubba?" she asked sharply, sensing there was more to his questions than what appeared on the surface. "You're about a subtle as a steamroller."

"Whoa!" he said, throwing up his hands in mock distress. "Don't get huffy. I'm just mingling and making conversation. You know, the mark of a good host."

Looking into his bland features, Pauline felt her irritation wane. Bubba was just Bubba. He had a big heart, was generous to a fault and loyal to his friends, but he could be a real pig when he wanted. She let her gaze sweep the crowd again.

"If you're looking for J.T., he's over at that table with the red and white umbrella, surrounded by his harem."

Pauline's heart took a nosedive. It didn't take her a second to locate the umbrella. Bubba was right. J.T. was surrounded by a bevy of girls, all hanging on to his every word.

She couldn't help thinking that he looked marvelous in his Air Force uniform, with its shiny silver buttons and the two stripes that signified he was an airman second class. He looked bigger than she remembered, as if he'd filled out and gotten even more muscular over the past few weeks.

She wasn't crazy about his hair, but the short style just gave a tough edge to his exciting good looks. Obviously, half the girls in Crystal Creek thought so, too.

They stood behind him and sat beside him and in front of him—redheads, brunettes, even a peroxide blonde or two. A couple even sat at his feet, rapt looks on their faces as he regaled them with some tale or another, that sexy smile on his face.

She was just starting to turn away, when J.T. glanced up and caught her looking at him. Was it wishful thinking, or did a hint of a smile claim the corners of his mouth for an instant before his dark eyebrows snapped together in a frown? The action sent her own fledgling smile plummeting to an untimely death. She felt as if a giant hand was squeezing every drop of blood from her aching heart.

Wondering why she'd ever imagined it was worth it to try and make up with him when he had the power to hurt her so badly, Pauline turned away, rummaging in her clutch bag for her keys. Coming here was a mistake. A big mistake. To heck with her plan to seduce J.T. She didn't need this kind of heartache.

She'd made it to the car and was reaching for the handle when a masculine voice stopped her. "Hey, Paulie."

Lifting a hand to cover her racing heart, Pauline whirled, her petticoats crackling. He stood so close that the fullness of her skirt was crushed between them. She wasn't aware of the paleness of her cheeks or the sheen of moisture that glazed her eyes. All she was aware of was the boy-turned-man standing before her, a reckless—somehow angry—look molding his features, a beer bottle dangling from his fingertips.

The urge to give in to the tears prickling behind her eyelids was strong. Almost as strong as the need to throw herself into his arms. Pride kept her from making a fool of herself.

"J.T." His name soughed from her lips in a breathless sigh.

"Hi, sweetheart. How've you been?"

His words were slurred the slightest bit. He was drunk, she thought in dismay... or so close it didn't matter. She was surprised. Other than the night she'd first gone out with him at Bubba's New Year's Eve party, she'd never seen him drink anything more than an occasional beer.

Oh, J.T., what's the Air Force doing to you?

"I'm fine," she told him with a false, bright smile. "How about you?"

"Great."

Smiling the smile that made her heart skip a beat, he reached out and trailed a finger along the band of fabric that edged the sweetheart cut of her bodice. Pauline's breath caught at the unexpected intimacy of the gesture.

"You look good," he told her in a husky voice. "You look real good."

"Thanks." Pauline couldn't help the hope that sprang up inside her at the heat radiating from his eyes.

"Where'd you get that tan?" he asked, grazing the swell of her breast with his knuckles. "Mexico?"

Her face burned with embarrassment and anger at the memory of her trip to Mexico. She shook her head.

"Lots of hours reading out by the pool. How'd you know I went to Mexico?"

"Everybody knows you went to Mexico," he told her. "Everybody knows everything about everyone else in Crystal Creek. Haven't you figured that out yet? Hell, the whole town is talking about what happened down there."

Pauline frowned. "Who told you?"

"Bubba. Surely you didn't think you could keep it a secret?"

For an instant, Pauline was furious that everyone knew about Matt, but her anger soon gave way to resignation. J.T. was right. Like any small town whose residents lived in one another's pockets, Crystal Creek had more than its fair share of gossips. It had always been that way and always would be, so there was no need getting upset over it. After all, she hadn't done anything wrong. Still, it was embarrassing to think that everyone knew.

Her face flamed again. "I never planned on keeping it a secret," she said, "but I certainly never expected Matt to say anything about it."

"Hell, sweetheart, you know how guys talk when they get together," J.T. drawled. "Dirty jokes, smutty stories, tales of conquest. It's the old locker room mentality."

But would any guy in his right mind brag about a girl kicking him right where it counted? she wondered. Wouldn't admitting that he'd been bested by a mere girl make Matt look ridiculous? She gave a small sigh. Oh, well, if he wanted the world to know what a jerk he was, who was she to argue?

"Actually, the trip wasn't that great," she said with a wistful sigh. "I'd like to go back some time with someone I really cared about and do it all again."

J.T., who was taking another swallow of beer, almost choked. Pauline gave him a couple of hard whacks on the back. "Are you all right?"

"I'm fine," he wheezed, taking the dainty, lace-edged handkerchief she offered. But he didn't look fine. He looked pretty terrible.

"I need to sit down," he said.

"Come on." Slipping her arm around his waist, she led him around the hood of her dad's Lincoln. When she opened the door for him, J.T. almost fell into the seat.

She rounded the car again and slid behind the wheel, glancing at him with sudden concern. "You aren't going to be sick, are you? My dad will die if you're sick in his car."

"I'm not going to be sick," he said. "Just take me home so I can die in my own bed."

Pauline started the ignition. "What about the party? What about Bubba?"

J.T. let his head fall to the back of the seat. "To hell with Bubba," he said with a venom she'd never before heard him use against his friend. "Bubba needs to learn to keep his mouth shut."

PAULINE WAS FOLDING clothes for her mother the next day when the phone rang.

"It's for you, Paulie," Deborah called. "J.T."

J.T.? Like a bird looking for freedom, Pauline's heart fluttered against her rib cage. She raced to the telephone, careened around the corner of the living room and then took a deep, calming breath before walking slowly to the sofa. She perched on the edge and raised the receiver to her ear.

"Hello," she said in her most sedate voice.

"Hi. It's J.T."

"J.T.!" she said, feigning surprise. "How're you feeling?"

His laughter had a tinge of embarrassment. "I've been better. I called to thank you for bringing me home last night."

"That's all right," she hastened to assure him.

There was a moment of strained silence while each of them tried to think of something to say. She wanted to see him. Should she ask him if he wanted to come over and watch some TV or play some Monopoly?

She heard him take a deep breath and blow it out. "So, are you dating anyone in particular?" he asked with studied nonchalance.

The question caught her off guard. Surely Bubba would have told him that she'd dropped out of sight for the summer. "No. Why?"

"I...uh...thought if you aren't busy tonight we could, uh, drive over to Fredericksburg for dinner at one of those little beer gardens and then go to a movie or...something."

Shock rendered her speechless. J.T. was asking her out? It was unbelievable. A miracle. Was it possible that he'd realized how much he cared for her while he was gone? That must be it. That had to be it.

When she didn't answer immediately, he rushed on. "Nothing special. I just wanted to do something to pay you back for ruining your evening last night."

She twined the spiral phone cord around her finger. "You don't have to do that," she said, not wanting to sound too eager.

"I want to," he insisted.

Her smile broadened, and she fell back onto the floral sofa in a cloud of rapture. "I was leaving anyway."

"Stop finding excuses, Paulie. I want to take you out. As friends. Maybe for old times' sake."

"Are you sure that's a good idea? Our old times weren't always so good," she reminded him.

"Not always," he agreed. "But they weren't all bad, either, were they?"

"No," she said. "They weren't."

"What time should I pick you up?"

Pauline knew she should hold out a little longer, but her eagerness to see J.T. again urged her to follow her heart. "If we're going to Fredericksburg, we should probably leave here about six."

"I'll see you then," he told her. "Bye."

"Bye." She cradled the receiver, gave a squeal of excitement and did a cartwheel in the middle of the living room floor. J.T. had called *her*. She hadn't had to connive and scheme to spend some time with him. This was better than anything she could have come up with herself. He must still care, if he'd asked her out.

Now all she had to do was make him realize just how much he did care. And get him to admit it. He would, she vowed. This time he'd say he loved her.

"I WANT YOU Paulie," J.T. breathed against her breast, encased in the flimsiest, laciest strapless bra she owned. "I want you so much."

Just as he'd suggested that afternoon, they'd had dinner in Fredericksburg, but instead of going to the movies, J.T. had suggested the drive-in. *Cat on a Hot Tin Roof* was playing. Pauline had already seen it, but she adored Paul Newman, so she had agreed. She and J.T. had often done some pretty heavy petting under the guise of watching a movie, and her plan, like Liz Taylor's, was to make her man realize how crazy he was about her.

Almost as soon as J.T. had parked his car in the back row and hung the speaker on the partially open window, he'd turned to her and taken her in his arms, putting a lie to his reason for asking her out. He'd kissed her with a thoroughness that stole her breath and set her heart to racing.

Greedily, they'd reacquainted themselves with the taste and texture of each other's mouths while their hands had touched, caressed, explored. Had his shoulders always been so hard, so wide? Had her waist always been so small, her collarbones so fragile?

Now, panting with her own need, she clutched his head closer, gasping when he used his mouth to nuzzle aside the wet lace and take one throbbing nipple into his mouth. She felt as if he were drawing every nerve ending she possessed to the ultrasensitive crest of her breast. Dear, sweet heaven, she was so hot. Perspiration dampened her skin. Desire dampened her cotton panties.

J.T. abandoned her breast and took her mouth in a hard kiss. "Do you hear me, Pauline?" he ground out between clenched teeth. "I want you."

A soft sigh escaped her lips. He still wanted her. Lord knew she wanted him. Her breasts felt full and achy; there was a delicious tingling between her thighs, one she'd felt often before when she and J.T. had gotten into heavy petting. But she'd never let him go this far before. She'd never let him touch her bare breasts before. If she'd known how good it felt, she'd have done it long ago.

"If there's one thing I've learned, J.T.," she whispered into his ear as she reached out boldly and touched him through the denim of his starched blue jeans, "it's that you have to take what you want."

J.T. needed no other encouragement. While she worked free the brass buttons of his jeans, he reached behind her and unhooked her bra, tossing it into the back seat with the stiff petticoats she'd ridded herself of earlier. The elastic neckline of the Mexican peasant blouse she wore with the brightly hued squaw skirt had long ago been peeled down to her waist. J.T.'s shirt was unbuttoned and pulled free from his jeans.

Muttering what sounded like a curse, he dragged her so close against him that not so much as a molecule of air separated their hungry young bodies. His bare chest rubbing against her breasts was the most erotic

sensation Pauline had ever experienced...well, maybe
it was second to the sensation of his lips on her breasts.

Before she could decide, his hand slid beneath her
skirt and she gasped in shock at a delicious pleasure
that grew and grew. It was only a matter of a few seconds before he was peeling off her underwear. His
hand fumbled between their bodies, and the next thing
she knew, there was a probing...and a sudden building pressure followed by a burst of exquisite pain as he
thrust inside her aching, wanting body. She cried out,
but J.T. swallowed the sound with a kiss.

Pauline was still trying to accustom herself to the
pain and the sensation of his body melded to hers
when J.T. clutched her tightly and ground his hips into
hers in a final powerful thrust. She thought she heard
him gasp "You're mine, dammit" before he relaxed
against her.

An unbearable emptiness settled inside her. Was this
what the hubbub was all about? Feeling bewildered
and curiously dissatisfied, she lay in J.T.'s arms,
fighting the urge to cry. When did the good stuff happen? Or was it only good for men? How could all
those incredible feelings J.T.'s touches and kisses ig-
nited end in nothing but pain and a suspicion of having been denied something so close you could
almost—but not quite—get your hands on?

A few minutes later, when J.T. began to kiss her
again, she wondered if she hadn't made a really big
mistake.

"ARE YOU SAYING that J.T. wasn't a good lover?" Cynthia asked in blatant shock.

Carolyn smiled wryly. "How was it Pauline put it later, when they could finally joke about it? Something about when J.T. tumbled over the edge of ecstasy, he'd forgotten to take her with him."

"Unbelievable," Cynthia reiterated with a shake of her head. She lifted her glass to take a swallow of tea.

"Not really. You have to remember they were both virgins. Besides being as dumb as a fence post about what it took to satisfy a woman, I imagine J.T. was a bit trigger-happy."

Cynthia nearly choked on the mouthful of tea she'd taken. Wiping her streaming eyes, she thought of her husband's infinite patience, how he could spend hours just kissing and touching her, how, even when they were joined in the act of love, he could hold off his own climax until she was begging him to let go and give them both the release they craved.

When she had her coughing under control, she asked, "Are you sure you're talking about J.T.?"

"Yes, J.T. I know you're dotty about the man, and I don't doubt he's refined his performance over the past thirty-five years, but let's face it, not many of us are sex machines when we first start out."

"WHAT TIME did she start out?" J.T. asked, taking another look at his watch.

"About nine-thirty or so."

He glanced at the kitchen clock that said twelve-fifteen and glared at Lettie Mae, who was cleaning up the kitchen with patent unconcern.

"Where do you think she is?" he asked.

"I don't have any idea."

"Are you sure she was taking Jennifer to the doctor?"

Lettie Mae turned to look at him over the rims of her glasses. "That's what she said."

"To Nate Purdy?"

"Uh-huh."

"Call and see if she's been there," J.T. commanded.

"You call. She's your wife."

J.T. got up and went to the wall phone near the sink.

"No sense calling now," Lettie Mae said, turning on the dishwasher. "Doc Purdy always shuts down from twelve till one."

Giving a disgusted snort, J.T. headed for the back door.

"Now where are you goin'?" Lettie Mae called to his retreating back.

"To Nate Purdy's office."

Meanwhile, back at the ranch . . .

"NOT MANY OF US are sex machines when we start out."

Cynthia thought about what Carolyn had said and dredged up her first sexual excursion from the pits of her memory, where she'd banished it. If she remembered correctly, it had been a disaster, even with a partner who claimed some experience.

Then, remembering the misunderstanding between J.T. and Pauline about her trip to Mexico, Cynthia laughed.

"What's so funny?"

"I was thinking about Pauline's incident with Matt. You know—J.T. talking about Matt and Pauline going all the way, and Pauline thinking J.T. was talking about her letting Matt have it in the groin. Talk about not communicating!"

"Can't you just picture it?" Carolyn said with a girlish giggle. "Crystal Creek's version of 'Who's on First.'"

Cynthia laughed again. "So J.T. only asked her out to see if he could beat Matt's time, and Pauline had this scheme to seduce J.T., hoping he'd say he loved her and make a commitment."

"Crazy, huh? Oh, J.T. swore later that he didn't have revenge on his mind at all. He said that he never could resist Pauline, and when it was there for the taking, so to speak, he was darn sure going to take it. I don't think she really tricked him. I think it was about tit for tat."

The look on Carolyn's face grew thoughtful. "The only problem was that J.T. was so inexperienced, he couldn't tell Pauline was a virgin."

CHAPTER FOUR

September 1958

"ARE YOU FEELING okay, honey?"

Pauline, who was home from Texas A&M for the weekend, looked up from the scrambled eggs she was pushing around her plate with a slight grimace. "I'm fine, Mama. Just tired."

"Well if you and Patty hadn't stayed out till all hours, you wouldn't be so tired," Deborah said in her most sensible "mother" tone. "I'll bet you girls stay up all night at the dorm, too, don't you?"

Pauline sighed, a sound that didn't escape her mother's ears. "Sometimes, if we have a lot of studying to do," she confessed.

"You aren't still pining over J.T., are you?" Deborah asked with a frown.

Pauline stared down at the eggs on her plate and swallowed hard. "No, Mama."

"Well, thank goodness. J.T.'s a good boy, but it looks like you'd see by now that he just isn't worth all your fretting."

"You're right, Mama."

Deborah picked up her purse from the kitchen counter. "I have to run into the store for some things.

Your daddy wants Lettie Mae to fix a pot roast for lunch tomorrow, and Mr. Parnell at the A&P has them on sale. How does that sound?''

Pauline shrugged and pushed aside her plate.

Deborah walked to the table and placed her hand on Pauline's forehead. "You don't seem to have any fever. Are you sure you feel okay?"

"I'm fine," Pauline said, forcing a smile to her lips. "You go on. I'll clean up the kitchen while you're gone."

Wearing a wry smile, Deborah felt Pauline's forehead again. "Now I'm sure you're sick." She dropped a kiss to Pauline's shining head. "The kitchen is Lettie Mae's domain, but I appreciate your offer."

"How's Lettie Mae fitting in?" Pauline asked.

Lettie Mae's mother, Viola, had cooked for the Randolphs for as long as Pauline could remember, and throughout the years, on Saturdays and holidays, the cook had brought her daughter along to play outside the kitchen door when there was no one to watch her at home.

Pauline and Lettie Mae were the same age, and they had spent many hours playing together and exploring the wonderful world of the ranch. They'd grown close, the way children do who spend a lot of time together. Like Pauline, Lettie Mae had graduated this past spring, but she'd received her diploma from the all-colored school on the other side of Crystal Creek.

Recently, Viola had been forced to take an extended leave from the Randolphs' employ when she'd undergone back surgery. In a bid to hold on to her job, she'd convinced Deborah that her daughter could carry on in her place, and Lettie Mae had come to work for the Randolphs about the time Pauline left for college.

"She's a marvel," Deborah said with a shake of her head. "Cooks just like Viola. Even your daddy doesn't complain—and that's something."

"I'm glad she's working out. Where is she, anyway?"

"She took a carafe of coffee to Steven's office in the barn. His coffeepot went out on him, and you know what a mood he's been in lately." Then, remembering that Pauline had been away for almost six weeks, Deborah shook her head. "No, I guess you don't."

She smiled again, a halfhearted attempt. "I've got to get out of here. I have a million things to do this afternoon."

"See you later, Mama," Pauline said, smiling as Deborah left through the back door. As soon she was gone, Pauline's smile faded. Her mom was a nervous wreck.

Though it had taken her being absent for six weeks to see it, Pauline knew that Carolyn's statement back in the spring had been correct. Her dad wasn't happy. Neither was her mother. She didn't think they were fighting or anything, but there was a problem here, something festering and painful, like an aching, throbbing tooth.

"What you mopin' around here for, girl?"

Recognizing the voice, Pauline leaped to her feet. Lettie Mae stood in the doorway, one hand propped on her trim hip, and a wide smile on her pretty face, looking very nice—very professional—in the black uniform and white apron she wore.

When Deborah and Steven first married, Pauline's grandmother had told Deborah that making the servants wear uniforms would help them to remember their place, make them understand that though they might be valued employees, they were separate from the family.

"Lettie Mae!" Pauline squealed, leaping up from her chair and rounding the table, a gleam of pleasure in her eyes. The two young women embraced and held each other at arm's length, wide grins on their faces.

"You look wonderful!" Pauline said, admiring Lettie Mae's slender figure.

"I wish I could say the same about you," Lettie Mae said with her legendary bluntness. "What's ailin' you, girl?"

Pauline's smile faded. "I'm just tired. College is a lot harder than high school."

"Hmm." Lettie Mae's sharp, dark eyes searched her friend's face, as if she hoped to discover the truth of Pauline's claim there. "Are you still seein' that Mc-Kinney boy?"

"Sort of," Pauline hedged. "He was home on leave for a couple of weeks in August before he went to San Antonio for his officers' training school. We've talked on the phone. I've written."

But he never writes back, and when I talk to him, he sounds distant . . . almost like a stranger.

"Hmm," Lettie Mae said again.

Hoping to divert Lettie's attention from herself, Pauline asked, "What about you? Are you and Clark still going steady?"

"Uh-huh," Lettie Mae said with a slow smile and a nod. "Actually, we're engaged, but I don't have a ring."

Clark Larson, who was four years older than Lettie Mae, played piano for a local jazz group. He and Lettie Mae had grown up next door to each other, and to everyone's surprise, their friendship had grown into love.

"Is he still playing with that band?"

Lettie Mae shook her head. "They broke up right after graduation. A couple of the guys said they couldn't make a livin' playin' at second-rate clubs, so Clark went down to New Orleans. He's playin at some club on Bourbon Street and savin' his money so we can get married at Christmas."

Pauline looked stricken. "You aren't moving away, are you? What will Mama do for a cook?"

"I figure Mama will be able to come back to work in another month or so. Besides, I'd travel to the ends of the earth to be with Clark."

"You're crazy about him, aren't you?" Pauline noted in a wistful tone.

"He's been a part of my life for as long as I can remember," Lettie Mae said in a soft voice. "I can't imagine life without him."

"Well, from the sound of things, you don't have to worry about that," Pauline said. "When's the wedding?"

"I'm not sure. Just some time around Christmas." Lettie Mae gave Pauline another of those scrutinizing looks. "More to the point, I think, is when is yours?"

Pauline couldn't hide her surprise. "Mine?"

"Yes, yours. I do suppose Mr. Hotshot-Airman-Second-Class J. T. McKinney plans to marry you since you're carryin' his baby."

Pauline actually staggered back a step. Her face drained of what little color it possessed, making the dark circles beneath her eyes more pronounced. "Baby?"

"Well, it's true, isn't it?" The look in Lettie Mae's eyes said without words that there was no sense in Pauline denying the obvious.

"How did you know?" The question was an anguished whisper.

"Honey, I been seein' my mama and my older sisters breedin' since I was a child. A woman's got a certain look about her when she's pregnant, that's all. Does your family know?"

Pauline shook her head.

"What does J.T. say?"

"He doesn't know, either."

Lettie Mae literally threw up her hands. "My grief! Don't you think you oughta tell him? And your parents, too? It ain't like you can keep it a secret, you know. How far along are you, anyway?"

Pauline shrugged. "It had to have happened while J.T. was home the first part of August." Pink stained her cheeks. "The first time was the night of his welcome-home party, and—'' her color deepened even more ''—he didn't leave until two weeks later.''

"Hmm. You could be almost two months gone, then.''

Tears filled Pauline's eyes. "What am I going to do?''

"First thing you're going to do is tell your mama. The sooner the better. And then you're going to tell J.T.''

Pauline knew Lettie was right, but recalling J.T.'s coolness on the telephone, she couldn't help wondering what would happen when she broke the news to him. Or her parents.

IT WAS A NIGHTMARE. Pauline's father raved and ranted and cursed. In one breath he threatened to kill the cocky little SOB, the next he threatened dire things to certain vital portions of J.T.'s anatomy. He threatened to call Calvin McKinney and force him to make J.T. "do the right thing."

Pauline cried and trembled in fear and foreboding.

Deborah almost fainted at the news; she, too, cried copious tears. She asked Pauline how she could shame them that way, asked how she expected any of them to hold up their heads in the community for the rest of their lives, told her that what she had done was very wrong and that only bad girls "slept around."

Tearfully, Pauline told them she loved J.T., that she didn't sleep around. He was the first, the only and the last. Even though her conscience had pricked her every time they made out, she lied and told her mother that it hadn't seemed wrong. And even though the times she and J.T. had made love hadn't been anything to jump up and shout about, she would have died rather than admit it to anyone.

Hearing her daughter's defense of her actions, Deborah had succumbed to a fresh bout of tears. In a mood somewhere between anguish and anger, she said that if Pauline felt that way, that obviously what had happened was all her fault. She was a bad mother if she hadn't instilled any more moral conscience than that—a complete failure, in fact.

Pauline had shrunk back into her corner of the sofa, a bundle of nerves and shame and degradation. Dear God, she wondered, how could any reaction J.T. might have be worse than this?

J.T.'S MAIL two days later was the usual: a postcard from Bubba, who was in New Orleans with Martin...having a ball in the French Quarter, a letter from his mother and one from Pauline. The letter from his mother could wait; it would be the same old who-was-doing-what stuff. The letter from Pauline was a different matter.

Even the sight of the pink stationery filled him with conflicting emotions. As usual, the faint scent of her perfume rose from the paper, stirring up fragments of memory that made his heart pound with a heady recollection of how she felt, all malleable and quiescent beneath him, of how she tasted and how he'd lost himself in the softness of her body. That memory invariably brought along its companion: guilt.

He'd gone home in August with the idea that he'd lose his virginity, and by darn, he had. Having sex with Pauline had made him feel like a million bucks...like a man.

Still, he knew he shouldn't have done it. He should have been more in control. Oh, he knew she thought she loved him, and he was positive he wanted her, but the two weren't the same. The problem was, he was addicted to her kisses, to the taste of her mouth, but even as he led her to believe things between them were okay that first night, he'd known he was going to hurt her.

He'd tried hard to forget her and the night they'd shared. He'd reasoned that it would probably take another girl to oust Pauline from his thoughts. It hadn't taken long to discover that he could have almost any female he wanted. The problem was, that even when one of those other girls was kissing him, he'd still found himself wishing she were Pauline. He'd soon find himself back at her house, in her arms, taking what she so willingly gave and hating himself for his weakness....

When he left for San Antonio, J.T. had consoled himself with the old "out of sight, out of mind" platitude, but then the phone calls and letters had started...and the old feelings had returned.

He stared down at the letter that had just arrived. He started to put it aside, but then, unable to help himself, J.T. tore open the envelope, drew out the small rectangle of folded paper, and read:

Dear J.T.,

I hope this letter finds you well. I wanted to call, but the last time I tried, you weren't in. I guess you didn't get my message, because I never heard from you. I couldn't take that chance now, because I have something very important to tell you. I'm pregnant. I've started feeling pretty sick, and so I had to tell my parents. To say they weren't happy with either of us is an understatement.

I know you were trying to warn me last spring that this might happen, but I never believed it could happen to me. I guess I never thought beyond the fact that I love you and that I want to be with you.

I don't know what to do. I'm afraid the whole world will find out and people will talk about me behind my back. I need you, J.T. Please call as soon as you can and tell me what we're going to do.

I love you,
Pauline

For a moment, J.T. was so stunned he couldn't think. He wasn't sure he was even breathing.

"Pregnant," he said aloud. The word stuck in his throat like a tough piece of meat. How could she be pregnant? Oh, he knew how, but . . .

If you want to dance, you have to pay the fiddler, son, and don't you ever forget it.

How many times had he heard Grandpa Hank spout the old adage? A hundred? A thousand? Well, he'd found out the hard way that it was true.

J.T.'s head whirled in confusion. The tightness of tears he hadn't shed since he was a kid rose in his throat. He felt sick. He wanted to puke. To bury his face in his hands and cry like a baby. He wanted to scream at the unfairness of it all. He wanted to run out of the barracks and through the gates of Randolph Air Force Base so fast and so far that no one could find him—not the Air Force, not Pauline...not even himself.

He drew a deep breath and blew it out, hoping the action would calm the erratic beating of his heart and clear his mind. He had to think, had to weigh his options and see what could be done to salvage the mess his desire for Pauline had gotten him into.

Though she'd never mentioned marriage, that was what she meant when she said he should let her know what they would do. He couldn't contemplate an abortion. He'd heard too many stories about guys who'd taken their girlfriends to Mexico and how something had gone wrong and the girl'd nearly died. As much as he didn't want this baby, as much as he didn't want to marry Pauline, he couldn't wish for anything bad to happen to either of them.

But *marriage*. Even in his wildest dreams, he couldn't picture it. At least with his Air Force stint, he knew he'd get out eventually. But marriage was *forever*. He couldn't imagine being tied down, never having the freedom to go out with the guys again, coming home to a wife and a squalling baby. Being responsible for two more people when he was just getting used to the idea of being responsible for himself was a terrifying thought.

He was still wrestling with the problem that night when it occurred to him that maybe Pauline had made a mistake...maybe the baby wasn't his. Everyone knew she'd made it with Matt in Mexico. Maybe this baby was Jeffries's kid and not his at all.

J.T. remembered all the times in the past when Pauline had manipulated him into doing what she wanted by exploiting his weakness for her with flirting and kisses. Maybe she was trying to pull a fast one. Yeah. Maybe she couldn't get Matt to 'fess up and marry her, so she'd decided to place the blame on good old J.T. *He* always did what was expected of him. Yes, sir. J.T. was a model of propriety. A solid citizen. A good, all round guy, ol' J.T. Nice. Upstanding. Gullible.

Hell.

Well, he had to do something, start somewhere. Even though he didn't like the tune, he might as well face the music. He'd call Pauline first, and then he'd break the news to his parents.

THE PHONE at the Randolph house rang three times before it was finally picked up.

"Hello."

Carolyn. Thank God. J.T. had been scared to death that Steven or Deborah would pick up the receiver, and he wasn't ready to talk to them just yet.

"Hi, Caro. Is Pauline there?"

"J.T.?" Carolyn said in a harsh, conspiratorial whisper.

"Yeah, it's me."

"What did you do to Pauline this time? All she and Mom do is cry all the time, and Daddy stomps around the house looking like he could bite nails."

J.T. swore under his breath. "Nothing that concerns you, kiddo," he said. "Will you get Pauline, please?"

"Okay," Carolyn agreed, but her tone implied that he might not like talking to her.

In a matter of seconds, Pauline was on the other line. "J.T.?"

Was it his imagination, or did her voice catch on a little sob? "Hi."

"I was afraid you wouldn't call."

Those were definitely tears in her voice. "How could you think that?" he asked, even though the idea had crossed his mind.

"Well," she said, "you haven't returned my last two phone calls, and you hardly ever answer my letters. Even when you do, you don't really...say anything."

J.T. felt that familiar miasma of guilt rise up in him. "What am I supposed to say?"

"That you miss me..."

He did, and that was a fact, even though it galled him to admit it...even to himself. And he darn sure wasn't going to admit it to Pauline, not when he wasn't sure whether she was trying to put one over on him.

"That you love me," she added.

"Pauline..."

"Dammit, you do love me, J.T.!" she cried, the mild curse shocking him more than the sudden burst of anger. He'd never heard Pauline utter even a small oath before.

"Why won't you admit it?" she asked in a tear-thickened voice. "I thought for sure that if I could get you back, if we made love, you'd tell me."

"Is that why you were so willing?" he asked in disbelief. "Just so I'd tell you I loved you? My God, Pauline, what kind of fool do you take me for?"

She began to laugh, but there was no humor in the sound. Instead, her laughter held bitterness and the slightest vestige of hysteria. "Maybe it was the reason, but guess what? The joke's on me, isn't it? Because you didn't tell me. Not once in the eight times we made love."

"I said—"

"You said you wanted me," she interrupted. "You made that very clear. But you never once said you loved me, so who's the fool, J.T.? You tell me."

Even though pain stabbed J.T.'s heart at the misery he heard in her voice, he was compelled to know the truth. "Maybe we've both been fools," he said, his voice as taut as his tightly strung nerves. "But I don't intend to be made a fool of anymore. Not by you or anyone else."

"What are you talking about?"

"Is this my baby?"

The question hung in the silence growing between them. No sound came through the phone lines. Not so much as a breath or a snippet of static. When she spoke, her voice was so cold it sent shivers down J.T.'s spine.

"You bastard."

She sounded sincere, but denying that there had been anyone else was easy enough. The memory of Bubba telling him about Matt's claim triggered a deep-rooted jealousy that ate at J.T. like a dog gnawing on a piece of raw meat. He wanted to come right out and ask her about Matt, but he wasn't sure he could take the truth if she had. "I had to ask," he said.

"No, J.T., you didn't."

He let that lie. "What do you want to do?" he asked at last.

"What do I want to do? What do you think we should do?"

"I suppose we ought to get married." There! He'd said it.

"I don't know if that's such a good idea or not," she said in a frosty tone. "I don't think you have a very high opinion of me, and at the moment, I certainly don't have a very high opinion of you. I don't think a baby should be brought up in that kind of environment."

"But we have to get married," he said. Even as he spoke the words, he wondered how he'd gone from ambivalence to almost begging in a matter of seconds. "What will people think?"

"Don't worry, J.T. They won't be talking about you. You won't be the one walking around town with a big belly, having everyone point their fingers at you.

Girls are the ones whose reputations suffer. Boys have to sow their wild oats.''

The picture she painted made him feel sick. He passed a shaky palm over his perspiring face. He couldn't imagine Pauline's dainty body heavy with child. And he couldn't bear the thought of the people of Crystal Creek whispering behind her back, which was exactly what would happen. No guy he knew had suffered for getting a girl pregnant, but the girl's reputation was ruined forever. It hurt to imagine Pauline carrying around that stigma for the rest of her life.

"If we don't get married, everyone will think I'm some kind of creep who won't own up to my responsibilities," he argued.

"Oh, and we can't have that, can we?" she said, sarcasm dripping from every word. "Well, I don't want a man who'll marry me just because he has to."

What do you want? he wanted to yell. He felt beaten, whipped. Down for the count. "What do you want, Pauline?" he asked in a weary voice.

"I want a husband who'll provide for me and the baby."

"I'll do that."

"One who loves me."

J.T. pinched the bridge of his nose tightly with his thumb and forefinger and squeezed his eyes shut. "I do care for you, Pauline."

It was as close as he could come to saying what she wanted. As it turned out, it was enough.

"Okay, J.T.," she said with a sigh that sounded as spent as he felt. "When do you want to do it?"

"Let me talk to my folks and I'll see what can be worked out with the Air Force. I'll call as soon as I can."

"Okay," she said and hung up.

J.T. sighed and dialed his parents' number, collect. Lord, he hated to think what they would say. . . .

THEY SAID PLENTY. Calvin raved, ranted and cussed and demanded to know what kind of girl Pauline was, anyway. He threatened to pay for her to go away and have the baby and put it up for adoption. He threatened to call and tell her and her family that she was a no-account and had messed up a good boy's life.

J.T. listened and grew coldly angry. He told his dad that Pauline was a decent girl. She was spoiled, maybe, but a nice girl, nevertheless. He told his dad to butt out, that it was really none of his business.

Emily cried copious tears, with harsh, racking sobs that tore at J.T.'s heart even through the phone lines. Hadn't she told him to respect the girls he dated? To treat them the way he'd want a sister to be treated? Hadn't she warned him that there were girls out there who would try to trap a man into marriage by doing exactly what Pauline had done?

Though he had no ready rebuttal for her comment about a girl trapping a guy into marriage, J.T. informed her that he did respect Pauline. Lack of respect had nothing to do with it.

That sent his mother into a fresh bout of weeping. It was her fault. She hadn't been there for him. She wasn't a good mother. She was a failure.

To which J.T., sick of the whole ordeal, replied uttered a blistering curse and asked for his dad to be put back on the line.

He told Calvin about the rumors regarding Matt and Pauline. Cal heaved a deep sigh.

"But there's a fifty-fifty chance it could be yours?"

"More like a seventy-five- to ninety-five-percent chance, I'd say," J.T. admitted grudgingly.

"Damn, son, did you do anything else while you were home?" When J.T. didn't reply, Calvin went on. "If there's that great a chance Pauline is carrying your baby, I don't see any way out except for you to marry her."

J.T.'s sigh mimicked his dad's. "I was afraid you were going to say that."

"A gentleman always does the right and honorable thing, son," Calvin told him. "As Grandpa Hank would say, 'You made your bed—you'll have to lie in it.'"

Which, in J.T.'s mind translated to: if he wanted to dance, he'd have to pay the fiddler. Oh, yeah, whichever version you chose—lyin' in the bed you made, or payin' the fiddler—the old maxim definitely held true. But even with the tantalizing picture of Pauline lying in the bed they'd made together night after night, he was still afraid the price was just too darn high.

IMMEDIATELY after J.T. talked to his parents, a flurry of phone calls back and forth between San Antonio and Crystal Creek occurred. J.T. spoke to Steven, who told him in a coldly polite tone that he hoped J.T.

knew what a good girl he was getting, and how he wished they'd behaved more circumspectly, and that he hoped he understood what a responsibility he was taking on.

A tearful Deborah begged him to be good to Pauline and said she'd help however she could. Promising he'd do his best, J.T. hung up.

Calvin told Pauline that what was done was done, and there was no looking back. He said he hoped she knew what a fine young man she was getting, and how he hoped she would be supportive of J.T. in whatever he undertook in the future. A woman had the power to make or break a man.

Emily told her that she wished it hadn't happened, but that she welcomed her as a daughter-in-law and would do her best to make her transition to the Double C as smooth as possible. Promising she'd do her best, Pauline hung up.

Then the parents talked to each other. Amid digs and sly comments that were evident even through their veneer of cordiality, they worked out tentative plans for a small wedding that would be held at the Randolph ranch as soon as J.T. could get home and they could satisfy Texas law with their blood tests and marriage license.

There was talk of where they'd live.... "On the Double C, of course," maintained J.T.'s parents.

Of whether Pauline would finish the semester at a local community college ... "She really should, you know," said the Randolphs.

If they should have Howard Blake, the Baptist minister, officiate "under the circumstances," or if a justice of the peace would do. "If I can't have Reverend Blake, I'm not getting married," declared Pauline.

To J.T.'s amazement, his dad told him that they were still trying to resolve a minor skirmish over where the newlyweds would spend their first Christmas.

"Who the hell cares!" J.T. yelled through the phone lines. He just hoped the marriage lasted until Christmas... which was only three months away.

When J.T. and Pauline finally got to speak to each other again, they both felt as if their future had been yanked out of their hands, but neither of them said anything. There was something vaguely comforting in knowing that this much at least was being handled by other people.

THEY WERE MARRIED ten days later by Reverend Blake in the backyard of the Randolphs' home, with only family and a few close friends in attendance. The mid-October weather cooperated by not being too hot. Deborah's fall flower gardens were a riot of color. J.T. was resplendent, if a bit pale, in his dress uniform; Pauline looked unbearably pretty, if a bit pale, in a white sheath dress with three-quarter length sleeves and a boat neck.

Her something old was the pearl necklace that her parents had given her at her eighth-grade graduation. Her something new was the dress her mama had bought at Neiman-Marcus, as well as the plain gold

band J.T. slipped onto her finger next to the dia-
mond-and-emerald engagement ring he'd given her
when he first got home. Her slip was borrowed from
Patty Helms and her something blue was the satin
ribbon adorning the bouquet of white roses she carried.

She even had the requisite "penny in her shoe" for
good luck, but when she looked up into J.T.'s set features, she prayed that satisfying the old conventions
would be enough to guarantee their happiness.

"You may kiss your bride."

The words that ended the simple ceremony were
spoken by the smiling Howard Blake. They elicited a
sharp sob from Deborah Randolph and a soft sniff
from Emily McKinney. Steven Randolph sat in stony
silence; Calvin drew Emily close to his side.

J.T. looked into Pauline's guileless blue eyes. Pauline. His bride. His wife. Till death parted them. Like
a man in a daze, he slipped his arms around her and
pressed his mouth to hers. Pauline uttered a little cry
and melted against him, her lips warm and hungry and
clinging.

Lord, she felt so good, tasted so wonderful. It had
been so long since he'd kissed her. Too long. He could
kiss her for hours . . . days. . . .

"Ahem!"

The sound of the reverend clearing his throat intruded on J.T.'s thoughts. Feeling his face flush with
the heat of embarrassment, he set Pauline away from
him. He glanced out at the crowd. Carolyn smirked.
Pauline's dad looked as if he'd like to smash in J.T.'s

face. Her mom was sobbing into her hankie. His own parents looked as if they wished the ground would open up and swallow them. Grandpa Hank gave a shake of his graying head, and looked off at the hills.

How long had he and Pauline been kissing, anyway? he wondered, his anger at himself—and her—on the rise. Damn! Didn't he have any control when it came to her? Did she only have to kiss him a time or two to undermine his resolve and make him forget that he swore not to let her use those drugging kisses to wrap him around her little finger?

Releasing Pauline's hand, he shot a helpless look at Howard Blake, searching for some indication of what to do next. The minister smiled and indicated that they should turn toward the guests.

"Ladies and gentlemen, may I present Mr. and Mrs. John Travis McKinney!"

Mr. and Mrs. John Travis McKinney. It was over. Really over. He and Pauline were married. Laughing, crying, people got to their feet and gathered around, smothering them with hugs and kisses and bombarding them with good wishes and tidbits of advice for a long and happy life.

IT SEEMED as if they ate cake and drank punch and opened gifts all day, though J.T. reckoned that in reality it was only a couple of hours before he and Pauline were registering for the night at the Austin Hilton, compliments of his parents.

Other than the prescribed comments about how nice everything had been, neither had spoken a word during the fifty-minute drive to the city. But then, they hadn't said a whole lot more the entire time J.T. had been home.

When they got to their room, a sumptuous meal—compliments of Grandpa Hank—awaited them. Too nervous to eat during the days preceding the wedding, they stuffed themselves on steak and shrimp and strawberries and champagne while an Austin radio station played popular music.

"How do you do that so easy?" Pauline asked, watching him peel a shrimp with swift, economical movements.

"It's easy. Watch." He peeled another and offered it to her. She opened her mouth, and J.T. popped in the shrimp. When her tongue touched his fingertips, he jerked his hand away as if he'd been burned.

"Want some more wine?" he asked, to cover the awkwardness of the moment.

She shook her head. "No thanks. Too much makes me silly, and I'm not sure it would be good for the baby."

The voice of Conway Twitty singing "It's Only Make Believe" wafted throughout the room. It was a song J.T. and Pauline had danced to many times while they'd been dating. *Their song.* When Conway got to the part that said his only prayer was that some unknown girl would care for him someday, J.T.'s new wife looked at him with a fetching tenderness.

J.T. steeled himself against that look. He'd seen it before... usually just before Pauline began to perform her feminine wiles. His appetite fled. "It's not going to work, Pauline."

"What isn't going to work, J.T.?" she asked, all wide-eyed innocence.

"You fluttering your eyelashes at me and turning me into a puddle of butter at your feet. You aren't going to control me the way you do everyone else in your family."

"I don't know what you mean."

J.T. scooted back his chair. "Sure you do. You can tease and wheedle and manipulate the events and the people around you until they're willing to give you anything you want or forgive you of any sin. Well, not me. I'm not so easy... or forgiving."

Shock molded her pretty features. J.T. decided to leave while he was ahead. He sketched her a quick salute. "Good night, Mrs. McKinney. Sweet dreams."

He went into the bedroom and turned down his side of the bed. Then he stripped to his shorts and crawled between the clean-smelling sheets. He wasn't sure how long it was before Pauline tiptoed into the bedroom and lay down next to him. He knew she was crying, but he steeled his heart against the insidious assault and refused to say anything. The last thing he heard before he finally fell into a troubled sleep was the sound of her sniffles.

He awakened some time later with the sun streaming through the cracks in the drapes, to the sound of Pauline throwing up.

Welcome to the wonderful world of marriage and fatherhood, J.T.

Pauline emerged from the bathroom in a couple of minutes, wiping her nose and her streaming eyes, her face so devoid of color it was frightening. There was reproach in her eyes.

Aw, hell! Why did she have to act like it was all his fault?

He vacillated between wanting to pull her down onto the bed beside him and hold her, and the equally strong need to take her by the shoulders and shake some sense into her. He did neither.

He left for Randolph Air Force Base later that morning, acutely aware that he was responsible for the misery she was going through. He left without saying he was sorry for his part of what happened.

"Wow! They did get off to a rocky start, didn't they," Cynthia said. She sat at the table while Carolyn cleared the dishes and Jennifer sucked greedily on a bottle of formula.

"Rocky hardly begins to describe it," Carolyn said.

"It's hard to picture Pauline as a spoiled little conniver, when all I've heard the past sixteen months is what a wonderful person she was, and it's certainly hard to imagine the J.T. I know as the same person you're telling me about."

"Life has a way of changing you," Carolyn smiled. "Sometimes something can happen that turns you completely around."

J.T. RECOGNIZED the truck barreling toward him as Tyler's, and pulled his truck to a stop. Though J.T.

was anxious to find Cynthia, he supposed there was nothing to do but turn around and go back to the ranch.

"Where you headed?" his older son asked.

"I was going into town to look for Cynthia."

"Why on earth would you do that?" Tyler asked. "I haven't been married long, but I've already learned that you don't come between a woman and her shopping."

"She wasn't going shopping. She took Jennifer to the doctor."

Tyler, who was crazy about his baby sister, frowned. "What's wrong with Jen?"

"I'm not sure. She had a bad night. What are you doing over here?"

"Ruth went to a luncheon of some kind in Austin, and there's not a damn thing to eat in the house," Tyler said. "I was hoping Lettie Mae had some hot leftovers."

"There's plenty of chicken casserole."

Tyler grimaced and gave a slow shake of his head. "A cattleman eating chicken. What's the world coming to?"

"You're not a cattleman. You're a vintner. If you don't want what's left, you'll have to fend for yourself. You know Lettie isn't going to pander to your whims."

"If she did, it'd be the first time," Tyler said dryly. "Come on back and visit with me while I eat."

"I need to find Cynthia."

"Uh-oh. What's going on?" Tyler said, noting the determination in his dad's eyes.

"Nothing."

"Don't give me that. Something happened or you wouldn't be hell-bent on going after her."

The muscle in J.T.'s jaw tightened. "If you must know, we had an argument and there are some things I need to set her straight about."

"Ah." Tyler gave a sage nod. "Same song, second verse, huh?"

Beneath the brim of his Stetson, J.T.'s eyes narrowed. "I don't see that that's any of your business."

"Maybe not, but I never saw an argument that couldn't be put off."

J.T. sighed at hearing Lettie's words thrown at him the second time. "So I've been told." He put the truck in gear. "Let's go. The sooner you eat and I get rid of you, the sooner I can get on with my life."

Tyler grinned. "Meet you at the house."

Meanwhile, back at the ranch...

CYNTHIA, oblivious to J.T.'s determination to find her, was still more involved in the past than the present. "When did things start turning around for Pauline and J.T.?" she asked.

Carolyn considered the question thoughtfully. "Not any time soon. I think it was after Tyler was born, as a matter of fact."

Cynthia's mouth quirked in a teasing grin. "Since they had three kids, I guess it's safe to assume the marriage lasted until Christmas?"

"Oh, yes, but probably only because J.T. was gone and they couldn't fight. He did come home for Christmas leave, though, and as usual, when they were together, things started heating up."

Cynthia propped her chin in her palm. "How?"

"Well, Pauline was almost five months pregnant by then, and J.T. was forced to face the reality of the situation. Until then, he'd been able to go on his merry way and pretend that nothing had changed.

"Coming home and finding Pauline ensconced in his room at the Double C—the house Ken Slattery lives in now—brought it all home with a vengeance."

CHAPTER FIVE

December 1, 1958

THE FIRST OF OCTOBER seemed like aeons ago instead of the two months it had actually been. Pauline couldn't believe that J.T. was still so angry with her. She knew he blamed her for the marriage, for tying him down—but it wasn't as if she got pregnant by herself, for goodness' sake!

As soon as she'd taken J.T. to the bus station the morning after their wedding, she'd driven to her parents' house and started packing her things. Her mother thought she should stay at the Rocking R with her family; J.T. had insisted she move to the Double C.

Feeling very adult now that she was a married woman, and eager to pick up the reins of her new life, Pauline told her parents that she would rather stay with J.T.'s family until the new house Calvin was having built for them was ready.

She couldn't say that the time spent with the McKinneys had been bad. Emily made every effort to make things easier for her, allowing her to rearrange and add her things to J.T.'s room so she'd feel more at home.

In return, Pauline—who might be spoiled but who had a penchant for neatness and an impeccable Texas upbringing—kept the room straight, always offered to help with the dishes and kept her own clothes washed and ironed.

She didn't really mind doing her part around the Double C, because she could honestly say that Calvin and Emily made her feel right at home. She knew her being there must be strange to them, but if they felt put out at having her there, they never let on. Pauline also remembered her mother's parting words.

"Calvin and Emily McKinney are proud people. They're probably blaming you for trapping J.T. into marriage, so you've got to put your best foot forward. You don't want the McKinneys thinking you're lazy. If you pitch in when you're needed and treat them with respect, they'll soon see you're good enough to be called a McKinney."

For once, she had the feeling her mother was right.

While the town breathed a collective "Aha!" gossiped about the suddenness of J.T. and Pauline's wedding, marked their calendars and counted down the days until she went into labor, she did her utmost to act as if nothing was out of the ordinary.

At her parents' request, she was finishing up the semester at the community college in Hillsboro three mornings a week, and helping Eva Blake with some hospital visitation and secretarial work over at the Baptist church when she was needed. The regular secretary had recently moved and had yet to be replaced.

The pastor's wife and Pauline had hit it off when Pauline enrolled in Eva's speech and drama classes her junior and senior years at Crystal Creek High. As far as Pauline was concerned, Eva Blake was the best drama teacher the school had ever had the good fortune to hire. But the unlikely friendship between the eighteen-year-old and the twenty-seven-year-old former actress grew from Eva's empathy for Pauline's situation.

When the Randolphs had confided Pauline's predicament to Howard Blake before asking him to perform the wedding ceremony, the handsome young minister had been extremely understanding and had counseled both Pauline and J.T. about the sanctity of marriage and the responsibility that was before them.

After Pauline, who had been expecting threats of hellfire and damnation, expressed her relief to her mother, Deborah told her about the scandal that had surrounded the young preacher and his wife when they'd married back in '51.

Howard, just out of seminary, had gone to the national Baptist convention in Dallas and had come home married to Eva, who was several months pregnant. He'd almost lost his job over the scandal.

As usual, rumors flew. Some said that he'd kept her in Dallas as his mistress; others that he'd gone up there a few months earlier, gotten drunk at a party and...well, you know. Still another variation was that the baby wasn't his at all. There was a lot of speculation, but no one knew the truth except Eva and Howard, and they made no effort to clear up the situation.

When Eva lost the baby late in her pregnancy, the rumors had stopped.

Hearing the story, Pauline felt her heart ache for the minister's wife, who had always been so kind and helpful to her when she was in school. She took consolation in the fact that Howard and Eva Blake now seemed like the happiest of couples, and had the respect of the entire community.

She wondered how long it would take her to reach that status.

There were other small changes in Pauline's life. Aside from commenting that they bet J.T. was dynamite in bed, Patty and Lola accepted the situation as no big deal. Pauline was something of a novelty, and they made it a point to visit on the weekends they were home from college. Though always glad to see them, Pauline soon discovered she didn't have much in common with her friends anymore. While she tired easily and could never get enough sleep, they were perky and vivacious, bouncing on the bed, laughing and joking about what had happened at college and drooling over new guys who had caught their eye.

They regaled her with gossip: Patty and her boyfriend were back together and so were Dottie Little and Duff Jones. Martin Avery was seeing that slutty young widow of Lloyd Johnson's—you know Lloyd... killed in the accident at the quarry a year or so ago—and Bubba Gibson had started dating Mary Riles, a junior who was four years younger than he was. Other than the news about Dottie and Duff, Pauline couldn't have been less interested.

In return, she showed them the progress on the house and the things she and her mother were making for the baby. Patty and Lola oohed and aahed and said "How sweet," and went back to talking about what a good kisser so-and-so was. Had she seen *Marjorie Morningstar?* Wasn't Natalie Wood wonderful?

Pauline confessed that she hadn't been to a movie in a while, since the night she and J.T. had pretended to watch *Cat on a Hot Tin Roof* at the drive-in, and asked if either of them knew what had happened on "Search for Tomorrow" the day before. She'd missed the popular soap opera because she had a doctor's appointment.

Lola had looked at Patty and then at Pauline. They didn't watch soap operas, they informed her. Pauline felt the chasm between her and her friends widening every time they came to visit.

Pauline started spotting in her fourth month, and Grover Purdy sent her to bed. Pauline worried that if she lost the baby, J.T. might want to end the marriage. Thankfully, the spotting stopped in a couple of days, and she breathed a sigh of relief. She was instructed to rest every afternoon, giving her a perfect opportunity to write to J.T., which she did every day without fail.

If she received one reply a month from J.T., she counted herself lucky. His letters were always short and to the point; he answered her questions, congratulated her on the grades she was making in school, told what was going on in his officer's training.

In her most recent letter Pauline had written that she'd only gained six pounds because she'd been so sick, but that she'd probably be in maternity clothes by the time he got home at Christmas, because everything was just getting too tight around the waist. She also wrote about her parents' Christmas plans, and about some ideas she had for their house, a two-story affair that was big enough for at least two families.

J.T. ignored her comment about the pregnancy and gave her instructions to check with his mom about her plans for Christmas before agreeing willy-nilly to what her folks had arranged. He also cautioned her not to change the carpenter's plans for the house unless she consulted with his parents first. She needed to make sure her ideas were feasible and not too costly.

The fact that he wanted her to check with his parents before making any changes to the house was galling. She might be spoiled, and accustomed to getting her own way, but, according to her mother, she had a surprising eye for spotting the kind of architectural detail that enhanced a house's charm, as well as a knack for using color, two gifts that could combine to lift a house above the ordinary.

And though she was growing genuinely fond of J.T.'s mother, the very idea of being told to check with her before deciding what they were going to do for Christmas made Pauline feel like a child, not an adult. Why did they have to plan their Christmas around *his* family's festivities—why not around hers?

But what really made her furious was the way he refused to acknowledge her pregnancy, either in a letter or verbally. How long did he think he could ignore the fact that they were going to have a baby?

She couldn't help unburdening herself to her mother one day at lunch.

"Why is he acting like this?" she asked, after she'd listed all her complaints to Deborah.

Deborah put down her fork, rested her elbows on the table and laced her fingers together. "Because he's terribly young, Pauline. And so are you. For all that you dated for several months, you really don't know each other that well. And you've known each other as dates, not mates."

Pauline realized her mother was right. She was beginning to see that her mother was often right ... and about a lot of things.

"J.T. has no way of knowing that you won't mess up the house his family is shelling out good money for. But he knows his mother's taste and trusts her to make the right choices. It won't hurt you to ask Emily's opinion. She'll be flattered, and when she sees your ideas will work, she'll be pleased and pass on the information to J.T."

Pauline mulled that over. "Okay. I see your point. But what about the way he ignores anything I say about the baby? How can he just pretend it doesn't exist?"

"Oh, Paulie," Deborah said on a sigh. "This is much harder. I can only guess what's going on in his mind, but I imagine that, like you, he feels frightened by all that's happened to him the past few months.

The service, marriage...a baby. These are all big responsibilities. I imagine he feels as trapped as you do.''

"I don't feel trapped.''

"No?'' Deborah asked with a disbelieving lift of her eyebrows. "Not even when Patty and Lola are going out on the weekends having a good time shopping for clothes and looking for guys?''

Pauline thought about her thickening waistline, her hardening tummy and the way it was becoming almost impossible to find something she could fit into. And she thought longingly about the scrumptious jade and navy plaid skirt and matching angora sweater she'd seen in the J.C. Penney catalog.

"Maybe I do...sometimes,'' she admitted.

Deborah reached across the table and gave her daughter's hand a hard squeeze. "I wish things could have been different,'' she said after a moment. "I wish you and J.T. had waited, but since you didn't, we all just have to make the best of things.''

"I know. I'm trying.''

"I know you are. I guess your dad and I spoiled you and Carolyn, and it's too late to go back and change that. But you're a good girl, and J.T. is a good boy. One of the biggest obstacles in this marriage is that you're both so young.''

"I'm getting older by the minute,'' Pauline joked.

"I know.'' Deborah sighed. "You're going through some adjustments now, and when the baby comes, there will be more to get used to. And then, just when you think you've got everything figured out, J.T. will come home for good, and you're going to have to do even more adjusting."

"Do you have to paint such a gloomy picture?" Pauline asked with a wry smile.

Deborah gave a shaky laugh. "I don't mean to sound gloomy, honey, but I believe in being realistic. Marriage isn't all sunshine and roses. Sometimes it's hard work and hard times and disappointments. Even though this marriage between you and J.T. started off with a less-than-perfect beginning, it will work if you want it to."

That was the problem. Pauline wasn't sure J.T. wanted the marriage to work. And disappointments? She was already becoming familiar with those, too.

"I wrote and told J.T. about our plans for Christmas, and he said I should ask his mother what her plans were." Pauline's eyes flashed with irritation. "I don't think it's fair for him to put his family's wishes before mine."

Deborah forced a smile. "As I remember, where and how to spend our first Christmas triggered one of the biggest fights your dad and I ever had." She patted Pauline's hand. "There should be some fair way to satisfy everyone."

"I don't see how."

"Don't the McKinneys always have a big party to open their presents on Christmas Eve?"

"I think so, but so do you."

"We have a party, but we don't open our gifts until Christmas Day. Why don't you spend Christmas Eve with the McKinneys and Christmas Day with us? That should make everyone happy, don't you think?"

Pauline wasn't sure what it would take to make J.T. happy, but she agreed with her mother that her idea sounded as if it might work.

"It's called compromise, honey," Deborah said with a smile. "It's something you should—and will—become very adept at."

Compromise. Pauline wondered if J.T. had ever heard of the word.

The phone rang, and while Deborah went to answer it, Lettie Mae came out of the kitchen carrying two pieces of devil's food cake with seven-minute frosting.

"Thanks, but no thanks, Lettie Mae," Pauline said with a smile. "I'm trying not to gain too much weight. Everyone says it's so hard to lose after you have a baby."

Lettie Mae rolled her eyes. "I think it depends on the person," she said. "So how's married life treatin' you?"

"Okay," Pauline hedged.

Lettie Mae shifted her weight to one leg and rested a slender hand on her hip. "Not so good, huh?" she said in that knowing way of hers. "What's wrong? Doesn't J.T. cotton to married life?"

A sigh that was a cross between disillusionment and self-pity fluttered from Pauline's lips. "He doesn't really want to be married—to me or anyone."

"Then you've got to make him want to be."

"How?" Pauline asked, surprised by the idea.

"Be extra nice to him when he comes home for Christmas. Do things that will make him feel special."

"Like what?"

"I don't know," Lettie Mae confessed. "Go slow tryin' to patch up whatever's wrong between you. Don't rock the boat. And for goodness' sake, don't pick any fights." She brightened suddenly. "Maybe you should try to make the time he's home real romantic."

"Fat chance. J.T. won't even touch me."

Lettie Mae looked stunned. "My grief, girl! What did you do to him to make him shy away from you like that?"

Pauline sighed. "I don't know. He says I manipulate him and everyone else in my family."

Lettie Mae cocked her head to the side and pursed her full, shapely lips. "Come to think on it, I have seen you flutter those eyelashes of yours and beg and promise until you get your way—and on more occasions than I care to think about."

Pauline's look of surprise was genuine. Knowing how the people around her viewed her was a real eye-opener, especially when those people were the ones closest to her. "Well, if I do, it doesn't work with J.T.—not all the time, anyway."

"I don't know what to tell you, girl, but I know you as well as anybody around here, and I know that you ain't got a mean bone in your body. You're also one of the most generous people I know."

At least I'm not all bad, Pauline thought with wry amusement. "A lot of good that does me."

"Maybe you should just be yourself. J.T. is bound to realize that you're really a nice person sooner or later."

"Maybe so," Pauline said, touched by Lettie Mae's concern. "Tell me what's going on with you and Clark. Is the wedding still on?"

"Uh-huh," Lettie Mae said, a wide smile splitting her pretty face. "He's comin' in this Friday night in time for the Christmas parade."

Crystal Creek's Christmas parade had been an annual event ever since the town was established in 1847. Through the years the parade had changed from a horse-and-buggy affair with drunken cowboys whooping and hollering and shooting it up amid squealing, corset-clad ladies from the long-defunct Cactus Rose bordello and pious candle-carrying, piñata-bursting celebrants. It was now a well-planned, much-publicized gathering of most of Crystal Creek's seven thousand inhabitants, not to mention visitors from the nearby towns and countryside.

The parade had become more organized through the years, but it had begun to take real shape during the Depression. When the carousel that dominated the town square had been dismantled because money was so scarce the townspeople couldn't afford the price of a ride, Ellen Pollock had joined with Elvira Gibson and decided that something should be done to boost community spirits. They had determined to make the then-lackluster parade something the citizenry could be proud of, and together, through the years, they had.

The parade now boasted dozens of floats built by every class in Crystal Creek's high school, plus those outfitted by the Lions Club, the Rotary Club, the Garden Club and every other club and organization imaginable, including the local rodeo riders who provided the nostalgia of the horse-and-buggy days. There was the Christmas Queen float, complete with her throne and court, set amid mounds of glittering scenes of fake snow.

There were marching bands, prancing dance teams, cheerleaders waving pom-poms and legions of baton twirlers in short outfits glittering with thousands of sequins. There were food booths, arts and crafts and fireworks, but the culminating event was the flipping of the switch and the lighting of thousands of strings of Christmas lights.

They were draped in fancy designs over the streets, along the sidewalks and across storefronts. And they were swagged through the fragrant branches of the giant cedar that sat in the middle of the square where the carousel horses had once pranced in slow and stately splendor.

The Christmas parade, traditionally held the first weekend of December, was *the* event of the year in Crystal Creek—bigger and more exciting even than the Fourth of July fireworks display—unless you counted the year Brock Munroe's Aunt Millicent had ridden down Main Street in a two-piece swimsuit, each foot planted firmly, Roman style, on the back of a matched set of bays, while the crowd, both scandalized and impressed, hissed and booed and oohed and aahed.

The Randolphs had never missed the Christmas parade, and Pauline, who had been last year's Christmas Queen, fully intended to be there this year, too, even though J.T. wouldn't be home in time for the festivities.

"I'm glad Clark will be home to go with you," she said to Lettie Mae, unaware of the wistfulness in her voice. "Have you set a time for the wedding?"

"Sunday afternoon at 2:00 p.m. over at Mount Zion Baptist Temple."

"Oh, Lettie Mae! You're having a church wedding!"

"You bet I am. Mama made my gown, and Clark has a new navy suit."

"Did you have a shower?" Pauline asked, still lamenting the fact that she'd missed a lot of the fun generally associated with getting married.

Lettie Mae nodded, and excitement danced in her eyes. "We got a lot of good stuff. Sheets, towels—even a percolator and a new mixer. Clark's already found us an apartment in New Orleans."

"You're moving, then?"

"Well, sure," Lettie Mae said with a shrug. "Clark can't make a living playing jazz in Crystal Creek, now can he?"

"I suppose not," Pauline agreed.

For a moment, they both recalled the fun times they'd shared as children. And they both felt a sadness that those days were gone.

"Pauline..."

Pauline glanced up and wondered at the look she saw in Lettie Mae's eyes—something that wasn't quite worry, but wasn't quite pleasure. "Yes?"

"I have something to tell you."

"What? You look pretty serious."

Lettie Mae's wide mouth trembled the slightest bit, but she lifted her chin to a defiant angle. "I'm gonna have a baby, too."

"You are?" Pauline breathed. She couldn't have been more surprised if Lettie Mae had said she was the Virgin Mary.

"I guess it happened when Clark was home last time. I...I haven't told anyone else, but I wanted you to know." She threw her hands into the air in a gesture that betrayed her indecision. "I don't know why. I guess I wanted you to know that you weren't all by your lonesome."

"That was Hilda Barnard," Deborah said, breezing into the room, oblivious to the fact that she was intruding on a very personal moment. "She wanted to know if I could help with the Ladies Auxiliary booth at the parade Friday night. I told her I'd be glad to."

Pauline shot Lettie Mae a glance that said she wished Deborah's timing had been better.

Deborah spied the cake Lettie Mae had baked and smiled. "Oh, dessert. Thanks, Lettie." She sat down and began to eat the cake, blissfully ignorant that she'd interrupted a moment of shared confidences. "What were you girls talking about?"

"Lettie Mae's wedding," Pauline said.

"You should see her dress, Pauline," Deborah said. "Viola did a superb job."

Pauline looked at her friend. "I know you'll be beautiful." She rose and went to give Lettie a hug. "You know I wish you the very best."

Lettie Mae's smile was almost smug. "I already got the very best," she said.

FRIDAY NIGHT was respectably chilly for the time of year, cool enough to put the townsfolk in a festive, holiday mood. The citizens of Crystal Creek pushed and jostled, vying for prime spots along the street so that they could get an unimpeded view of the parade's passage. Though there was no alcohol allowed, a good portion of the populace had started their celebrating earlier in the afternoon—if the whoops and yells and general rowdiness was any indication.

Pauline stood sandwiched between her parents and J.T.'s, clutching her present for Lettie Mae to her breasts. She'd spent an entire week working on her gift. Under Emily's tutelage, she'd made yards of white hairpin lace. Then she'd cut off the hems of a top sheet and pillowcases and hand-sewn the lace insertion—which was no small task. The white cotton sheets looked elegant with the delicate addition, and Pauline was proud of herself for having done the work. J.T.'s mother had been pleased that she'd undertaken the job and praised her for her workmanship. Pauline only hoped Lettie Mae and Clark liked her efforts.

As usual, the parade was small-town Texas at its best. Though she enjoyed the bands and the floats and the cheerleaders doing their flips and jumps and flirting with guys along the street, Pauline felt a twinge of something she couldn't quite put a name to.

She had been out of high school for less than a year, and yet she felt older, separated from those girls as surely as if she'd crossed some invisible line. She supposed that, in a way, she had. And there was no going back to those carefree, somehow innocent days of her girlhood. She was a woman. Married. Soon to be a mother.

She watched as Carrie Farrington—this year's cheerleader captain—jumped from the shoulders of one of the other girls, turned a flip in midair and landed nimbly on tiny feet encased in pristine white bucks. With a sigh, Pauline wondered if she'd ever have that much energy again. Would she ever feel really good again? Would she ever want J.T. to make love to her—assuming he ever wanted to?

"Oh, I wish J.T. could be here!" Emily exclaimed. "He always loved the parade."

Pauline concurred with the comment, and let her thoughts drift back to her earlier conversation with J.T. She had talked to him just before leaving for the parade and told him that she'd asked his mother about a change in the bathroom, which Emily had agreed sounded "quite pretty."

She'd also told him her mother's idea for an equitable way to split their time between the two families at Christmas, and mentioned that Emily thought the arrangements would be an excellent compromise. J.T. had agreed that it sounded okay to him, too.

She told him she'd bought him a Christmas present—she'd looked for weeks for the tiger-eye cuff links. He said he had all of his shopping to do yet. She told him she missed him. He said he'd be home soon. She told him she'd been thinking about names for the baby. J.T. said he had to go, someone wanted to use the phone.

They'd hung up, and she'd run into their room and cried for what seemed like hours, while Calvin and Emily frowned at each other worriedly.

"Two wrongs don't make a right," Calvin had muttered to his wife, even though he'd been the one to give J.T. the spiel about duty and doing the honorable thing.

"It was J.T.'s decision, Cal," Emily had reminded him. "He wanted to do this. Whatever their problems are, it's none of our business."

To which Calvin McKinney had gritted his teeth and stomped from the room.

Both he and Emily had been extremely solicitous to Pauline the rest of the day, drawing her out at dinner and exclaiming over the handiwork that she'd done for Lettie Mae, though in private, Calvin expressed concern that their new daughter-in-law might be getting a tad too friendly with the servants.

Pauline had taken extra special pains getting ready for the parade, hoping to hide the lingering traces of her tears beneath her new pancake makeup and to mask her pallor under an extra dab of rouge. But when she regarded the clownish result in the mirror, she'd scrubbed her face and reverted to her normal makeup. She wouldn't pretend to be something she wasn't—in this case, happy.

Tired of putting on a front, weary of living a lie, she had donned the new maternity dress her mother had purchased in Austin a month before. The outfit was a two-piece faux suede in a flattering rust hue. The top had a round neck, three-quarter-length sleeves and brass buttons.

It had taken her a couple of minutes to figure out how to do up the straight skirt, with its cutout for her expanding stomach and the strings that tied around the waist, but she finally managed it.

Turning this way and that, she eyed herself in the cheval glass that had been J.T.'s grandmother's and decided that she looked okay...for a pregnant woman. Then, drawing a deep breath and squaring her shoulders, she grabbed her tweed coat and leather purse. Let them talk, she had thought in a brief flare of anger. Let them count. As Bubba would say, she just didn't give a tinker's damn anymore.

"Oooh...look!"

The soft croon of wonder that interrupted Pauline's thoughts now came from Carolyn, who was gazing up at the canopy of lights in typical eleven-year-old awe. Turning on the lights was the culmination of the parade, and Pauline realized with a bit of surprise that she had been so caught up in her problems she'd missed most of it. All that was left of the evening was to exclaim over the new additions to the light displays around town and to meander up and down Main Street sampling the various foods and purchasing the many wares the local clubs had for sale.

"I'm supposed to meet Lettie Mae over by the newsstand to give her her gift," she told her parents. "I'll take Carolyn with me if you want."

"Sure thing, sugar," Deborah said. "Daddy and I will buy you a hot dog when you get back, so hurry, okay?"

Pauline promised she wouldn't be long, and she and Carolyn started off for their rendezvous. Lettie Mae and Clark were waiting for them, and Lettie Mae took the proffered gift with a smile of thanks. Pauline stepped forward and started to hug Lettie, but her friend turned away, taking Clark's arm instead.

"Clark, you remember Miss Pauline, don't you?" she asked, smiling up at him with pride and love.

Miss Pauline? Lettie Mae never called her Miss Pauline. But that was at home. This was public. With a surge of understanding, she knew why Lettie had refused to be drawn into an embrace. Another shaft of sorrow worked its way into Pauline's already aching heart.

"Hi, Miz Pauline."

"Hello, Clark. It's been a long time," Pauline said, extending her hand in greeting.

"It sure has."

Clark's handclasp was firm. His attitude toward Lettie Mae, as they visited for a few short minutes, bordered on adoration. Why couldn't J.T. look at her that way? Like he wanted to kiss her silly.

Feeling like a fifth wheel—a common occurrence lately—she and Carolyn left the happy couple and went back to join her parents and her in-laws. Lettie was lucky, Pauline thought with a bit of envy. Clark was handsome, successful and obviously crazy about her.

An hour later, Pauline was stuffed with hot dogs, fresh-roasted peanuts, cotton candy and candied apples. She, Calvin and Emily were making their way slowly back to the car when there was a sudden sickening squeal of tires, the screech of locking brakes and a loud, metallic crunching that signaled a car accident.

A universal gasp rose from the people milling around the booths. Like lemmings drawn to the sea, the crowd surged toward the sound of impact, which seemed to Pauline to be a block down and around the corner, on Third Street. She and J.T.'s parents did likewise.

J.T.'s dad, who'd worked closely with a medic in the Second World War and knew a lot of first aid, elbowed his way through the crowd. Emily and Pauline followed close behind.

A battered pickup that she recognized as belonging to Brad Powers, Crystal Creek's star basketball player, had plowed into the driver's side of a new white '59 Chevy. The car wasn't familiar, and there wasn't enough light coming from the streetlight to see who was inside either vehicle. She could see that no one was moving. Pauline felt her stomach lurch in a sudden rush of nausea.

In the commotion of gawking, curious people—all of whom were afraid to take the initiative—she saw Grover Purdy push his way through the crowd. J.T.'s dad met him and together they began to check the victims, starting with the occupants of the pickup. She watched as Doc checked the driver and then went around to the passenger side. He gave a sorrowful shake of his head. A rumble of disbelief swept the crowd.

"Who's in there with Brad?" someone shouted.

Before the physician could answer, someone edged up behind him and looked over his shoulder. "Oh, my God! It's Tim Holloway." Again the crowd gasped in disbelief.

Shock made Pauline's knees grow weak. Brad and Tim. Both a year younger than she was, their lives snuffed out so quickly...so senselessly. She felt herself sway slightly and fought back an encroaching darkness.

Emily must have noticed. Her arm went around Pauline's waist. "I don't think you should be here," her mother-in-law said. "Seeing all this can't be good for you."

Pauline nodded. She started to turn away, when someone in the crowd cried out, "Hey, Doc! There's someone moving inside the Chevy."

Abandoning the pickup, Calvin McKinney and the doctor rounded the car and opened the passenger door. Sick fascination kept Pauline rooted to the spot.

She watched as Doc Purdy and J.T.'s dad moved the victim from the mangled car to the brick street. Calvin straightened, giving Pauline an unobstructed view of the doctor, who was working over his patient with calm efficiency.

When she saw who was lying there, Pauline crumpled to the ground in a dead faint.

"J.T.?" CYNTHIA ASKED, her eyes wide with surprise.

"No," Carolyn said. "Lettie Mae. Clark was with her but he died before they could get him to the hospital. Lettie Mae had a concussion, a broken leg and a crushed pelvis. She lost her baby."

"Dear God," Cynthia breathed, cradling Jennifer close in a sudden burst of love and thankfulness. "I had no idea."

"No one outside the doctor, our family and hers ever knew about the baby," Carolyn said, "so please keep it to yourself."

"Oh, I will. What was wrong with Pauline?"

"Grover Purdy checked her out and couldn't find much wrong. Her fainting was probably just shock at seeing Lettie Mae in such a bad way."

"What caused the accident?" Cynthia asked.

"Brad and Tim had been drinking—heavily, according to some of their friends. They were speeding, and didn't stop at the four-way intersection. Lettie Mae and Clark were halfway across the street when Brad's truck broadsided them."

Cynthia mulled over what she'd been told. "And Lettie Mae never married anyone else?"

Carolyn shook her head. "No. The doctors all agreed that there was no way she could ever carry a baby full term, and back then, if a woman couldn't have a child, she was only considered half a woman."

"How asinine."

"Archaic." Carolyn's smile grew wistful. "Aside from that, Pauline said that Lettie Mae claimed no man could ever measure up to her Clark."

"She must have really loved him."

Carolyn nodded.

"It's sad to think of her being alone all these years...sort of giving her life for the McKinneys. I mean, she's still an attractive woman."

"Don't waste any time worrying about Lettie Mae being lonely or martyring herself for the Mc-Kinneys."

"What do you mean?"

"She might not have married, but she's had her little flings through the years—if you know what I mean," Carolyn said with a knowing wink.

"Lettie Mae?"

"You said it yourself. She's very attractive for a woman in her mid-fifties. She has a great personality. Men like her, and she likes men. She's never been promiscuous, but she has had her affairs. As a matter of fact, she's seeing Mose Gilchrist who works down at the quarry right now."

Cynthia's shock was obvious. "I never would have guessed."

"One thing about our Lettie Mae. She's the soul of discretion."

THE SOUL OF DISCRETION was, at that moment, cursing the day she'd ever come to work for the McKinneys. She was supposed to meet Mose in an hour, and if the McKinney clan didn't clear out of her kitchen, she'd be late.

First, J.T. had shown up with Tyler in tow just as she got the dishes cleared away. The oldest McKinney son was making serious inroads on the remains of her casserole when Cal burst through the door, waving a postcard he'd received from Ken and Nora, who were honeymooning in Hot Springs.

Now he eyed the casserole, went to the cabinet and grabbed a plate.

"That's it!" Lettie cried, untying her apron and tossing it to the countertop.

"Whoa, there," Cal said, snaking a strong arm around her waist and drawing her to his side. "Who put the burr under your saddle?"

"You did."

Cal looked stricken. "What did I do?"

"You stepped through my back door."

Cal looked at her blankly.

"I have a date," she snapped, "and I can't even get ready for you dadburn McKinneys."

Tyler grinned. "Better make your casserole to go, little brother. Dad's chompin' at the bit to head out, too."

"Where are you going?" Cal asked.

"To finish his fight with Cynthia," Tyler said without giving J.T. a chance to answer.

Cal looked thoughtful a moment, then plopped into a chair and began to spoon up a healthy portion of chicken and rice. "Bad move, Dad. I'd advise against it. Let her come crawling back to you."

"Isn't there a song by that title?" Tyler asked, pointing his fork at Cal.

"If there isn't, there should be."

Disgusted by their cheery exchange at his expense, J.T. pushed his chair away from the table with all the force Cynthia had earlier that day. Placing his hands on his lean hips, he regarded his two oldest offspring.

"You know, it's simply amazing that I've managed to get this far in life without the two of you to guide me."

Cal looked at Tyler with raised eyebrows. "Eat faster, bro," he said with a grin.

Meanwhile, back at the ranch...

"How did Pauline take the news about Clark and Lettie Mae?" Cynthia asked Carolyn.

"Not well. It shook her pretty badly to come face-to-face with death that way. You know, when we're young, we think that nothing bad can happen to us. Seeing three people near her age die and a close friend lose everything dear to her went a long way toward making Pauline realize that life is precious, something to be cherished and lived to the fullest. And I think that, for the first time, she realized that youth doesn't necessarily equate with invincibility and began to understand what love—real love—was all about.''

CHAPTER SIX

December 20, 1958

J.T. WAS DUE HOME, and Pauline was too worn-out to be more than marginally nervous about seeing her new husband again. It had been two weeks since the accident and, against everyone's advice—what would people say?—she had visited Lettie Mae in the hospital every day of her stay in Crystal Creek's small medical facility.

All night, every night of the first week, Pauline had sat by Lettie's side, trying to ease Viola's burden, since it was hard for her to sit for long periods since her back surgery.

Pauline was there when Grover Purdy told Lettie Mae that Clark had died, that she'd lost her baby and that she would never be able to have another one. She had witnessed Lettie Mae's cries of despair and all-consuming grief, and watched her slide into a great gulf of depression during the days that followed.

The accident made Pauline excruciatingly aware that something could happen—to her, to her family, to J.T. . . . to the baby she was carrying. When she'd had the bout of spotting in November, she had been more inconvenienced than afraid, more concerned about the possibility that she might lose J.T. than she had been about the possible loss of her child. But she'd felt movement since then—the slightest fluttering of butterfly wings—silent proof of the life growing inside her.

She thought of J.T. going up in an airplane, not just several thousand feet up in the air, but *miles* up in the heavens, and shuddered to think what could happen. But she didn't know how to tell him about her fears. And she wasn't sure he would care how she felt.

WHEN J.T. STEPPED OFF the bus, Pauline was waiting for him. Somehow, he'd expected his parents to be with her. He wasn't sure he was ready to face her alone after almost three months apart. His mouth grew dry. His heart began to pound. He cursed under his breath.

It was ridiculous that a single glimpse of a one-hundred-pound wisp of a girl could turn him into a mountain of misgivings—about who he was and what he wanted. Ridiculous that she could make his heart race by just standing there and looking at him with those big blue eyes...big blue eyes with dark smudges of weariness beneath them. Big blue eyes that held not one smidgen of their usual lively sparkle. Big blue eyes that looked as if they'd come face to face with something too terrible to even think about.

Pauline hadn't written so often lately, and he assumed she had tired of their one-sided correspondence. Maybe, he thought, as he studied her pale face, she was just worn-out from spending so much time at the hospital.

Both Pauline and Emily had written to him about the accident. Pauline had told him about Lettie Mae's loss and how distraught she was. She'd told him that she was worried about Lettie Mae.

Emily had written about Lettie Mae's loss, about Pauline's vigil at her friend's side and how distraught Pauline was. She'd told him she was worried about Pauline and how she feared her daughter-in-law was doing too much "in her condition."

Now, even with the distance of several yards separating him from Pauline, he could see that his mother's concern was valid. His heart thudded with each slow step he took toward her. She stood waiting, unsmiling. Something about the look on her face reminded him of the sadness she'd exuded the night of her graduation, when he'd tried to tell her he wasn't ready for a serious relationship. It was a look of loss, of helplessness.

But J.T. knew all too well that his bride was far from helpless. If she so desired she could turn the tables on him and have him eating out of her hand again. Or, more aptly, devouring the sweetness of her lips again.

Was this a pose? he wondered suddenly. Was this sadness, this air of suffering a new stratagem to bring him to heel? A different ploy? A new ruse in Pauline's nifty bag of tricks? As the old saying went, "Once bitten, twice shy," and he'd been nipped by Pauline several times. He renewed his vow not to let her get to him. His manhood was at stake, for cryin' out loud.

Still, J.T. realized that he missed her saucy smile and the twinkle of devilry in her eyes. Though he chafed under the harness of this unwanted marriage, he felt an almost uncontrollable urge to draw her into his arms and offer what comfort he could.

He stopped a few feet from her and set his duffel bag down on the sidewalk, uncertain under the circumstances how to greet her. Should he be cool, controlled? Should he give her a husbandly peck for the benefit of the people sitting in the café and watching his arrival with avid curiosity?

Opting for the second choice, he leaned over and brushed the softness of her cheek with his lips. The scent of her perfume washed over him, crushing him beneath the wave of a thousand memories...her laughter, her smile, the way her body felt against his...beneath his.

He drew back, and Pauline turned her face so that their lips passed within a quickened breath of each other. The urge to lean forward and taste her mouth lured him like the song of a siren or the inevitable pull of the tide. The very fact that he wanted to kiss her so badly set off a warning alarm in J.T.'s head. He straightened.

"Hi," she said with a small, awkward smile.

Was that disappointment in her eyes? "Hi."

They stood in an uncomfortable silence, unsure what to say or do next. Even though she was wearing a three-quarter-length tweed coat, J.T. could tell her pregnancy was starting to show. Confronted with his past sins, another wave of doubt washed over him.

How was she? Really? Emily seemed concerned about her. Bubba had written that she looked okay, but . . .

"How was the trip home?" she asked, the question derailing his troubled thoughts.

He picked up his duffel bag. "Fine. Crowded. There are a lot of servicemen headed home for the holidays."

"I imagine so." She started walking toward the car, and he had no choice but to follow.

"How've you been?" he asked, looking sideways at her as they passed the pool hall where they'd argued the previous summer.

"Pretty good." She grimaced. "Dr. Purdy thinks I'm doing too much."

"Are you—with your baby and all?"

He wondered at the tightening of her lips. "Maybe. But there's so much to do. I've been trying to help Viola all I can with Lettie Mae. But Reverend Blake finally got a secretary, and that's helped, especially since I've been spending so much time at the hospital."

"How is Lettie Mae?" J.T. asked.

"Physically, she's better. If she keeps improving the way she has been, she should be home by Christmas." She looked at him with those sorrow-filled eyes. "Emotionally, I think it's going to take her a long time to heal. She was crazy in love with Clark."

"She's young and pretty. She'll find someone else in no time."

"I don't think so." Pauline glanced over at him. "You know she lost her baby, too."

J.T. stopped as abruptly as if someone had called a halt. "She was pregnant?"

Pauline nodded. "And she'll never be able to have another baby."

To a guy who didn't want a child to begin with, it didn't sound like such a bad thing.

Pauline walked around the hood of a baby blue 1959 Chevrolet. Long and low-slung, with huge fins, the car had enough chrome to warrant sunglasses if you looked directly at it, and enough glass to discourage parking in all but the most secluded places.

"Nice car," he said, reaching to open the door. "Whose is it?"

"Mine."

"Yours?" he exploded, leaning his forearm on the top of the car. "Who gave it to you?"

Pauline looked at him over the top of the car. "My dad."

"Why didn't you tell me?" J.T. stormed.

Pauline's eyes were a turbulent blue. "Probably because I knew you'd act just like you're acting. Why are you behaving like such an idiot? The car is a wedding present from him and Mom."

J.T.'s finely shaped mouth curled into a snarl. "A wedding present! Sheets are wedding presents. Coffeepots are wedding presents. Not cars." He pointed an accusing finger at her. "Tell the truth, Pauline. You wanted it, and you batted those big blue eyes at him, and he got it for you because he's a sucker who just can't tell you no. Isn't that right?"

Pauline's eyes glittered with fury. "That's right, J.T., honey," she cooed, batting her eyelashes at him furiously. She got in the car and slammed the door so hard the Chevy rocked on its shocks. Immediately, she started the engine, and J.T. had no choice but to climb in beside her. He was barely seated when she put the coupé into gear and pulled out of the parking space. J.T. jerked his foot inside and slammed his own door.

"What the hell do you think you're doing?" he yelled.

She shot him a withering look, but her eyes held a suspicious sheen. "I'm driving us home in the car my daddy bought me because I'm a spoiled brat who manipulates everyone around me so I can have whatever my little heart desires," she rattled.

She compressed her lips and slammed on the brakes at a four-way stop, slinging J.T. forward. With a curse, he stretched out a bracing hand toward the dash. From the corner of his eye, he saw Pauline reach up and wipe at her cheek.

She was crying. Dear Lord, he hadn't been home five minutes and she was already crying. It promised to be a long ten days. He wished he was back at Randolph Air Base and the regimented life he'd resented having to embrace. He was beginning to think that having someone tell you what to do and when to do it made life a lot simpler.

Looking straight ahead, he shot another sidelong glance at Pauline. Silent tears ran unchecked down her cheeks. He supposed he had come down on her a little hard, but dammit, a car was a serious gift, even from family. Would everyone think J.T. McKinney couldn't afford a car for his wife? Didn't she know that men had pride? Didn't she have any idea that she was tromping all over his?

"Look, Paulie," he said, his voice softer. "I guess I shouldn't have yelled. But we don't need your dad to buy you a car. If you need a car... if you want a car, tell me. I'll buy it for you."

"How?" she said with a mighty sniff. "With that piddly check you get from the Air Force every month?"

The sarcastic comment was a direct hit to his ego. He wondered if girls were born with the innate ability to home in on a man's weakest spot, born knowing how to fight dirty.

"The McKinneys may not have as much money as the Randolphs," he informed her icily, "but we can damn well keep our wives in clothes and cars."

"Well, the next time I want anything, I'll just have to remember to bat my eyelashes at you, won't I?" she retorted in a smart tone.

J.T. didn't say anything else, but he gritted his teeth until his jaw knotted. December twenty-ninth couldn't come soon enough.

PAULINE HAD her tears under control by the time they reached the ranch. Calvin and Emily met them at the door, and Pauline prayed they wouldn't notice her smeared mascara. As J.T. was hugged by both of his parents, she couldn't help comparing the warm, loving welcome he received from them with the one she and he had shared, which had been cordial at the very best. She felt her lips tremble. Even that cordiality hadn't lasted any longer than a snowflake in hell.

When she'd met him at the bus stop, she had longed to throw herself into his arms and tell him that she loved him. But pride had kept her glued to the spot. He had to make the first move the next time. She couldn't count the times she'd professed her love to him, but she knew exactly how many times J.T. had told her he loved her: zero.

He'd said he cared for her, that he missed her, that he wanted her, but never that he loved her. Pauline had made a promise to herself that she wouldn't say the words again unless she had some indication that the feeling was reciprocated. It was a promise she intended to keep.

In honor of J.T.'s homecoming, Emily was cooking his favorite meal—fried chicken, mashed potatoes and cream gravy, purple-hull peas and cream-style corn that she'd cut and scraped from the cob herself. In the meantime, she had brewed a fresh pot of coffee and had a batch of warm brownies waiting to "hold him over."

J.T., who was starving for home cooking, tucked into the midafternoon snack with a gusto Pauline envied. Her appetite had been almost nonexistent since the accident.

"Pauline, honey, do you want a brownie?" Emily asked, turning from the coffeepot.

The warmth in her mother-in-law's voice was almost Pauline's undoing. She swallowed hard and blinked harder. "No, thank you. I think I'll go lie down a while."

She barely made it to their room and got the door closed before she burst into tears that she muffled by burying her face in a pillow. What would it take to make J.T. love her? Why couldn't he accept the fact that they were married and going to have a baby, and just pick up and go on with his life the way she was trying to do?

Pauline didn't know how long she cried, but she must have finally dozed. The sound of the door opening roused her. Sleepily, she pushed herself to her elbows as J.T. entered the room.

He stopped dead in his tracks. His eyes made a slow survey of the room that had once been his domain—from the frilly eyelet bedspread she'd bought to the matching priscilla curtains hanging at the window. A pile of stuffed animals sat in the corner next to the baseball bat he'd hit three home runs with in his senior year. An Elvis Presley poster was thumbtacked to the ceiling. A too-tight bra Pauline had taken off earlier was draped over the post of the pineapple bed. A stack of romance comic books rested on the desk next to his football trophy. His jaw dropped. His disbelieving gaze met hers.

"What in the hell have you done to my room?"

The clipped coldness of his voice was enough to make her sit up and swing her feet to the floor. "I just brought some of my things, so I'd feel more at home."

"You've ruined my room."

So, she thought. It was *his* room, and *her* baby. Pauline had had enough. She stood and straightened her shoulders. J.T.'s eyes moved to her stomach. He paled a bit beneath the lingering traces of last summer's tan. Good. She hoped he got puking sick. She had, often enough.

"I haven't ruined your room, J.T. I've just changed *our* room. I live here, too, you know." She raised her left hand and waggled her fingers at him, a false, bright smile curving her mouth. Her diamond blinked in the winter sunshine. "We're married, J.T. Not that that's any big deal."

"Oh, yeah?" he snarled.

She thrust out her chin. "Yeah."

"Well, for your information, there are a lot of girls out there who'd love to change places with you."

"Well, for *your* information, that's only because they don't know what a jerk you are or how lousy you are in bed!" she cried.

As soon as the hurtful words had flown from her lips, Pauline wished she could call them back. They hung in the air between them like some dark miasma. J.T. looked as if she'd struck him, as indeed, she had. Another mighty blow to his ego.

"What's wrong with me in bed?" he demanded, his eyes dark with fury, his mood even darker.

"Nothing," she said, turning away.

He grabbed her by the shoulders and spun her around. She glared up at him; he glared down at her. "Don't turn your back on me. You started this, and you're damn well going to tell me what you mean."

"All right, J.T., but remember—you asked for this." She took a deep breath and plunged. "Nothing happens."

"What do you mean, nothing happens? I thought our sex was pretty darn good."

"For you, maybe."

His smile was grim. "Well, I didn't see you stopping me after that first night, so it must have been all right."

Weary beyond words and knowing that her marriage, her very life, lay on the line, Pauline felt her anger die a sudden death. She knew her accusations hurt, knew she was killing what tiny bit of feeling he might have for her, but she also knew that if she and J.T. stood even a small chance of making it, they needed to be honest with each other.

"I knew the first time wouldn't be very good, but I kept hoping it would get better," she told him. "It didn't." He started to say something, but she held up her hand to silence him. "The kissing and touching is good—it's wonderful—and I thought it would end in something even more wonderful, but it didn't."

His scowl deepened.

"You went off like a Fourth of July firecracker and that was it." She closed her eyes and pasted on her best throes-of-passion face. "'That was great, baby,'" she groaned in her best John Travis McKinney imitation. She opened her candid blue eyes. "But it wasn't great. Not for me. It was more like wham, bam, thank you ma'am. I felt cheated, J.T. I kept thinking there ought to be more, and there's supposed to be, if a woman has a considerate lover."

J.T.'s face was as red as the velvet bow on the wreath of holly Emily had hung on the front door. He reached out and grasped her chin in a rough grip.

"Maybe I need more practice," he said harshly, swooping to take her lips in a bruising kiss that reminded her of Matt Jeffries's hateful attempts at seduction.

For the first time since she'd met him, Pauline couldn't find it in her to respond. She felt like crying. There was no tenderness in J.T.'s kiss, not the tiniest bit of love. It was punishment for what she'd said, pure and simple.

He released her so abruptly that she staggered back and would have fallen if it hadn't been for the edge of the bed. Tears burned beneath her eyelids, but she refused to let them fall. Without thinking, she wiped her lips with the back of her hand.

"You do need practice," she whispered.

"And maybe I ought to ask who you've been practicing with."

Her face paled. It was the second time he'd implied that she'd been with someone else. "What are you talking about?"

"I'm talking about you being such an authority on what makes a good lover. I'm wondering how you became such an expert."

Pauline sank down onto the bed. "I'm going to pretend you didn't say that, but if you must know, I read Alfred Kinsey's *Sexual Behavior in the Human*

Female.'' Her voice trembled and she fought back her tears. She refused to let him see her cry again. ''Why are you treating me this way, J.T.? I'm your wife—remember?''

''It looks like you don't intend to let me forget it.''

She laced her fingers together over her abdomen in a deliberate action that drew attention to her growing belly. ''You're right. I don't. A fool could see that you don't care about me or this baby. All you're worried about is how your life has been ruined. But you're the one who got to run away from it all. You're the one who gets to go off and play soldier and forget I'm even alive for days on end. Well I have news for you. This is as much your mistake as it is mine, and I have no intention of letting you forget.''

So much for Lettie Mae's advice, Pauline thought, on a wave of despair. Instead of not rocking the boat, instead of romance, instead of working out their problems slow and easy, she'd just thrown down the gauntlet.

Rather than pick it up, as she expected, J.T. turned and started back out the door.

Sorrow rose up inside her on black wings of regret. When would she ever learn not to let him goad her? When would she learn to turn the other cheek the way Reverend Blake had admonished the congregation a few weeks ago?

''J.T.?''

He stopped and pivoted toward her, his chin set at his don't-mess-with-me angle, the muscle in his cheek working. Pauline wanted to beg him not to be angry with her. Wanted to tell him she was sorry for saying what she had, sorry for whatever it was that she had done to turn him against her so, but pride forbade her. Instead she did what her mother had told her she would become very good at.

"I want to ask you a favor."

The look in J.T.'s eyes went from anger to wariness. "What kind of favor?"

"I want to call a truce while you're home."

He laughed, but the sound held no humor. "Yeah, kick me in the gut and then call a truce. That's just like a woman."

A sigh escaped her lips. "It's Christmas. It's supposed to be a happy time, not a time for fussing and fighting. I'm sorry for hurting you, but I'm not sorry for telling you."

J.T. scraped a hand through his short hair. "Well, that makes a hell of a lot of sense."

"If you think about it, you'll see that it makes a lot of sense. I'm tired of fighting with you, J.T. Frankly, I just don't have the energy to fight. Don't you think we owe it to our parents to make this Christmas a good one?"

For a moment, he didn't say anything. Then, he gave a grudging nod. "Sure. We'll call a truce. It's Christmas." Turning, he left the room.

Pauline watched him go with a heavy heart. Compromise. It would be interesting to see if it really worked.

PAULINE WAS RIGHT, J.T. thought as he took a staple from his mouth and set it against the treated fence post. All the fight had gone out of her. Him, too, for that matter. They both dragged around the house like strangers. Weary, battle-scarred strangers.

He cocked back the hammer and swung it against the post—once, twice, securing the barbed wire with two angry blows.

He knew his parents had heard his and Pauline's argument three days before, and it was all he could do to look them in the eye. He wasn't sure which was worse: having them know Pauline thought he was lacking as a lover or having them know how bad things were between them. Calvin had tried to talk to him a couple of times, but J.T. always cut him short. He couldn't bring himself to unburden himself about sex to his dad.

He was still steaming over what Pauline had said. *Wham, bam, thank you ma'am,* he mouthed in disgust as he had a thousand times since the argument. A firecracker, huh? Which translated to *pfft...bang,* and it was over. Which meant he had no staying power. Which meant he didn't satisfy his wife. Which meant he was less of a man.

He still wondered if Pauline was telling the truth. Had she gotten so knowledgeable by reading that Kinsey book or by messing around with Matt Jeffries? He'd confront the sorry bum if he was in town, but, like J.T., Matt had gone into the service. The Army. Who knew when he'd be back?

Firecracker. J.T. whacked another staple into the post. Okay, so most of his knowledge was the locker-room variety. He'd joked and bragged along with the best of them, and no one, not even Bubba, had any idea that Pauline was his first.

Wham! Bam! He was supposed to be cool, suave. How could he find out if Pauline was right without blowing his cover? More important, *who* could he ask? Who was understanding, knowledgeable and most important, not a blabbermouth? Too bad he wasn't Catholic; he could talk to the priest.

What about Howard Blake? The thought came from nowhere. Yeah. Reverend Blake was pretty cool. Maybe he could point him in the right direction. He and his wife seemed happy, and the Mrs. was a voluptuous, ripe-looking woman. Ol' Howie had to be doing something right. Surely, he thought, with growing hope, Baptist preachers were like lawyers and priests, sworn to keep the confidence of their flock.

THE DOOR to Howard Blake's office opened. "Come on in, J.T." the minister said with a friendly smile.

J.T. picked up his Stetson from the chair next to him, followed Howard into the office and sat down in the leather chair across the wide expanse of polished mahogany. The desk was piled with various Bible translations, several commentaries and concordances and a picture of the minister's wife and their son.

"I was working on my sermon," he said, rubbing the side of his straight nose with a blunt forefinger.

"I'm sorry I interrupted," J.T. said, half-rising. "I can come back another time."

"Sit down," Howard said, leaning back in his chair and putting his stocking feet on the desktop. "I have plenty of time."

J.T. eased back down, took the brim of his hat between the tips of his fingers and swung it back and forth between his denim-clad knees.

"What can I do for you, J.T.?" the preacher asked in a voice that exuded friendly concern.

What could he say? J.T. wondered. How could he find the words to tell the reverend about him and Pauline?

"Are you and Pauline having problems?"

J.T. looked up sharply. The man must be psychic. He exhaled a harsh breath. "To put it mildly."

"Why didn't she come with you?"

"She doesn't know I'm here."

"I see," Howard said with a slow nod. "Do you want to tell me about it?"

J.T. shrugged. "I don't know where to start."

"How about the beginning?" Howard suggested with a smile.

Over the next hour, J.T. told the pastor about his relationship with Pauline, including her machinations, his addiction to her kisses, her supposed fling in Mexico with Matt and what had happened between them when he'd come home from boot camp. He told Howard how Pauline could wheedle until she got her way. He told the minister about how trapped he felt—

both by his marriage and by his being forced to join the armed forces.

Howard Blake said very little. Mostly he listened. He was a real good listener, J.T. thought, as he finished relating their latest argument, complete with Pauline's accusations.

Drained, relieved, ashamed and embarrassed, J.T. leaned back in his chair with a sigh. "I can't believe I just told you all that."

Reverend Blake smiled his friendly smile. "Feel better?"

"Yeah," J.T. said with a nod. "I do."

"Good. I think it's safe to say that you feel Pauline trapped you into this marriage, yet you said that you'd decided that if she'd 'do it' with Matt, you might as well get yourself what she was willing to give. Don't you think that's wrongly placing the blame on her? Shouldn't you accept at least part of the fault yourself?"

J.T. nodded. "I guess so."

"And now you're wondering how Pauline knows so much about a woman's feelings during intercourse and thinking that maybe the rumors about Matt Jeffries are true?"

"She claims she read that book by that Kinsey guy. *Sexual Something or Other in Women*, but I don't know what to believe."

Howard smiled and reached for a pencil. "*Sexual Behavior in the Human Female.*"

"Yeah, that's it."

"Have you asked her outright about Matt?"

J.T. studied his booted feet, and shook his head.

"Why not?"

He lifted his gaze to the preacher's. "I'm not sure I could stand it if it was true."

"Why is that, do you suppose?" Howard queried in a gentle voice. "Are you jealous?"

"Yeah," J.T. said, with a belligerent lift of his chin. "I guess I am."

"Why are you jealous . . . since you say you don't think you love her? Isn't that a little contradictory?"

"Maybe. Yeah, I guess." J.T. shook his head in confusion. "I don't know. I feel like a rat going round and round in one of those mazes, you know?"

"Maybe you ought to give your feelings for Pauline a little more thought," Howard suggested, rolling the pencil between his palms. "Let's get back to your argument. I guess you were pretty angry over what she said about your skills as a lover."

"Angry, yeah." J.T. met Howard's gaze squarely. "But I think it hurt my pride more than it made me mad."

"I think with a man it amounts to the same thing," Howard said with a grin. "Hurt a man's pride, and he responds in anger. It's the nature of things."

"Was she right? Is a woman supposed to . . ." J.T. shrugged and searched his mind for a word the minister would find acceptable.

"Climax?"

J.T. almost fell out of his chair. "Uh . . . yeah."

"Definitely." Howard smiled. "A lot of women experience multiple climaxes during the course of one session of lovemaking."

"No shit!" J.T. exclaimed. Then, horrified at what he'd said in front of the preacher, he murmured, "I'm sorry, Reverend Blake. I wouldn't offend you for the world."

"No offense taken," Howard said. "What you have to remember, J.T., is that sex is different for a man than it is for a woman. A woman in her underwear, or a swimsuit or a low-cut blouse, can be a strong sexual stimulus for a man. Men, more than women, are more apt to engage in the act without any involvement other than a certain portion of their anatomy.

"Women are different. Good sex to them starts up here." Howard Blake tapped his temple with the point of the pencil. "They like all the steps that lead up to the culminating act as much as they like the act itself. Women like the fondling, the whispers of love, the kissing, just like Pauline told you she did."

J.T. nodded, storing away all he was hearing so he could use it later.

"Another thing to remember is that some women take longer to reach a climax than others. The trick is for the man to be in touch with her feelings and know when she's ready, to learn to hold back and wait for her, if it's necessary. It's a wonderful sensation to reach together. And if you can't possibly hold out, don't just roll over and say good-night. You stay right where you are until you know she's been fulfilled, too."

"What if she...you know—" J.T. colored and shrugged "—goes first?"

Howard shrugged. "No problem. If you're skillful enough, you can bring her to fulfillment again and again."

"How do I do that?"

"Ask her what she likes, what feels good."

"Talk about it?" J.T. asked in surprise.

"Husbands and wives should be able to talk about anything."

"I can't see that ever happening."

"Then it won't. This marriage got off to a bad start. Maybe not a bad start, but a hard one. You and Pauline are both young. Ideally, newlyweds need time to adjust before children come into the picture. But you and Pauline haven't been able to get to know each other as man and wife because you've been away. And when you do come home for good, you'll have a baby. It's not the best of situations, but it can work."

J.T. listened intently to what Howard Blake had to say, but he wasn't convinced.

"You have to decide if you care for Pauline enough to give the marriage your best shot. If you do, then you'll have to work out your problems together—by talking, communicating, sharing your thoughts, your fears, your dreams and your goals. If you decide you don't care for her and that there's no way to work things out..." Howard's voice trailed away and he shrugged his broad shoulders again.

He didn't have to say the word. J.T. knew what he meant. Divorce. But J.T. knew that a divorce would rock the very foundation of the McKinney family.

A knock sounded at the door, and Howard Blake's new secretary told him he had another appointment. J.T. told him he'd taken up enough of his time and rose to leave. He was almost to the door when the minister called him back. He crossed the room, a book in his hand.

"Take this. It might help." He held a copy of *Sexual Behavior in the Human Female.*

Only marginally surprised that the preacher had a copy of the book, J.T. thanked him and drove back home, his mind filled with everything he'd learned . . . about Pauline, their marriage and, especially, himself. Howard Blake had given him a lot of food for thought.

"THAT MUST HAVE BEEN the turning point for them," Cynthia said, lifting her coffee cup to her lips. The dishes were done, Jennifer had been fed, burped, changed and was fast asleep. Cynthia and Carolyn were indulging in just another small piece of pie and a fresh pot of coffee.

"Not really. J.T. said he was really shaken up. He had a lot of soul-searching to do. He told me that he was an expert at fixing fences but that he wasn't sure what to do about the fence between him and Pauline. It was too tall to climb and too tough to tear down."

"What did he do?"

"He held to his part of the truce and watched and waited."

"For what?"

"To see if the changes he saw in Pauline were for real, and whether his feelings for her were more than lust."

"And did he?"

"Of course he did . . . eventually."

J.T.'s STOMACH was tied in knots. He'd made it half-way to town and had a flat tire, which, considering the way his day was going, was about par. He pushed through the doors of Nate Purdy's office just as they were opening up after lunch, and asked if Cynthia had been in.

"She was here, Mr. McKinney, but that was hours ago," the receptionist said. "Is something wrong?"

J.T. tried to smile. "Just a small family emergency. Did she say where she was going?"

"No, but I saw her car in front of the Curl Up and Dye when I went to the Longhorn to get a couple of doughnuts."

"Thanks," J.T. said with a smile. "Appreciate it." He felt his concern ebb and his irritation rise as he left the office. Dammit! Why hadn't she called?

Meanwhile, back at the ranch . . .

"DID THE CHRISTMAS holidays go smoothly?" Cynthia asked Carolyn.

"More or less. They were both treading pretty lightly around each other, until the day Pauline was straightening the angel on the tree and she and J.T. got into another big fight."

CHAPTER SEVEN

December 1958

J.T. SPENT every spare moment reading *Sexual Behavior in the Human Female*. The trick was to read the book Reverend Blake had lent him and not get caught... which was hard, considering he could no longer escape to his room for privacy. Instead, he read in the hayloft, in the bathroom, wherever he could snatch a few minutes of uninterrupted time. An academic work, the book was intriguing, nonetheless. J.T. grudgingly admitted that his knowledge about the sexual behavior of either sex was pretty rudimentary, as was all the other guys' he'd hung out with before getting married.

His relationship with Pauline the next few days was cordial, if a bit strained. They both worked hard at being civil, at compromising. When they were in the same room with his parents, J.T. felt as if the older couple regarded him and Pauline the same way they would a couple of carnival freaks: with a little wariness, and a lot of skepticism.

He had to admit, though, that his parents seemed to have taken to Pauline like pretzels to beer. And he had to admit that she seemed genuinely fond of her in-laws. She was helpful and polite. She pitched in with the housework and the cooking, doing whatever Emily asked with no questions, no complaints.

The problem was that, as hard as she tried, she couldn't cook. Everything she touched was either scorched, hard as a brickbat or so salty that a few forkfuls were guaranteed to raise a body's blood pressure. Like everyone else, J.T. attempted valiantly to eat her offerings—at least she was trying—but he felt like telling her to throw in the towel—the kitchen towel, along with her spatula.

The day after he got home, he, Pauline and his parents went to the new house, which would be ready for occupation soon after the first of the year. J.T. found to his surprise that he liked the ideas Pauline had incorporated into the existing plans.

The following day, he observed as, under Emily's tutelage, Pauline painted cookie tins and decorated them with ribbon and pine cones and chinaberries and roadside grasses she coated with silver and gold paint. He watched as she fitted the tins with cupcake papers and filled them with a variety of cookies she'd baked by the dozens—gifts for their friends—that she tagged "Merry Christmas from J.T. and Pauline." Strangely, though she couldn't cook, she had a knack for baking. Even more strange was his pride in her endeavors when they delivered the goodies to their friends.

When J.T. commented to his mother about how good the peanut butter cookies were, she gave him a pointed glance and told him to tell Pauline. Blushing like a seventh-grader, he had, and had been rewarded with a smile that bordered on brilliant. The tight band squeezing his heart eased the slightest bit.

He went with her to the hospital to visit Lettie Mae. The young woman was improving, but there was a soul-deep sorrow in her eyes that J.T. knew intuitively would be there for a long time to come. It would be in her heart even longer.

He watched Pauline fuss over her friend and knew, without a doubt, that in spite of what the townsfolk might say, friendship knew no color in Pauline's mind. It gave him a warm feeling of satisfaction to know that she was strong enough to stand by Lettie Mae, even in the face of disapproval.

Nights were the toughest. He was used to sleeping in a single bed, alone. The instant he felt Pauline's slight weight on the mattress next to him, he was awash in the clean scent of her soap and a tide of torturous memories.

Invariably, sleep was a long time coming, and as often as not, he awakened at some time during the night to find her snuggled close to him, as if she—or maybe he—sought the warmth and closeness in sleep they wouldn't allow themselves to seek during the bright light of day. He longed to draw her closer, ached to kiss her awake, hungered for something he couldn't put into words, something he was almost afraid to think.

But instead of acting on those wants, he always rolled over and willed the throbbing in his groin to go away. Pauline had made it very clear that she didn't want him. He supposed he could demand his conjugal rights, but the very thought was repulsive. So he gritted his teeth and counted sheep. He considered the nighttime hours as exercises in self-control.

J.T.'s grandfather was coming from Pearsall for the holidays and was due to arrive the day before Christmas Eve, which was also Hank's sixty-fifth birthday. Hank Travis always groused about his birthday, saying he got cheated on gifts because he was born so close to the holiday. Of course, there wasn't a lot Hank didn't grouse about, J.T. often thought, even though he dearly loved the crotchety old scoundrel.

Pauline had volunteered to bake Hank's birthday cake. Knowing he liked chocolate on yellow, she proceeded to make the cake from scratch the day Hank was due to arrive.

J.T., who pretended to be doing the daily crossword puzzle in the *Crystal Creek Record Chronicle,* was actually watching his wife perform yet another feat of domesticity. Still somewhat wary, he wondered if this new facet of her personality was put on.

Even as he thought the uncharitable thought, the tip of her tongue came out as she struggled to make the bag of frosting she was wielding do her bidding. J.T. wasn't aware of the grin that claimed his lips.

She looked adorable with one of his mother's aprons tied over her maternity smock, a smear of chocolate icing on her cheek. He wondered what she would do if he went around the table and took her in his arms and licked away the frosting. That would lead to kissing, and kissing would lead to...

"Damn!" he muttered.

She glanced over at him. "What?"

"Nothing," he lied. "I can't figure out this word."

He eyed her creation, the rich chocolate frosting, the pink roses, the swags of white and the message "Happy Birthday, Grandpa Hank." It looked pretty good to him. Pretty darn professional. "The cake looks nice."

She glanced up sharply, as if the comment took her off guard. A soft rose bloomed in her cheeks. "Thank you."

Feeling that familiar awkwardness settle over them, J.T. folded the paper and put it aside. "I'm getting a headache," he fabricated. "I think I'm going to go lie down a while before we drive in to the furniture store."

All the parents and grandparents on both sides of the family were giving them money for Christmas to be used to buy furniture for their new house. Though he was dreading the trip, which sounded like just barrels of fun, J.T. knew it was one he'd have to make.

"There's aspirin in the medicine cabinet," Pauline said, licking some icing from her finger.

"Thanks," J.T. said. What he was really going to do was finish the Kinsey book. "See you later."

"Uh-huh," she replied, engrossed in her task.

An hour later, J.T. thoughtfully closed the book and slid it back beneath the bed, where it lay hidden beneath some copies of *National Geographic*. He'd take it back to Reverend Blake as soon as he could. He'd learned a thing or two, and that was a fact. The problem was, he wasn't sure he'd ever get up enough nerve to try out his newfound knowledge on his wife. He wasn't sure he could take the possible rejection.

As soon as the lunch dishes were cleared away, J.T. and Pauline drove to Harmon's Furniture Store. J.T. hadn't given much thought to decorating a house, but discovered over the next hour and a half that he did have definite likes and dislikes. He and Pauline discussed their purchases—weighing color and style against their preferences and their pocketbook—like adults. Not once did their differences of opinion flare into an argument.

Actually, their tastes were very compatible. J.T. only complained when Pauline tried to get too "frilly." They left the store with the assurance that the furniture would be delivered as soon as the house was ready, filled with a sense of accomplishment . . . of being very grown-up. Both were proud that they'd managed to spend a couple of hours together without resorting to barbed comments or dirty digs. J.T. attributed it to the control he had learned in the Air Force; Pauline gave credit to that wonderful new trick . . . compromise. They both felt very married.

"How about a piece of pie over at the café?" he asked as they headed for the truck. J.T. refused to let Pauline squire him around in her new car.

She looked a bit surprised, but nodded. "That sounds nice. Thanks for asking."

MacBride's Café was full of midafternoon shoppers who were taking time out for a little rest and refueling. Christmas might take its toll on the patrons who were busily shopping for just the right present, but Fanny MacBride would reap the benefits. They took the only available booth, near the front door, and ordered pie and Cokes. They had just been served when the door opened and in walked Dottie Little and Matt Jeffries.

Dottie's face was red-cheeked; Matt, who looked striking in his Army uniform, tried to look suave as he surveyed the crowded room. Pauline had only seen him a couple of times, from a distance, since the summer fiasco.

Her first thought was to wonder what on earth Dottie Little was doing with Matt? Had she and Duff broken up again? It wasn't that Pauline didn't like Dottie. She did. Or at least she always had until the younger girl had moved in on J.T.

Dottie slipped off her coat and draped it over her arm. She looked cute in a straight skirt that fit smoothly over her shapely derriere and a matching Ban-Lon cardigan that was buttoned down the back and showed off her magnificent breasts. The crocheted angora lace collar she wore with the sweater was closed with a pearl button. It added a touch of femininity...not that Dottie needed that. Pauline felt fat and frumpy, a little jealous and more than a little threatened, feelings she didn't like at all.

"There's your old buddy, Matt," J.T. said with a tight smile. "I didn't know he was coming home for Christmas."

"Neither did I," Pauline said. "I see he's with your friend, Dottie."

"Yeah, Dottie looks great, doesn't she?"

"Very nice," Pauline said in a prim tone. An idea hit her with the suddenness of a lightning bolt. "There aren't any seats left. Why don't we ask them to join us?"

It wasn't that she was anxious to spend any time with Matt, but it would be a chance to squelch any ideas Dottie might have about J.T. once and for all. And since Matt was such a good-looking guy, maybe she could stir up a spark of jealousy in her indifferent husband while she was at it.

"Are you crazy?" J.T. snapped.

But it was too late for him to do anything but make a verbal objection. Pauline was already waving. "Hi, Dottie!" The couple turned. Pauline motioned them over. "The place is packed. Why don't you sit with us?"

Matt shot a glance at J.T., who was glowering at his wife. The expression he bestowed on Matt wasn't much better. Looking uncomfortable, Dottie cast her date a questioning glance.

"Sure," Matt said with an agreeable smile. "Why not?"

Pauline got up and moved next to J.T., so that the newcomers could have the other side of the booth.

"Hello, Matt...Dottie," J.T. said. Pauline couldn't help noticing that his expression softened when he spoke to the voluptuous Dottie.

"Hi," she said with a subdued smile.

"How have you been, Dottie?" Pauline asked. "I swear, I've been so busy at home, I've lost track of what's going on in town." Without giving Dottie time to answer, she turned to Matt. "How's the Army? And what happened to your forehead, for goodness' sake?"

She was referring to the angry red scar that bisected Matt's forehead and disappeared into his thick, blond hair. The question was enough to set Matt off. He talked nonstop about a Jeep accident he'd been in during his basic training. He'd gone through the windshield and severed an artery in his head.

As Matt rattled on about the accident, Pauline shot J.T. a surreptitious glance to see if her ploy was working. That muscle was knotted in his jaw, and his chin was set at a "watch-out" angle. Pauline frowned. She'd wanted to make J.T. jealous, but he was downright furious. She knew there had been a certain amount of competition between him and Matt in school, but she'd never thought it was more than surface deep.

"Anyway," Matt was saying, "by the time they got me to the infirmary, they decided I needed a pint of blood."

"Did they have any trouble locating it?" Dottie asked, a concerned look on her pretty face.

"Naw."

Beside her, Pauline heard J.T. mutter something that sounded like "Too bad."

Now that Matt's story was winding down, J.T. gave Dottie his full attention. "How's school?"

"Fine," she said with another hesitant smile. "How's the Air Force?"

"Different. I finish my officer's training soon, and then I'll start my pilot's training there at Randolph."

Pauline didn't like the way they were shutting her and Matt out of the conversation. She looped her arm through J.T.'s and leaned toward him, aware that her breast was pressed against his arm. She sighed, deeply, deliberately.

"I hope he gets to come home for the baby." She lifted her limpid gaze to his. "Do you think you will, honey?"

Annoyance flickered in J.T.'s eyes. "It's hard to say."

Knowing she was playing with fire, she offered him a seductive flutter of her eyelashes and turned her innocent gaze to Dottie . . . just to remind her of the situation. "I swear, sometimes I think I can't stand it until he gets home. It gets so lonesome being by myself, especially us being newlyweds. Why, when we get into our new house and his parents aren't around, I'll probably die of loneliness."

The look in J.T.'s eyes said he was more likely to murder her.

"You're getting a new house?" Matt asked.

Pauline offered him a flirtatious smile. "Uh-huh. We move in right after the first of the year. You'll have to come over and see it when we get settled."

Matt shot J.T. a challenging look and trailed his foot up Pauline's leg beneath the table. She jerked it away and glared at him. Matt didn't seem to care. "Doesn't J.T. mind if you entertain strange men while he's away?"

"I—" she began, but J.T. interrupted.

"I hardly ever think of you as strange, Matt," J.T. said, lifting his Coke glass in studied nonchalance. "A little arrogant, maybe, something of an SOB, but not strange."

Matt's smile faded. Panic assaulted Pauline. If looks could kill, she'd be a widow about now. Oh, Lord, this was getting out of hand. Why was it that all her plans went awry?

J.T. glanced at his watch. "Damn! Look how late it's getting. We've gotta run."

He reached into his pocket and put a couple of crumpled bills on the table to cover the cost of the pie and Cokes. Then he scooted over, literally pushing Pauline off the red vinyl seat. "My grandfather is coming in for Christmas." The explanation was directed to Dottie.

"I understand," she said as J.T. rose and put his arm around Pauline. "It was good seeing you, J.T."

"You, too, Dottie. Always."

He made no parting comment to Matt. Before Pauline had a chance to voice her own goodbyes, J.T. pulled open the door and ushered her out into the damp, cold day.

J.T. SEETHED all the way home, but he didn't say anything. *Control,* he reminded himself. *It's Christmas. Stay cool. But dammit! How dare Pauline pull such a stunt?* He knew she was trying to let Dottie know he was unavailable—as if Dottie cared. Even though they argued a lot, Dottie only had eyes for

Duff Jones. J.T. also realized that Pauline's actions were nothing but an effort to make him jealous, and she'd certainly succeeded. But why had she chosen Matt Jeffries to do it with? Was she trying to drive him completely out of his mind?

He ground his teeth in frustration. He wanted to shake her until her teeth rattled; he wanted to turn her over his knee and whale the daylights out of her, something Steven Randolph should have done more often during her formative years. He wanted to have it out with her and demand to know what the hell had happened between her and Jeffries in Mexico.

But he didn't do any of those things. It was Christmas. His grandfather would be there in a couple of hours. He and Pauline had a truce, and darn it, he wouldn't be the one to break it.

He heard her sniff. His anger faltered beneath the weight of the knowledge that he'd made her cry... again. How, he wondered with a pang of dismay, had the day—which had been so great just an hour before—turned so sour? He hardened his heart at the memory of her actions at the café. There was no way he'd let her weasel her way out of this one with a few well-timed tears.

When they reached the ranch, Pauline mumbled something about having gifts to wrap and escaped into the house. J.T. followed, going to their room, where he pulled his shirt from his jeans, collapsed onto the bed and covered his eyes with his forearm. What was going to happen to them? he wondered bleakly.

J.T. AWAKENED a couple of hours later and was surprised to see that dusk had homesteaded the room while he slept. His grandfather, who was supposed to arrive in time for dinner, should be there any minute.

He turned on the bedside lamp and started for the kitchen. As he passed the living room, he saw that the Christmas tree lights were on. The sight brought back a hundred memories. Hoping that a moment spent in remembrances by the tree would cheer him up, he stepped through the arched doorway.

The room was dark except for the glow of the multicolored lights draped over the branches of the fragrant cedar tree. Their reflection shimmered on the strands of tinsel that dripped in silver splendor from every branch and danced on the surface of the Christmas balls that hung in well executed abandon.

J.T. neared the tree, his stocking feet making no noise on the floral-patterned rug. Like a child, he marveled at the array of colorful packages spread beneath the tree.

Christmas was just two days away, and he still hadn't bought anything for Pauline. He didn't know what to buy her. As far as he could tell, she had everything a girl could want . . . including a new Chevy.

A movement from the far side of the tree caught his attention. He inched to the left and saw that Pauline was standing tiptoe on a kitchen chair, her arms stretched high above her as she struggled to straighten the angel perched precariously on the top branches. As he watched, she tottered, but caught her balance.

Fear that she might fall and do something to herself or the baby gripped him by the throat. "What the hell do you think you're doing?" he snapped.

With a sharp gasp of surprise, she turned so fast that she lost her balance again. For a couple of seconds, she swayed like a sailor riding the deck of a storm-tossed frigate, before she lurched forward with a high-pitched shriek.

J.T. was there in two running steps, reaching out to break her fall. As small as she was, her weight and his momentum sent him sprawling to the floor, where they landed in a tangle of arms and legs, Pauline draped on top of him.

Her hair lay across his face like a fragrant, golden cloud. Her breasts and her hard little tummy pressed against him. One thigh rode between his denim-clad legs. Every molecule of J.T.'s body was instantly aware that it had been a long time since he'd made love with her. The familiar stirring of desire left him feeling breathless, nervous and irritated.

Breathing heavily, Pauline raised her head and looked down at him. She might have been lying in the path of a prism that split the light into rainbow colors. Her face, wide-eyed and wary, was dappled in a soft red and yellow glow. Green and blue light shimmered in her hair.

Her tongue peeked from between her lips, wetting them in a gesture that sent J.T.'s pulse racing. His memories of her tongue invading his mouth were vivid, erotic. The recollection of the way her lips, all warm and pliant, had parted beneath his, sent the blood surging through his veins. Need, hot and heavy, settled between his thighs.

She knew. He could see it in the way her eyes widened the slightest bit, could tell by the way her breath hung in her throat. How could she not know, since the telltale portion of his body was pressed so intimately against hers? J.T. didn't know what to say. He was afraid to move.

"You scared me," she said, her voice the merest wisp of sound.

"You scared me," he retaliated. "What were you doing?"

"Straightening the angel."

"That's why women get married."

Unable to follow his train of thought, she frowned.

"Women get married so they'll have someone to take out the trash, bring in the newspaper and straighten angels," he told her, in an attempt to lighten the moment.

"Oh. I thought it was for this." Without warning, she reached down and pressed her palm against the bulge in his jeans, even as she dipped her head and took his lips in a brief kiss. J.T.'s libido shifted into overdrive. She didn't caress him. Instead, her hand just lay there in a possessive way, almost as though she were staking her claim. It was agony of the most pleasurable kind.

Taken at face value, it wasn't much of a kiss, nothing more than a soft, lingering touch of her mouth to his. It was the execution that threatened to knock off his socks. How she put so much into that brief kiss would always remain a miracle. Pauline rotated her partially open mouth against his for the span of a heartbeat while the tip of her tongue teased the crease of his lips. He lay quiescent and unmoving beneath her.

"You want me," she whispered with pleased surprise.

She was so close their breaths tangled. Under the circumstances, it was a statement he couldn't refute with any conviction. Smiling a smile as old as Eve, she ran her hand down the fly of his jeans. J.T. thought he might very well go slowly insane with wanting. Her eyes drifted shut, and she caught her bottom lip between her teeth.

He held his breath. Everything in him told him to stop her while he still could, stop her before he was sorry, but dear God, it felt so good.

"I like touching you," she whispered, opening her eyes to seductive slits. "Do you like it?"

Did he like it? Now that was a stupid question. And was he hearing right? Was she actually *talking* about this, like the Reverend Blake suggested?

"Touch me, J.T. I like for you to touch me."

J.T. lifted his hand and started to do just that when Pauline giggled softly. The sound of her laughter resurrected all his fears of not being able to please her. Grabbing her shoulders, he rolled her over until she was pinned beneath him.

"That's right, Pauline," he snapped. "Laugh. This is all just a big game to you, isn't it?"

Shock molded her pretty features. She grabbed a handful of his shirt. "No! J.T., I was laughing because—"

"Spare me!" he said, halting whatever denial she was about to make. "All you want to do is see if you can bring J.T. to heel, but I'm not going to let you make a fool out of me again."

Her eyes were awash in tears that glittered like the lights of the Christmas tree. "Why do you always think the worst of me?"

Without answering, J.T. levered himself up. He leaned back against the sofa, his legs drawn up, his forearm resting across his knees. He rested his chin on his arm and gave her a direct look. "Tell me why I shouldn't."

Pauline sat up on her heels and pushed her heavy blond hair away from her face. "Because I'm your wife. Because I've never lied to you. I may not be an angel, but I think I'm paying for my mistakes. If I'm guilty of anything, maybe it's being too honest."

"You tricked me into marrying you."

Her eyes registered her surprise. "Are we back to that? How do you figure I tricked you? By going all the way? By finally giving you what you'd made it abundantly clear that you wanted from me from the first time we went out, something you tried to get every time we went out? That's trickery?"

J.T. rose from the floor and seated himself on the edge of the sofa. "If it wasn't a trick to get me back, why did you finally decide to go all the way after we'd broken up?"

Pauline got to her feet. For the first time, she looked clumsy. "I've told you my reasons before, but you don't listen, J.T." she said, looking down at him with an expression that was a mixture of exasperation and weariness. "I did what I did because I loved you, and I was foolish enough to think that if I gave you what you wanted, I wouldn't lose you. Getting pregnant never entered my mind except in an abstract sort of way. I was silly enough to think that sort of thing only happens to other people."

J.T. recalled thinking the same thing himself back when he and Pauline were making out almost every night.

"And I assure you," she went on, "that I didn't set out to get pregnant on purpose." She sighed, and he could almost feel the irritation draining from her. "There's nothing so sneaky or so wrong in what I did, is there?"

J.T. didn't reply.

"Maybe I should ask about *your* motives. Why did you ask me out again after you were so dead set on breaking up with me?" She leveled a direct gaze at him. "And don't pretend it had anything to do with absence making the heart grow fonder."

The growing anger he heard in her voice and the fact that she'd turned the tables on him, were the last straws in a pile of feelings of hurt and anger that had been gnawing at him since Bubba had told him her and Matt. His control, the control he'd learned in the Air Force, the control he was so proud of, snapped. All the poison he'd kept bottled up for so long erupted in one cold, vituperative statement.

"I guess I figured that if you gave it to Matt in Mexico, I might as well get in line."

Even in the frail light of the room, J.T. could see the color drain from her face.

She approached him like a sleepwalker. "What are you saying?"

"You know what I'm talking about. Like you said, we've already gone over this once, so why act so surprised now? I'm talking about the fact that everyone in Crystal Creek knows that you and Matt had a fling in Mexico."

If possible, Pauline grew paler. "Who told you that?"

"Bubba. Matt told him."

"Well, it's a lie," she said, her eyes brimming with sudden tears.

"Yeah? Well, look at it from my perspective. How do I know this baby isn't Matt's? How can I be sure you didn't do what you did so you could palm off his kid on me?"

She moved so fast he never saw it coming, but he felt the pain as her palm contacted with his cheek in a sharp, stinging blow. His head whipped to one side, and he literally saw stars. Before he could regroup, she'd attacked in earnest, shoving him back onto the couch and planting her knees in his middle, raining a series of blows to his face and shoulders. J.T. was so astounded by her behavior that all he could do was hold up his forearms and try to deflect the wild flailing of her fists.

"Ouch! Dammit, Pauline, I—"

"You sorry, stinking bastard!" she cried, tears streaming down her cheeks. "Were you so dumb you couldn't tell you were the first? How could you think such a thing!"

A chance swing broke through his defenses and hit his lip. The sudden taste of blood was sharp and metallic. J.T. grabbed her wrists—no easy task—and tried to hold her still.

"Stop it, Paulie!" he commanded. "Stop it right now."

She stilled suddenly. A harsh sob ripped its way up from her throat. "How could you?" she asked again.

The question, whispered in a torment that was more convincing than words could ever be, sent a shaft of contrition straight through J.T.'s heart. He had no idea what it was that she'd owned up to that night at Bubba's when he'd thought they were talking about Matt; all he knew was that, at this moment, he believed in her innocence. Remorse, guilt and shame coursed through him, each vying for control of his emotions.

Without thinking of her reaction or the consequences, he let go of her wrist and slid his hand around the back of her neck. Wanting to ease the pain in her eyes, needing to assuage the hurt in his heart, he drew her head toward him at the same time he raised himself on one elbow to meet her halfway.

Like a high-strung filly, Pauline tossed her head and tried to pull away. "No!"

"Yes." Soft insistence laced his voice. He released her other wrist and slid his hand up under her skirt along her thigh. Just before their mouths met, she gave a sob, whether of acquiescence or helplessness, he couldn't be sure.

Her mouth tasted as sweet, as intoxicating as it always had. He couldn't get enough, he thought, as he kissed her again and again. He would never get enough.

He felt Pauline relax against him, knew she was starting to feel the magic. His hands went beneath her smock to her breasts, fuller—much fuller—from the pregnancy. Pauline gave a little moaning sigh. He was reaching behind her to unhook her bra when the doorbell rang, shattering the stillness and the mood.

They both froze. For a moment, they just looked at each other, and then the excited voice of Emily McKinney called, "I'll get it, honey! It's probably Dad!"

J.T. knew that to get to the front door, his mother would pass right by the archway that led from the living room. He looked at Pauline. Without a word, she jumped up from the sofa. J.T sat up and smoothed back his hair in an old familiar way before he remembered that he didn't have much hair to smooth anymore.

As Emily passed the living room, she glanced over and saw them sitting side by side on the sofa, like statues. She smiled uneasily.

The next few minutes passed in a blur. Hank came in grousing about the traffic, Emily told him to calm down, and kissed his cheek. Calvin helped Hank carry in the gifts he brought. It was at least fifteen minutes before Emily lured everyone to the kitchen for a dinner of home-made vegetable soup and roast beef sandwiches. J.T. said he wasn't hungry. He had plenty of food for thought that needed digesting. The family left him and Pauline alone in the living room.

Pauline seemed anxious to escape. She started toward the door, stopped and turned, framed in the aperture. "By the way, J.T. I wasn't laughing at you a while ago. The baby moved. I laughed because it's a relatively new experience and it gives me a strange feeling, like there's a butterfly inside trying to get out, or like he's trying to get me to pay attention or something."

There was a softness to her features as she tried to explain a feeling he could never experience, a sort of smugness in her eyes that J.T. found irresistible. He started to ask her why she'd called the baby a "he," but she turned away and left before he could. Feeling like an outsider, and ashamed for all he had put her through, he watched her go.

"WOW," CYNTHIA BREATHED. "They really had a rough time, didn't they? Instead of getting better, things just got worse."

"I'd say so."

"Did she ever explain to J.T. what she meant when he thought she was talking about Matt?"

"Not until after Tyler was born."

"I wonder why J.T. never told me any of this?"

Carolyn smiled. "You said it yourself. Most women don't like hearing about first wives. J.T. probably didn't want you to think he was still carrying a torch for Pauline."

"Probably," Cynthia agreed. "You know, as I listen to you, I can see them growing up, changing, trying to do what they thought was right with their immaturity and limited experience."

Carolyn nodded. "It was a much more innocent time back then. Talking about sex wasn't as common as it is now. Getting pregnant outside of marriage was still a big deal. There wasn't that much open communication between men and women."

"I'm not sure that's changed much, even now," Cynthia said with a wry twist of her lips.

"Sometimes I'd be inclined to agree." Carolyn looked thoughtful. "I think men were a different breed back then. Men who were brought up to be a man's man had little or no experience with dealing with a woman's ways. It's no wonder Pauline had J.T. tied in knots."

J.T.'S STOMACH was tied in knots. Where the hell was Cynthia, anyway? He pushed through the door of the beauty shop, and the buzz of conversation came to a sudden halt. Every eye turned toward him. Stetson in hand, he shifted from one booted foot to the other.

"Hi, Suzi. Have you seen Cynthia?"

"Yeah. She was in earlier for a haircut."

J.T. sighed. "Did she say where she was going?"

Suzi shook her head, and an older woman who was getting a manicure looked up. "I saw her car at the Longhorn."

"Are you sure?"

The woman raised pencil-thin eyebrows. "Of course, I'm sure. How many people in Crystal Creek drive a Lexus, Mr. McKinney...hmm?"

Meanwhile, back at the ranch...

"PAULINE *WAS* A GOOD person, wasn't she?" Cynthia asked, and as she admitted it, she realized that the knowledge brought no accompanying jealousy.

Carolyn smiled. "She was the best. Of course it took until I was grown for me to realize it. Do you want to know what he got her for Christmas?"

"I'm almost afraid to ask."

Carolyn's eyes sparkled with good humor. "A cookbook."

Cynthia's mouth fell open. "No!"

"I swear. He got her a Betty Crocker cookbook, an apron and a timer so she wouldn't overcook things."

"I'd have killed him."

"Pauline was furious. Actually, I think she was hurt because it was such an impersonal gift, not to mention that it was a slap in the face because she couldn't cook."

"What did she give him?"

"A beautiful sweater she knitted all by herself and some tiger-eye cuff links."

"She could knit?"

"We both could knit. Back then, it was still the thing for mothers to pass on those skills to their daughters. I was always the cook, but Pauline was the seamstress." Carolyn's smile was self-deprecating. "I was a mediocre knitter at best, but Pauline was good at it. She was excellent."

Cynthia listened to Carolyn's praise of her sister, and for the first time she was able to accept Pauline's virtues without suffering any feelings of inferiority.

"What happened to Matt?"

"He moved away after he got out of the army," Carolyn said. "Dottie and Duff got married, bought McBride's, and renamed it the Longhorn."

"Did this confrontation about Matt put an end to J.T. and Pauline's quarreling?" Cynthia asked.

"Oh, no. Fate wasn't finished with them yet. J.T. had a whole new range of emotions to go through."

"Tell me," Cynthia said, leaning forward eagerly.

"He left on the twenty-ninth just like he planned, and things rocked on as they had been, with the exception that he returned her calls and wrote more often.

"Pauline had some contractions and some more spotting around her birthday in February and had to spend more time in bed. She moved into the new house about the middle of January.

"Mama was worried about Pauline being there alone, and she didn't think she should be doing the housework since she seemed prone to miscarry, so she sent Virginia over to stay with Pauline's and do the housework."

"Virginia Parks?"

"Yes," Carolyn said with a nod. "Pauline just took it easy, tried to fix things up and wrote a lot of poetry. She told me once that looking back on that time, she felt as if she was in limbo, just waiting."

CHAPTER EIGHT

February – April 1959

JUST A WEEK before Pauline's birthday and just ten days before she was sent to bed for more cramps and spotting, Texas and the whole country were stunned by the plane crash near Mason City, Iowa that took the lives of Buddy Holly, Richie Valens and the Big Bopper. The young people of Crystal Creek were horrified. It was unbelievable, they murmured. Tragic. They were all so young.

The news chilled Pauline's heart and reminded her of the car accident that had taken the lives of Lettie Mae's Clark and their baby. It reminded her once more that something could happen to J.T. when he was flying in those Air Force planes.

Despite the bad news, there were good signs as February advanced—warmer days and crocuses and daffodils springing up overnight in greening yards. Near the middle of the month, Mattel introduced a new doll, a flaxen-haired siren with blood-red nails and a ponytail, who wore a striped swimsuit and high heels. Pauline promptly bought Virginia's daughter, Belle, a Barbie and set about making her a whole wardrobe of clothes from Deborah's sewing scraps.

The task kept her mind off the plane crash and the fact that J.T. was going up with an instructor in the big planes now.

Like the spring and the new life unfolding throughout the Hill Country, the life inside Pauline grew. It seemed that every day brought a new experience, a new dimension to the drama that was her life: terrible cases of heartburn, which Emily laughingly attributed to the baby's hair growing; the baby stretching inside her until she felt that its feet were somewhere in her throat. It had hiccups, Dr. Purdy said, a condition that was normal in unborn babies.

Pauline wished J.T. was there to share some of those moments with her, wished that the pregnancy was over and her life could get back to normal...whatever that might be.

By March the bluebonnets and Indian paintbrush started making their annual appearance along roadsides and in fields. The hope spring carried on its soft breezes put Pauline in a dreamy, reflective mood. While Patty and Lola experimented with the newest campus rage—telephone-booth stuffing—and tried white lipstick, Pauline stayed up late, listening to her favorite songs, writing love letters to J.T. that she never mailed and filling a loose-leaf notebook with free verse poetry about her love for J.T., the hopelessness of her feelings and the despair that hopelessness engendered.

And as she set the perfect, tiny stitches in the perfect, tiny clothes she created for Belle's new Barbie doll, she fantasized about a daughter of her own. Unlike Belle, who was sturdy, plump and blond-haired, the daughter Pauline and J.T. had created would be slim, with dark eyes and dark hair like J.T.'s. She would name her Lynnette, and call her Lynn. Lynn McKinney would be mannerly like her mama, and fiercely proud and determined like her daddy. It went without saying that she would be beautiful, the apple of her daddy's eye.

April seventh was a day that would live forever in Pauline's mind. She was awakened by cramps that got worse throughout the day, making her tense and nervous, fearful that the spotting was going to start again. She considered the possibility that she was in labor, but her mother had said her back would hurt, and hers didn't.

The day went steadily downhill. She cooked purple-hull peas from her mother's freezer for lunch, and made them way too salty, as usual. Hungry for fudge, she whipped up a batch and beat it for a full thirty minutes, to no avail. Clearly, it wasn't going to get hard. Disgusted, she and Belle ate the gooey confection with spoons from the pan until they both felt queasy from too much sugar.

Deciding that the best thing she could do was as little as possible for the remainder of the day, Pauline went out on the porch to watch Belle play with her Barbie. Pauline was sipping a cool drink when she heard the ringing of the phone.

In a few seconds, Virginia pushed open the screen door. A strained look marred her pleasant features. "It's for you, Pauline."

Pauline lowered her feet from the footstool. "Who is it?"

Virginia couldn't quite meet Pauline's eyes. "Someone from Randolph Air Force base. Something about J.T."

Fear tripped down Pauline's spine, leaving her feeling chilled to the marrow. Memories of the deaths resulting from Lettie Mae's accident and from the February plane crash that had taken three vital young lives rose from the dark corner of her mind, where she'd tried so hard to banish them.

Feeling as if she were a hundred, and the bulk of her pregnancy weighed at least a thousand pounds, she pushed herself up from the rocker and made her slow and clumsy way into the house. *Please, God, don't let anything have happened to him.*

The receiver lay on the end table. Pauline reached out an unsteady hand, but drew it back at the feel of the cold, hard plastic. Then, swallowing her trepidation, she grasped the receiver tightly and raised it to her ear.

"Hello." Her voice sounded small and insignificant.

"Mrs. McKinney?"

"Yes."

"This is Lieutenant Colonel James Marston. I'm your husband's commanding officer at Randolph."

"Is something wrong with J.T.?" she blurted, having no patience for the niceties and formalities, when all she wanted to know was the bottom line: was J.T. all right, or wasn't he?

"There was an accident this morning, while he was out with his instructor."

An accident! Pauline's mind screamed. Planes didn't have accidents. They crashed. Before Lieutenant Colonel Marston could tell her more, her stomach gave a sickening lurch and blackness rose up in front of her with the suddenness of night descending on the desert. Her head drooped to the side, her knees buckled, and the telephone receiver slipped from her numb fingers and clattered to the floor.

PAIN TORE AT PAULINE with careless claws. She drew up her knees and groaned in agony. Voices whispered somewhere nearby. It was as much the sound of the voices, the sound of her own voice as it was the pain that awakened her. She opened her eyes slowly and grabbed her abdomen with both hands. It was as hard as a rock. Even while she tried to compare this pain to the cramping that had accompanied her spotting, the torment passed. She realized that she was stretched out on the sofa, barefoot. Someone had put a pillow beneath her head.

"Are you okay?"

The voice was her mother's. Pauline raised herself to her elbows and saw that Deborah was sitting in the wing-back chair on the other side of the coffee table, a cup of coffee in her hand, watching her with a frightening intensity. Emily stood nearby, her fingers knit together. She heard Virginia's voice in the kitchen.

"What are you doing here?" Pauline asked, relaxing against the pillow.

Deborah set the saucer on the coffee table and stood, coming to kneel at Pauline's side. "Virginia called me about J.T., and told me you'd fainted. I called Emily. We got here as fast as we could."

"J.T.!" Pauline cried, swinging her feet to the floor quickly, too quickly. The room swayed; so did she.

Deborah's hands pressed at her shoulders. "Lie down, sugar. J.T. is fine. Emily spoke with him not ten minutes ago."

Pauline's gaze flew to her mother-in-law's. Emily smiled and nodded. "He was still pretty groggy and in a lot of pain, but he's going to be fine."

"What happened?"

"When I called for details, they said there was an electrical fire in the cockpit. There was no real blaze, but it got so hot that the zippers on J.T.'s flight suit burned blisters wherever they touched."

Pauline winced.

"He and his instructor had to eject from the plane. Evidently, J.T. landed wrong and broke his leg. Considering what could have happened, a broken leg isn't such a big deal." Emily's smile widened. "As a matter of fact, the nurse I spoke with said he'd be coming home to recuperate for a few weeks."

Pauline felt herself go limp with relief.

"Maybe he'll be here when the baby's born," Deborah said. "Won't that be nice?"

Pauline nodded and rubbed a weary hand over her face. Without warning, she began to cry, and Deborah drew her into a close embrace. "I was afraid something would happen to him," she confessed.

"Ever since Lettie Mae's accident, I've been afraid something would happen to J.T."

"Why?" Deborah asked, flashing Emily a concerned look.

"Because until then, I never believed anything bad could happen to me or the people I loved. Now I know it can."

Emily joined Pauline and Deborah on the sofa. "We all learn that sad truth sooner or later, Pauline. But you can't borrow trouble, either. You just have to live one day at a time."

"I know you're right, but—" Pauline doubled over with a sharp gasp of pain.

"Are you all right?" Deborah asked in an urgent voice.

All Pauline could do was nod. She'd dismissed the other pain as a product of her dreams and stress. But this was no fantasy. This was real . . . and excruciating.

"It's the baby." Emily's voice held firm conviction. "This isn't like the cramping when she had the spotting. This is labor."

"I think you're right," Deborah concurred.

Labor? The baby! The words whirled in Pauline's mind, making her dizzy with dread and fear. It wasn't time for the baby. It was too early.

"Are you sure this is it, Mama?" she asked, grimacing through the pain. "My back doesn't hurt at all."

"Not everyone's back hurts," Emily said. "Mine never did."

Pauline's eyes widened. Great. How was a body supposed to know what was going on if the people with experience in these matters couldn't get their stories straight? As the pain eased, her panic abated the slightest bit. Maybe it wasn't labor. Maybe it would go away. Maybe... A horrified look spread across Pauline's white face.

"What is it?" Deborah asked in a sharp voice of concern.

Pauline looked at her mother in total shock and complete shame. "I just wet all over the sofa."

The look on Deborah's face was something between relief and humor. "You didn't wet on the sofa. Your water broke."

"But it's our new couch!" Pauline wailed. "J.T. will kill me."

"J.T. will never know. I'll have it cleaned," Emily said in a brusque tone. "Deborah, do you know Dr. Purdy's number off hand?"

Deborah Randolph shook her head. "Maybe we'd better just drive her in. It wasn't long between those pains."

Pauline's gaze volleyed back and forth between her mother and her mother-in-law. They were both so calm. How could they be so calm?

"I've changed my mind," she said, gripping her mother's hand. "I don't want to do this."

"Well, it's a little late for that now," Deborah said matter-of-factly. "Come on, sugar, let's get you outside. Sometimes walking helps"

"She's right," Emily said, patting Pauline on the shoulder. "I'm going to call and tell Dr. Purdy's nurse that we're on our way. Where are your towels, Pauline? We'll need some for the car."

"In the closet in the bathroom," Pauline said more calmly, trying hard to take her cue from her mother. "Maybe I'd better go pack my bag," she added. "I thought it was too early."

Just as she finished the sentence, another pain hit, threatening to tear her in half. Holding on to her mother for support, she walked her way out of it, her wet skirt clinging to her legs. When the contraction passed, Emily looked at Deborah.

"Let's don't worry about your bag," Emily said. "I'll come back for it later."

The next thing Pauline knew, she was being hustled into her mother's car and seated on a pillow of fluffy towels. Emily got into the back seat, and Deborah spun out and tore off down the gravel road as if all the hounds of hell were chasing them.

The trip to Crystal Creek was made in record time, and the next thing Pauline knew she was being dressed in a hospital gown and confronted with the embarrassing, requisite drill that accompanied giving birth. One thing was certain. Having a baby went a long way toward dispelling any modesty she might have.

She'd only been in the small labor room a few minutes when Dr. Purdy came in, a smile wreathing his lined, weary face. "Hello, Pauline."

"Hi, Dr. Purdy."

"How're you feeling?"

"Fine."

"That's good. I spoke with your mother before I came in, and she said to tell you not to be afraid."

"I'm not afraid."

"That's my girl." He examined her and told her she was dilating nicely, and gave her a shot to help her with the contractions that were starting to come even more rapidly. Pauline lost track of time. All she was aware of was that, near the end, the pain never stopped.

When she woke up, she learned that she had given birth not to Lynnette McKinney, but to a six pound, two-ounce boy. She and J.T. had a son.

He looked like his daddy, she thought, with all that dark hair. His eyes were blue, but her mother assured her that all babies were born with blue eyes and that the color was subject to change. Pauline cuddled the baby close, and counted his fingers and toes. Since J.T. had never shown any interest in choosing a name, she decided to call him Tyler. Everything would be all right now, she thought, as sleep claimed her. She would soon have her figure back; J.T. would come around.

The worst was over.

"OBVIOUSLY, everything worked out okay with Pauline and Tyler," Cynthia said when Carolyn paused in her tale to take a sip of her iced tea.

Carolyn nodded. "Thankfully, it didn't take them too long to get Pauline's blood pressure stabilized, but it could have been serious. Tyler had a spastic stomach. The minute the formula hit it, he threw it all back up. They tried a lot of things, but as I recall, none of it helped much." She shook her head. "I was just a kid, but I can remember Pauline being so worn out back then."

"I can relate to that."

"I know. That's why I'm telling you all this." Carolyn's eyes held a faraway look as she examined her memories of the past. "She changed after she had Tyler. Everyone could see it. It was like someone waved a wand, and the old Pauline disappeared and the new one stood in her place."

SHE'D CHANGED, J.T. thought, as his booted feet carried him the three blocks from the beauty shop to the Longhorn Café. Cynthia was a different person since she'd had Jennifer. The old Cynthia would never have gone off this way without calling and telling him where she was. J.T. could feel his worry give way to irritation. There was no sense in anyone being so discourteous.

The bell on the door of the Longhorn tinkled as he went inside.

Kasey Bradley, who was taking an order, looked up and waved. He waved back, and motioned her over.

"Hi, Mr. McKinney," she said. "What can I get for you?"

"Nothing, thanks. I was wondering if you'd seen my wife."

"Yeah," the waitress said with a nod. "She was in before lunch." Kasey smiled. "Oh, Mr. McKinney, that baby of yours is a doll."

"Thanks." But J.T.'s mind wasn't on Jennifer. "Did Cynthia say where she was going?"

"No," Kasey said, a thoughtful look on her face. "But I mentioned to her that Aunt Eva had been sick and could use a visit, and I had the impression she was going to stop by and see her."

"Eva Blake?"

"Uh-huh. You know she's been having some problems with her heart."

"I'd heard. How long ago was Cynthia in here?"

Kasey looked at the clock. "Two, two and a half hours ago, at least. Is something wrong?"

"Not really," J.T. said, rising. "Just a minor emergency. Thanks, Kasey."

"Any time. Sure you won't have some chocolate pie?"

But J.T. was already out the door. "Maybe next time," he called over his shoulder.

Meanwhile, back at the ranch...

"WHAT DID YOU MEAN about Pauline changing?" Cynthia asked Carolyn, after her hostess had refilled their tea glasses.

"Pauline had always been pretty independent, but she got worse. When she was released from the hospital, she was supposed to go to Mama's for ten days. That's the way they did it back then—lots of bed rest and all that. When I had Beverly, I thought of that time with Mama as a crash course in motherhood. You know the one—'Everything You Need to Know about Raising a Baby in Ten Days.'"

Cynthia laughed. "I wish I'd had it."

"Well, after a week, Pauline decided she was ready to go to her house, and there was nothing to do but pack up her stuff and take her. Once she got home, she refused to ask anyone for help."

"Why?"

"Years later, she told me that she felt as if she had to prove herself to everyone. To our parents, to J.T.'s parents and to J.T. She was afraid that if she leaned on anyone, it would seem that she couldn't 'cut it,' as she put it."

Cynthia thought about her own actions since Jennifer's birth, the way she'd been so determined to do everything herself, and for much the same reasons Pauline had. She had wanted to prove to J.T., to his children and to the whole darn town that J.T. McKinney's new wife wasn't just an expensive plaything.

"I think Pauline and I had more in common than I realized."

"You do. There was something else that I remember thinking was really strange back then."

"What's that?"

"Almost as soon as she went home from Mama's, she gave away a lot of her clothes. Perfectly good clothes. She brought me all her hair ribbons and said that she was a wife and mother now, she couldn't go around looking like a silly teenager. And then she went into Crystal Creek to Betty's Beauty Bar and had all her gorgeous hair cut off, just like you did. Boy, was J.T. mad." Carolyn grinned. "But I'm getting ahead of myself."

CHAPTER NINE

April 1959

EVEN THOUGH he'd taken a pain pill before they left and slept the better part of the journey from San Antonio to Crystal Creek, J.T. was in a fair amount of pain by the time he and his dad pulled into the Rocking R, where he, Pauline and the baby would be staying the next few days. All he wanted to do was take another pill, go to bed and sleep until his leg stopped hurting.

When he entered the room that had been Pauline's before they married, he was instantly aware that there was something strangely sterile and empty about it. Then he remembered that all the pictures cut from movie magazines, and all the high school memorabilia had been taken from the walls and shelves and transferred to his room at the Double C. Pauline's attempt to hold on to her old life.

He could hardly remember those carefree, fun-filled days that constituted his life just a year before. This was his life now, this girl—this woman—lying there with her hand beneath her cheek, her long blond hair spread across the rumpled pillow.

The sudden, unexpected surge of joy that rose in J.T. was powerful, frightening. He was stunned at just how much he'd missed her.

Funny how cramming for a college exam had seemed so stressful and demanding back then. Now he knew what stress was. Stress was sitting in a cockpit as hot as Hades and knowing that you were as close to dying as you'd ever been.

J.T. heard a shuffling sound from the bassinet that sat a few feet from the bed. With the aid of his crutches, he hobbled over, trying his best not to wake Pauline. Tyler, now a week old, lay sleeping on his side, a small pillow rolled against his back.

Awestruck, J.T. could only stare down at the baby, and try to comprehend the swell of emotions coursing through him. He was looking at his son, the child he and Pauline had created between them. It was unbelievable to think that this tiny scrap of humanity was the result of those passion-filled nights they'd spent in the back seat of his mom's car.

"J.T."

The sound of Pauline's voice sent him spinning around on his crutches so fast he almost lost his balance. "Hi."

"Hi."

Her smile was soft, tentative. Confused by the strength of his feelings, both about himself and his life, uncertain about who he was, where he was going and his place in the new scheme of things, he stood his ground, taking solace in the only thing the past few months had left intact. His pride.

"Are you okay?" Her gaze—concerned, somehow almost maternal—swept him from head to foot, as if she needed to see for herself that he was indeed all right.

"Other than hurting like hell unless I'm full of pain pills, I'm fine. How about you?"

"I'm okay," she said. Her smile was self-deprecating, humorless. "I sat down wrong the day I came home from the hospital and broke a stitch loose, which wasn't much fun, but other than that I'm doing pretty well."

J.T. hardly heard. Stitches? From what? He didn't know she'd have to have stitches . . . down there. He swallowed. What he didn't know about having babies would probably fill a room.

"How long will you be home?" she asked.

"Until the nineteenth of May."

Was that a flicker of pleasure in her eyes? "Have you seen Tyler?"

"Uh, yeah." J.T. rested his weight on his crutch and waved a hand toward the bassinet. "I was just looking at him. He's really . . . little."

"That's because he was a month early."

Guilt, again. "I know. I'm sorry."

"It's not your fault. I'd had problems off and on all during the pregnancy. It's just one of those things that happens." She looked almost embarrassed. "I was so worried about you when they called about the accident."

J.T.'s jaw tightened at the memory of that morning, and his palms grew damp, but he didn't reply.

"I'm glad you're okay," she said, her voice soft and sincere, "and I'm really glad you got to come home for a while."

"Me, too." J.T. realized with a start that he was. It was a heck of a lot better than the alternative, he told himself. But deep down inside, he knew that he was glad to be there because he was glad to see her.

As a welcome, it wasn't bad. Unfortunately, things got worse. Tyler developed colic, which meant that Deborah was in and out of their room at all hours of the night, doing her grandmother thing so Pauline could rest and regain her strength.

The little guy had good lungs; he'd give him that, J.T. thought, as he lay awake beside his wife night after night and stared sleepless at the ceiling.

J.T. thought a lot about his son as he tossed and turned, his leg hurting and his conscience smarting. He wondered if Tyler would be a serious sort of guy like him, or a fun-loving hell-raiser like Pauline. He wondered if he'd be around to see.

FIVE DAYS PASSED. Gradually, Pauline began to regain her strength, and some of her usual vitality. Her relationship with J.T. was something between careful consideration and wary respect. It could have been worse.

Twelve days after Tyler was born, a week after Pauline brought him home from the hospital, she began to feel restless. The time spent at her mother's seemed interminable and, though she couldn't deny that it was nice having someone get up with the baby while she slept, she couldn't rid herself of the feeling that she and J.T. and Tyler should be in their own place. Maybe if they were alone, something would happen to break the spell of inertia binding her and her husband.

Pauline didn't know what she expected from J.T. She just knew that he was different than he'd been when he left. After their argument in December, his attitude had changed somewhat for the better, a change that had manifested itself in his letter writing and phone calls, signs that implied that he believed nothing had happened between her and Matt.

She had assumed—wrongly, now it seemed—that when he got home and saw the baby, he would realize as she had that between them, they had created a wonderful thing. She'd hoped that he would finally see that he loved her, but so far, nothing had been said.

On the surface they were getting along just fine. J.T. no longer carried that chip on his shoulder and no longer found fault with every breath she took, but she sensed a new, different sort of distance between them. Impossible as it seemed, J.T. seemed to have separated himself even more from her, while trying to get closer on some level. She didn't like to admit that she held back some, too, a sort of punishment for his lack of interest in the past.

Pauline had taken her new concerns to her mother, a move that was the deciding factor in her decision to go home. Deborah had listened to Pauline with a sensitive ear and sorrow in her heart.

"All I want is a happy, stable life like you and Daddy have," Pauline said at last.

Like a cloud blocking out the light of the sun, a shadow crossed Deborah's eyes. She reached out and brushed Pauline's wispy, too-long bangs from her forehead. "Oh, sugar, what you want is a fairy-tale marriage, and they just don't exist."

"Why not?" Pauline asked, tears in her voice, in her eyes.

"Because no matter how much two people love each other, they're going to argue sometimes. Things happen. Men lose their jobs. Babies get sick. People die. We make decisions—bad ones and good ones—and once those decisions are made, we have to live with them, or live them down, just like Tyler."

"I didn't *decide* to get pregnant," Pauline said.

"Maybe not, but you thought if you gave J.T. what he wanted, he'd stay with you—didn't you?"

The hot color that rose in Pauline's cheeks was answer enough.

"So you slept with J.T., and you got caught. You found out that this was something you couldn't pout, fib or finagle your way out of, and now you're living with that mistake as well as living it down."

Pauline sighed. She'd learned that, for sure. "I know you're right, but when I look at Tyler, it's hard to think of him as a mistake."

Deborah smiled. "I know."

"Do you think I'll ever live it down?"

"In time," Deborah said with a nod. "People have long memories, but they'll look back at you one day when you're my age and say, 'Remember when Pauline Randolph got in trouble with that McKinney boy? I wouldn't have given you a nickel for their chances of making it, but just look at her. She's head of the P.T.A., works hard at the church and raised a fine boy.'"

Pauline's mouth curved up at her mother's pretend scenario, but the smile had a bittersweet edge. "Do you give a nickel for our chances?"

"Oh, Paulie! Ask me something simple," Deborah said with a sigh. "I don't know what the future holds for any of us. I know that things aren't right between you and J.T. I think the problem is more that he resents losing his freedom than it is he doesn't care for you."

Though that was a somewhat positive observation, Pauline's eyes filled with tears.

"I will tell you this. The secret to happiness is to try and keep a positive attitude. Try to make the bad times good."

"It sounds like a lot of work."

"It is, sometimes. But you need to remember that life is filled with choices. We choose how we react to any given situation. If our house burns to the ground because of an electrical failure we can vow revenge on the electrician, or we can pick up the pieces and rebuild."

"I guess the same holds true for marriages, huh?" Pauline asked in a wistful tone.

"I'd say so. One thing you've got to remember, Paulie. Contrary to what some people say, marriage isn't always a fifty-fifty proposition. Sometimes it's ninety-ten.''

It was at that moment that Pauline made the decision to take her family home. It was at that instant she made the conscious decision to grow up. It was time she stopped relying on her parents so much. Someone in the family had to be responsible. Someone had to be the adult. It was up to her.

When she announced her decision to Deborah, she didn't miss the fleeting sorrow that crossed her mother's face. It was as if Deborah knew that Pauline's asserting herself had taken her life and the mother-daughter relationship in a new direction.

DEBORAH AND STEVEN and Carolyn moved Pauline, J.T. and Tyler home—lock, stock and bottle warmer. After they brought in all the baby paraphernalia and made sure J.T. and Pauline were comfortable and the baby was asleep, Deborah gave Virginia explicit instructions and took a reluctant leave, urging Pauline to call if she needed her.

Pauline promised and promptly got out of bed and started cleaning out closets and dresser drawers. She sacked up all the dresses she deemed too short or too tight, along with her bobby socks and her poodle skirt and instructed Virginia to give them to the Salvation Army. She boxed up all her romance comic books and movie magazines for the nursing home and set them aside her stuffed animals for the children's wing at the hospital. She gathered up all her hair ribbons for

Carolyn, and called Betty's Beauty Bar for an appointment.

When Pauline came home from town the next day—Tyler had stayed with his Grandma Emily—she was sporting a new hairdo, a sleek style reminiscent of Elizabeth Taylor's in *Cat on a Hot Tin Roof*.

J.T. was sitting in the porch swing, his leg in its plaster cast resting on the railing, when she got out of the car and carried Tyler up the front steps. Even from several yards away, she could tell that J.T. was hardly aware of the car's approach. She could also tell that he hadn't bothered to shave.

His eyes were focused on the craggy hills in the distance, but it wasn't the lush new grass sprouting from the rocky crevices or the crisp white clouds adrift on the blue of the sky that held his attention. His mind was riveted on some thought, some memory that robbed his dark eyes of everything but a dull flatness.

A shiver of apprehension slithered down her spine. "J.T.? Are you all right?"

The sound of her voice brought him out of his trance. His gaze slewed toward her. She saw him stiffen. The emotions that chased one another across his handsome face were evident. Surprise. Disbelief. Anger.

"What the hell have you done to your hair?"

Pauline fought back the sharp retort that sprang to her lips. No more fighting over silly things, she reminded herself. She was an adult. She could discuss this rationally. Sensibly. She raised one hand and touched the curl resting against her cheek in a self-conscious gesture. "I cut it."

"I can see that," J.T. said, his eyes wide and disbelieving. "Why?"

There was more emotion in his voice than she'd heard since he got home. Why was it that a stupid haircut could get a reaction out of him when his child's constant crying didn't seem to faze him? she thought in disgust. "I'm a mother now, J.T. I don't need to go around looking like a teenager. Besides, somebody in this family has got to face reality."

J.T. looked as if she'd slapped him. "What do you mean, somebody has to face reality?" he snapped, his face red.

Pauline wished she could take back the words. They must have erupted from some place deep inside her where the truth of her relationship with J.T. was festering. She hadn't meant to say them—had she?

She drew a deep, steadying breath. "I just meant that all this is real. I'm a wife, now. A mother. I'm not a kid anymore." She met his gaze squarely. There was confusion in his eyes and a keen interest in what she was saying.

"The past few weeks have taught me that the responsibilities I've taken on are not only real, they're frightening. Having Tyler put things into perspective for me. All this is more than people gossiping about me and me losing my figure. And it isn't going to go away—at least not for the next eighteen years."

Some emotion she couldn't define flickered in J.T.'s eyes.

"There's no going back to the way things used to be, so I've got to learn to cope with the fears and the problems the best I can. And if that means cutting my hair to make life easier, then that's what I'll do. I'll do whatever it takes, J.T."

The last was not only a statement of intent, it was a plea to let him know that she was willing to go the extra mile to make things right with him, to bring back the smile to his eyes.

When he didn't reply, she stood there for a moment, trying to think of something to say that might salvage the deteriorating conversation, one of the few they'd had since he'd come home. Unable to think of anything, she heaved a soulful sigh. So much for honesty. Nothing got through to J.T. Nothing.

"I'm taking Tyler in. It's time to start dinner."

J.T. didn't hear. He was already caught up in whatever thoughts were taking him farther and farther away from her.

WHEN J.T. HEARD the screen door slam shut, he gave a sigh of relief and scrubbed a trembling hand along his whisker-stubbled jaw. Being around Pauline was harder than he'd anticipated. Motherhood agreed with her. There was a softness, a sort of serenity about her that had been lacking before. He supposed she had, as his mother would say, mellowed. The difference in her would have been obvious to a blind man.

She was good with Tyler. Patient. Conscientious. Traits that spilled over to him. Since he got home, she had been eager to see that his every need was met.

Were her sudden need to purge her life of every vestige of youth and the cutting of her hair outward signs of a newfound maturity? It had been something of a shock when he went into their bedroom the night before and saw her childhood all boxed up and ready to be discarded. There was something sad about seeing the bears and dolls thrown aside willy-nilly. Something final. She was doing what Howard Blake said he should do—pick up and go on—but her actions left him with a feeling of alarm. Unable to put a name to the fear, he shoved it back into a corner of his psyche, where he relegated all the things he wasn't ready to face.

It was one thing to be at the base and not have to deal with his mistakes, but another to be in daily contact with the wife and child—the life—he wasn't ready for. The life she was facing—if not without fear, at least with bravery. The knowledge that she had found the courage to do what he couldn't ate at him like a canker.

J.T. gave the swing a shove that jerked his bad leg and made him grind his teeth in agony. He welcomed the pain. He deserved it. The more certain he became that this new Pauline was the real thing, the more certain he became that he'd been a jerk. A fool.

And now, he had to deal with not only his reprehensible behavior and his fear of trying to make things right, but a new fear as well.

Gut-deep, heart-stopping fear.

The kind that grabbed you by the throat and choked the air from your lungs. The kind that turned your

insides upside down and threatened to make you puke.
He was training to be a pilot, to fly miles up in the air,
and the very thought of even climbing to the top of
one of those rocks out toward the horizon was enough
to make him want to bawl.

Flying was supposed to supply him with the freedom he didn't have in his life. It was supposed to offer him an escape. And it had, until the accident. Now,
the memory of what had happened on April seventh
haunted his every waking hour and made him question the cornerstone of his manhood.

How could he tell a woman who had found the
courage to face her past, present and future that he
was terrified to go up in a plane again? And worse—
that he was even more terrified of *not* finding the guts
to go up again.

Even if he could dredge up the courage to go to
Pauline, what could he offer her? A man who was half
a man? A man paralyzed by fear? The man she
claimed to have fallen in love with hadn't wanted his
freedom taken away, and he hadn't wanted to get
married, but he hadn't been a coward. But a coward
was what he'd become.

If he lived to be a hundred, he'd never forget that
day. He and Haskill, his instructor, cruising a clear
azure sky, a perfect day for flying. They weren't flying at an altitude high enough to make wearing their
oxygen masks a necessity, and they'd been out about
twenty minutes when the unmistakable odor of an
electrical fire first tickled J.T.'s nostrils.

When he mentioned it to Haskill, the instructor had grown suddenly serious and radioed the base. It went without question that they would try to make it back. No pilot wanted to ditch his plane and walk home, something that had as much to do with ego as with the fact that the T-33 they were flying cost a fair amount of pocket change.

As the heat and the stench of burning wire filled the small area, the cockpit seemed to shrink. The claustrophobic feeling had escalated on the return trip. J.T. felt his flesh burning, and looked down to find that the zippers of his flight suit were so hot they'd burned his skin.

Heat and thin tendrils of smoke curled around him, fighting him for every molecule of oxygen. He pulled his mask up over his face and wondered if the fire and brimstone of hell would be any hotter. All he could think of was that he was going to die without seeing his child. He was going to die, and Pauline would never know that she was right. He did love her. J.T. prayed as he'd never prayed before.

They were five minutes into the return trip when Haskill announced, "We're not gonna make it. Blow the canopy."

Blow the canopy! They were going to eject. A fresh surge of fear raced through J.T.'s veins. This was a scenario that had never played through his mind. There was a handle on either side of his seat. Either or both would send the canopy flying away from the plane. J.T. automatically stretched down his right hand, took the handle in a firm grip and rotated it. As the canopy blew up and away, fresh air, blessedly sweet, blessedly cold, rushed in at him.

"Let's go!" Haskill shouted. His mind numb, functioning on automatic pilot himself, J.T. triggered the small explosion that sent him rocketing up and away from the plane.

And then he was falling. . . .

For a few glorious seconds, his relief to be outside the confines of the plane was so great that he didn't care. Then, above his relief and fear, he heard Haskill screaming something. A degree of sanity returned. His rip cord. He was supposed to pull his rip cord.

His free-fall was halted by a sudden jerking of his shoulder harness, and he began his slow descent to the ground. He saw the plane hit the earth in a roiling, boiling ball of flame that spewed metal for hundreds of yards. It was sobering to realize that he might have gone up in flames just like the plane.

J.T. was thanking God for sparing him and thinking that he wasn't sure he could ever climb inside another cockpit, when he hit the ground. The loud crack of snapping bone and his anguished cry were the last sounds he remembered hearing until he woke in the hospital to the news that Pauline had given birth soon after she heard about the accident. He had a son. He was a father.

BY THE TIME Pauline, J.T. and the baby had been home for a week, she was beginning to doubt the wisdom of leaving her mother's house. With Deborah taking responsibility for most of Tyler's care, Pauline had been blissfully unaware how much work was involved in caring for a newborn with colic and a new husband who was a moody stranger.

Setting her alarm for fifteen minutes before Tyler's feedings so that she could give him the phenobarbital drops became an established ritual. It often took her more than an hour to give Tyler his bottle, which, more likely than not, he spit up. Then he promptly got a stomachache. Many were the nights that Pauline cried right along with Tyler while J.T. slept. She wasn't sure she would ever be rested again.

There was the formula-making every morning, the washing and sterilizing of twenty-four-hours' worth of bottles, the never-ending pails of diapers to be soaked, washed and rinsed in vinegar water and then hung out on the line to dry, not to mention Tyler's bath—which he hated—and the hand-washing of all his baby clothes.

She realized that motherhood was a very demanding job and found a new respect for her own mother. Pauline did adore Tyler, though. He was a beautiful baby, and on some level, she knew the colic would pass. She vowed she would do her best for him.

Though Virginia did the major cleaning, Pauline refused to let the housekeeper do the ironing, and insisted on cooking all of J.T.'s favorite meals herself. For every disaster she created, she told herself that at least she was trying. She hoped J.T. would see that she was doing her best to make a go of their marriage. She kept hoping he would decide to do the same.

The only attempts to "put one over on him" as he once would have claimed, were her subtle endeavors to make him aware of her as a woman. Regardless of how little sleep she got, she put on her makeup every morning and fixed her Liz Taylor hairdo. She wore J.T.'s favorite perfume and brushed against him whenever it was possible...in an unobtrusive way, of course. So far, nothing had worked. Considering her bone-deep weariness, she was giving the marriage everything she could...just as she'd said she would.

If anything, J.T. had grown even more distant in the two weeks since they'd come home. He had started drinking beer every night, too, something she hated, something he'd never done before.

"I really wish you wouldn't drink so much," she'd said one evening, when he popped the top of another beer.

J.T. looked at her, the old cockiness back in his eyes. "It helps the pain," he told her. "It helps me sleep."

"You have medicine for that," she reminded him.

"Back off, Pauline. How much beer I drink is none of your business."

Pauline started to tell him that it was very much her business, but stopped the sharp retort that sprang to her lips. She refused to argue with him. J.T. grabbed the truck keys from the countertop and hobbled to the door on his crutches.

He was leaving again, going off in the automatic-transmission pickup to God-knows-where. She realized that her need to know his every move got on his nerves, but she couldn't seem to help herself. She worried about him since the accident. What if he had one beer too many and fell, reinjuring his leg? How would she know where to find him?

"Where are you going?"

"Away from here."

To Pauline, the callous statement meant that he'd rather be anywhere other than where she and Tyler were. As he stomped out of the house, she realized that she'd made a terrible miscalculation in forcing the issue between her and J.T. She'd wrongly imagined that if they got married, everything would be all right. She had thought that if she got pregnant he would offer to marry her. She would give him a son, and in return, he would realize he loved her, and they would live happily ever after.

She saw now, belatedly, sadly, that that line of reasoning had been founded on selfishness and immaturity. Things weren't ever going to work out between her and J.T. unless some drastic changes were made.

One afternoon, while Virginia was in Crystal Creek doing the weekly grocery shopping and when Pauline had just finished giving Tyler a bottle, there was a knock at the door. She and the baby were both crying—Tyler from pain, Pauline from frustration. Dashing the moisture from her eyes with impatient fingers, she found Eva Blake standing on the other side of the screen door.

"Hello, Pauline," the pretty minister's wife said, eyeing Pauline and the baby with a smile. "I thought

I'd stop by and see how you and Tyler were getting along. I didn't see you at church last Sunday."

"Eva!" Pauline exclaimed, over the sound of Tyler's crying. She and Eva had got past the "Mrs. Blake" stage when Pauline had helped with the hospital visitation in the fall. She shifted Tyler to one arm and pushed open the door. Her excited smile bordered on pathetic. "I was sleeping Sunday morning. Tyler had a bad night. Come on in. It's so good to see you. Would you like a glass of tea?" she said, aware that she was rattling.

"I'd love one, if it isn't too much trouble," Eva replied, entering the room with an almost imperceptible limp.

"Oh, no. I'm glad for the company."

Eva set down her purse on the fat arm of the sofa and held out her arms. "Let me hold the baby while you get the tea," she said, with a twinkle in her blue eyes.

"Thank you." Pauline handed over the crying infant and hoped she didn't sound too eager. "Would you like to sit in the kitchen? There's a nice cross breeze."

"That sounds wonderful." Eva followed Pauline into the kitchen and sat Tyler on her lap while Pauline poured the tea and added sprigs of mint from Virginia's herb garden to the glasses.

For the next twenty minutes, Eva caught Pauline up on what was happening in Crystal Creek. The senior play was a smash hit. Bubba Gibson's sister had the lead role. Graduation was scheduled for the twenty-seventh of May, which was just a little more than three weeks away. Howard was going fishing in Mexico with a friend from Arkansas. And though he knew it would be another year before she graduated, Bubba Gibson had proposed to Mary Riles.

There was a lull in the conversation, while Eva tried to think of any tidbit she might have overlooked. Pauline sat staring at a spot across the room, thinking that even though she was enjoying the visit, she'd rather be taking a nap while the baby slept.

"You're exhausted, aren't you?"

The question took Pauline by surprise. She nodded.

"I remember those days well. You're too tired to eat, too tired to do anything. Even too tired to make love."

"What's that?" Pauline quipped in a light tone, the mention of sex by the preacher's wife snapping her out of her lethargy, at least for the moment.

"That bad, huh?" Eva said. "Want to talk about it?"

Pauline shrugged. "I wouldn't know where to start or what to say."

"Then let me." Eva looked Pauline directly in the eye. "Things haven't been good with you and J.T. since you married. It's worse since he came home."

"How do you know?"

"It's a pretty simple guess. Just start at the beginning and tell me."

Pauline sighed. For the first time, she opened up with someone besides her mother, and talked about her relationship with J.T., including her fear for him every time he left the house. She ended with what she'd told him more than two weeks before about facing reality.

"I feel as if it's my fault things are in such a mess, and I don't know what to do. I know I'm grouchy, and I'm praying for patience—with J.T. and the baby—but I have a feeling that even if I were a saint, it wouldn't make any difference to J.T."

Eva laughed. "I guess you know that when you pray for patience, you're praying for tribulations," she said, paraphrasing Romans 5:3.

"I hadn't thought of it that way," Pauline said with a sheepish grin. "Oh, Eva, I don't know what to do."

"It sounds like you're doing all you can. You know, I'm not so sure this new distance, as you call it, has anything to do with you."

"What's it all about, then?" Pauline asked in surprise.

"I have a feeling J.T.'s behavior is all tied up with the airplane accident."

"What do you mean?"

"J.T. has always been a self-assured young man. Can you imagine how he must have felt, losing control of a situation that way? The accident made him acutely aware of his own mortality for the very first time. And he knows that when he goes back to Randolph in a couple of weeks, he'll have to climb right back into another plane, without showing so much as a qualm of fear."

"How do you know all that?"

"As far as what the Air Force will expect, that goes without saying. As for J.T.'s feelings, I'm just guessing. You have to remember that fearlessness is a vital part of manhood, Pauline. Even if a man is scared to death of something, he's supposed to bluff his way through life pretending he isn't." Eva rolled her eyes. "It's asinine, I know, but true. I think that under the circumstances, you're just going to have to give J.T. some time and space."

"WAS SHE RIGHT about J.T.?" Cynthia asked, her troubled eyes fixed on Carolyn, who had paused after this chapter of J.T.'s past.

"She hit it right on the button, J.T. told Pauline later. Eva Blake was a pretty sharp cookie. Still is, for that matter."

AT THE MOMENT, the "smart cookie" was opening the door to J.T., who was growing more irritable by the moment.

"Why, hello, J.T.," Eva Blake said, when she saw who was standing there. "What brings you here?"

"Hello, Eva," J.T. said. "I'm looking for Cynthia. Kasey said she was going to stop by and see you."

"Oh, dear. I must have missed her. I just got back from my sister's in Austin."

Somehow, the news didn't surprise J.T. He stood there while Eva called out to her housekeeper. Yes, the woman replied, Cynthia had been there, and when she hadn't found Eva at home, she'd gone to the church to say hello to Reverend Blake.

"I'm sure Howard knows where she went," Eva said. "Why don't you go over and ask him."

J.T. plunked his Stetson back onto his head, which was beginning to throb. "I'll do that, Eva. Thanks."

Meanwhile, back at the ranch . . .

"POOR PAULINE!" Cynthia said with a shake of her head. "Did the talk with Eva help?"

"Surprisingly, it did. It was sort of a catalyst. Pauline decided that things were bad, would probably get worse before they got better, and that it was time she did something. She figured that if J.T. left her, it wouldn't matter. As far as she was concerned, their marriage was no marriage as it was."

"What did she do?"

"She cornered him that evening and had it out with him. She laid all her cards on the table and put the ball in his court."

CHAPTER TEN

May 1959

THE POOL HALL was crowded. J.T., Bubba Gibson and Martin Avery were playing pool when Frank Townsend came in and was invited to join them. Frank, who was J.T.'s age, had moved to Crystal Creek during their senior year. His dad worked for the local co-op, and though J.T. liked the younger Townsend well enough, they'd never become close friends. Frank, a part-time rodeo rider who was working for Bubba's dad, was reputed to be a hell of a cowboy and a pretty salty saddle bronc rider.

He wasn't half bad at pool, either, J.T. thought as Frank called the last ball and it went spinning into the side pocket. J.T. wasn't sure if his own game was off or he was just worn out. He hadn't slept a full night since he'd stopped taking his pain pills. If Tyler's crying didn't keep him awake, he found himself lying there trying to figure out how he could resolve the problems in his life. So far, his weary brain hadn't been able to come up with one workable answer.

"I took Callie Michaels out last night," Martin said, raising his cigarette lighter to the tip of his Camel.

"Aaand?" Bubba drawled suggestively. "How was she?"

"Hotter'n a pistol," Martin said with a wink, snapping shut the top of his Zippo lighter with a flick of his wrist.

"Lord, I miss squirin' the dollies around," Bubba said with a mock sigh. A cocky grin split his attractive face. "I imagine half the girls in Claro County are wearin' black now that Mary's taken me out of circulation."

"You know it, ol' buddy," Martin said, slapping Bubba on the back. "Want to play another game?" He asked the question of the group in general.

"I suppose," Frank said.

"Why not," Bubba added.

J.T. really didn't want to play another game, but he didn't want to go home, either. He shrugged. "Sure."

"Well, don't sound so excited, son," Bubba drawled. "It can't be good for your health, you an old married man and all." He gave J.T. a considering look. "I been meanin' to ask—how is married life, anyhow?"

J.T. lifted his Coke bottle and wondered why he'd never before noticed how Bubba's eternal good humor and constant wisecracking got on his nerves. "Fine."

"Pauline makin' a good little wife, huh?" he asked with a sly grin. "Things still hot and heavy, or has the kid cramped your style?"

The muscle in J.T.'s jaw tightened. He had no intention of discussing his marriage with Bubba Gibson.

Frank must have seen the glitter of anger in J.T.'s eyes. "Rack 'em up, Bubba," he said, effectively defusing the situation. "Let's play."

"Okay, okay," Bubba grumbled in his good-natured drawl. He swiped his comb through his DA and reached for his pool cue. "When we get through here, we can drive over to the A&W and grab something to eat. Then I'll head over to the Blue Mound and pick us up a couple of six-packs and we can play some poker. How does that sound?"

"Another time," Martin said. "I'm going to go see Dave Grimes. He said he'd found me a Corvette motor for my Chevy, and you know how Callie likes drag racing."

"I thought your daddy told you to quit racing when you blew that last engine," Bubba said, breaking the balls with a sharp crack of wood against wood.

"He did." Martin's smile was unrepentant. "What he doesn't know won't hurt him."

J.T. listened to the talk and wished he hadn't agreed to another game. A year ago, he would have been having a good time, swapping stories about his sexual prowess—made up in his case, and, he realized with sudden insight, mostly made up in theirs, too—drinking with the guys, not that he ever drank much, and playing poker or pool. Checking out the girls at the swimming pool or the rodeo or the Crystal Creek Country Club dance.

Now the brags and the minor defiances sounded childish, immature. The entertainment sounded dull. The things he'd considered the hallmark of his freedom weren't so attractive after all. Didn't these guys know there was more to life than trying to con your parents and making out with a different girl at every opportunity? Didn't they realize that drinking and carousing and looking for a perpetual good time was a shallow existence at best? Did they have any idea what was going on in the real world? Had he ever been as narcissistic and self-centered as Bubba and Martin?

J.T. knew the answer to that last question. The thought didn't do much to improve his mood. "Count me out," he said. "I need to go when we finish this game. It's getting late and Pauline will have dinner ready."

"*Paawk...paawk...paawk, paawk, paawk,*" Bubba said, placing his hands under his armpits and flapping his arms like wings.

J.T. shot his best friend a deadly look.

Bubba slapped a hand over his heart and staggered backward. "Whoa..." he croaked. "Big Daddy's gettin' mad. Does she make you punch a time clock, ol' son?"

"No, Bubba, she doesn't," J.T. said, his voice chilly enough to raise goose bumps. "It's called consideration, but I doubt that word's in your limited vocabulary."

Even Bubba—especially Bubba—knew when to back off. J.T. had been his friend too long for Bubba not to recognize the warning signals. He sobered suddenly, dropping his good-time Charlie image like a hot coal. "Hey, I'm sorry. I was just teasin'."

J.T.'s anger dissolved like a spoonful of sugar in a cup of hot coffee. He shouldn't be angry. A year ago, he'd ragged Don Henry the same way when he'd married Sally Lundquist. What had seemed funny then was far from it now. J.T. knew that Bubba and Martin and the rest of the gang weren't at fault. They hadn't changed; he had.

He'd outgrown his old buddies, and that was a fact. He wondered when it had happened and realized that time had nothing to do with it. Circumstance did. Life had dealt him some pretty serious hands this past year, things that had forced him to make some life-altering decisions: to be drafted by the Army or join the Air Force; to marry Pauline or deny the baby was his; to accept his new responsibilities or pretend they didn't exist.

The latter had worked until recently.

J.T. put down his pool cue and reached for his crutches. "I gotta go."

"But we haven't finished the game," Martin said, a stunned look on his face.

"Sorry." J.T. headed for the door as fast as his crutches would allow. He barreled through the door and careered into someone—a female someone—almost sending them both sprawling to the sidewalk. He managed to keep his balance only by sheer will. When he was steady on his good leg again, he saw that he'd run into Lettie Mae.

"J.T.!" she exclaimed, recognizing him about the same time he did her.

"Hello, Lettie Mae," he said with a slow smile. "Fancy running into you like this."

Lettie's low laughter was warm and attractive. "How's your leg?"

"Getting better."

"I talked to Pauline after the baby was born, and she told me what happened. It's too bad."

"That's the breaks," he quipped, and they shared another moment of laughter. "How have you been?"

A hint of sorrow shadowed her eyes. "Physically, I'm doing just fine. Emotionally..." Her voice trailed away. "Emotionally, I feel like I could shatter into a million pieces like one of Miz Deborah's crystal glasses that got dropped on the floor."

"I know how you feel."

Lettie Mae nodded. "Maybe you do, at least in some ways. You know what that moment is like just before you realize you're about to meet your Maker."

J.T. nodded solemnly.

"Brushin' so close to death sort of puts things into perspective, doesn't it?"

J.T. thought about the instant in the plane when he realized he loved Pauline, and about the way his feelings toward his so-called freedom had changed. Staring death in the eye definitely put a new slant on life. "Yeah, it does."

"I miss him, J.T., and that's a fact." Tears glistened in Lettie's dark brown eyes. "I'm never gonna find another man like him, and that's a fact, too."

"Sure you will, Lettie. You're young and pretty. You've got your whole life ahead of you."

Lettie shook her curly dark head. "No. I'll never find another Clark, and—" her voice broke "—I'll never be able to have another baby. Think about how you'd be feelin' now if Pauline and the baby had died instead of gettin' better."

J.T.'s eyebrows snapped together in a frown. "What do you mean if they'd died instead of getting better?"

Disbelief spread across Lettie Mae's pretty features. Her eyes grew wide. "Do you mean your daddy or nobody told you what happened when the baby was born?"

Anger mingled with J.T.'s growing sense of despair. "Obviously not."

"They probably didn't want to concern you, you bein' in such a bad way yourself," she said.

Didn't want to concern him? Dammit! Pauline was his wife, and Tyler was his son. If something had happened, he had a right to know. He wasn't some kid who had to be coddled and protected. "Why don't you tell me?" he suggested.

"Miz Deborah said that Pauline's blood pressure wouldn't stabilize. They were afraid she'd have a stroke or something there for several hours."

A stroke! Old people with high blood pressure had strokes, not nineteen-year-old girls who were in the peak of health. He tried to imagine Pauline partially paralyzed from a stroke, the way he remembered his

Great-aunt Mollie had been, and his stomach clenched into a painful knot.

"They said she coulda died, J.T."

J.T. stared at Lettie Mae with bleak eyes. "What about the baby?"

"Well, he come early, and he was pretty small. That part coulda been worse, from what they tell me. But somethin' was wrong with his stomach. It was havin' spasms or somethin', and he couldn't hold down any formula. They had him sittin' up with pillows all around, hopin' that gravity would help hold down the milk. I guess they tried him on about every formula imaginable and he'd just throw it all back up."

J.T. shook his head in stunned disbelief. Pauline must have gone through hell...worrying...waiting to see what was going to happen. And then he came home and was so wrapped up in his own misery that he hadn't given her any kind of support.

"But they must have got things straightened out," J.T. said. "Other than colic, he seems to be doing okay."

Lettie Mae nodded. "They're giving him phenobarbital drops to settle his stomach. He'll outgrow it. But it was nip and tuck there for a few days. Miz Deborah said Mr. Steven even took out a burial policy on him."

J.T. felt the blood drain from his face. How could they have kept this from him? Whose idea was it, anyway? Were they all in on the conspiracy to keep him in the dark?

"Look, J.T.," Lettie Mae said, interrupting his dark musings. "Maybe this is none of my business, but I'm gonna say it anyway, because I love Pauline like a sister. She's been a better friend than most, and I want the best for her."

"Spit it out, Lettie Mae," J.T. commanded.

Lettie looked him squarely in the eye. "I know things between you and Pauline aren't the way they should be, and I know she's been spoiled, and she doesn't always do what's right, but then—who does? Maybe she tricked you into marrying her, but she's paid for that because she knows how much you resent her and the marriage."

"Yeah, well maybe I did resent marrying her. But what you said about the accident was right. When I thought I wasn't going to make it, I realized that I do care for her."

"Then for God's sake, tell her," Lettie urged, "and put the poor girl out of her misery. She's crazy about you."

Despair darkened J.T.'s eyes. "I've treated her so badly, she probably doesn't want to hear my excuses."

"Bet she does."

"I'm afraid." The confession shocked him more than it did Lettie Mae.

"I know. But you can't run far enough or fast enough to outrun fear, J.T. You found that out in that plane. Face it. Don't let some sort of false pride stand in your way."

Pride. J.T. acknowledged that his pride had played a huge part in the way he'd treated Pauline, especially after she'd told him he was lacking in the sex department. And now his pride was all tangled up in his fear of getting back into an airplane, and fear that was making him feel less a man.

Lettie was right, though. He'd have to face his fear, just as he'd had to when he'd known his plane was going down. But did he have the courage to face Pauline?

As if she could read his mind, Lettie said, "You've got to make things right with Pauline, or let her go. The way you're livin' isn't fair to either of you. Take it from me, life is too fragile, too short to be miserable a minute if you don't have to be."

The thought of losing Pauline or Tyler—through death or any other way—was unbearable. He turned away and headed for his truck.

"Where you goin'?" Lettie asked his retreating figure.

"Home to my family," he said without looking back.

AFTER MULLING OVER her talk with Eva Blake that afternoon, Pauline decided it was time for some changes. She intended to confront J.T. about the state of their marriage. She would confess her faults and take her part of blame for its failure, and she expected him to do the same. It was time they either resolved to work out their problems or end their misery. The thought of failure...of divorce...brought tears to her eyes. But it wouldn't really be a divorce, she reminded herself, since they hadn't slept together. An annulment would be sufficient to end the farce that was their marriage. Still, it was a depressing thought.

The afternoon passed. No J.T. Try as she might to tamp down her anger, it rose in slow degrees, along with the soaring May temperature. She told herself that she should be calm, cool and adult when she and J.T. talked, but she was tired of making all the conciliatory gestures. Tired of cooking and taking care of the baby while he roamed around the countryside doing whatever it was he did all day and while he slept, obviously undisturbed by the baby's crying, at night. She was tired of holding her temper, tired of being patient with his moodiness, just tired, period.

Along toward evening she took a bath to cool off physically, and donned a pair of pink pedal pushers and a matching gingham shirt that tied at her midriff. She noted with a sense of satisfaction that while her abdomen might not be as firm as it once was, she could at least wear the clothes she'd worn the previous spring, before the pregnancy.

For the first time since he'd been born a month before, Tyler took his bottle with a minimum of fuss and went right to sleep without the usual screaming. Pauline was glad he was cooperating. She didn't need any distractions while she had it out with J.T.

Weary of trying and failing with her cooking—something her husband didn't appreciate anyway—she opted for tomato soup and grilled cheese sandwiches for dinner. She scorched both.

It was almost dark when she heard the truck pull into the lane that led to the house. Pauline's mood was darker. She ladled up the now cold soup and put the burned grilled cheese sandwiches on plates. She was filling the tea glasses when she heard the thump-thumping of J.T.'s crutches on the back porch. Her heart pounding, she went to the screen door and pushed it open.

J.T. WAS SURPRISED when Pauline met him at the door. After talking with Lettie Mae, he'd decided that it was time to set things straight with Pauline. He'd behaved like a jerk, and it was high time he told her he was sorry, time he told her he loved her. He only hoped she still cared enough for him that an apology would be sufficient to mend all the wrongs between them.

As he thumped through the door, he gave her an all-encompassing glance. Her face had lost its youthful roundness, and the dark circles beneath her eyes gave her a weary look that he knew must be bone deep after so many sleepless nights. Why hadn't he offered to take turns with her? he wondered, marveling at his selfishness and lack of understanding.

"Supper's cold."

J.T. gave her another sharp glance. Supper couldn't be any colder than her voice. Great. She was angry about something, and he wanted to talk. At the moment, eating was way down his list of priorities. Aiming to appease her, he said, "It doesn't matter."

"It matters to me."

The blunt statement halted his progress to the table. He turned and looked at her with a bit of incredulity. She hadn't shown so much as a hint of anger since their big argument at Christmas. Something had happened, and she was spoiling for a fight. J.T. felt his blood stir in anticipation. Passivity had never been a particularly endearing trait as far as he was concerned, and especially not with Pauline. He liked her spitting fire, and he noted with restrained relish that the sparks of a major conflagration glittered in the depths of her blue eyes.

"If I'm going to go to the trouble to cook for you, the least you can do is be here when it's time to eat," she told him in an arctic tone.

"You're right," he agreed. "I'm sorry. I should have called to let you know I was going to be late." The apology was prompted by the memory of his comment to Bubba about consideration. "You tell me what time to be here, and I'll be here."

He could see that his amicable tone took her aback a bit, but she rallied with admirable quickness. "Six sharp," she snapped. "That should give you plenty of time to do whatever it is you do all day."

The irritation was back. He struggled to hold back a smile of pure pleasure. This was the real Pauline, the one who drove him crazy. The one he found so irresistible. He hadn't felt so alive in months.

"You're right. It should." Though he knew she wanted him to tell her what it was he'd been doing to pass the long days, J.T. deliberately kept his mouth shut, just to add a little fuel to her fire.

Acting as if nothing were amiss, he took his crutches from under his arms, propped them against the chrome edge of the red-topped Formica table and hopped to his chair, a couple of feet away. He lowered himself heavily into the padded vinyl seat and reached for the glass of tea. It was good and sweet and cold. He picked up his sandwich.

"We have to talk."

She sounded serious. He lowered his sandwich to the plate and gave her his undivided attention. She stood on the far side of the table, her fingers twined together.

"It's time we got some things settled between us."

"Okay."

For an instant her face wore that surprised look again, and then he saw her chin lift in determination. "I can't go on this way. I won't."

The exhilaration J.T. felt at thinking he was going to get to see the demise of Pauline's newfound "adulthood" died a sudden death. Anxiety took a toehold on his emotions. He'd expected to get raked over the coals for being late and questioned about his whereabouts the past week or so. He hadn't expected her to hint that their marriage was over. She didn't say that. But that was what she meant.

"We need to discuss the problems in our marriage like adults. We need some honesty."

J.T. didn't answer. He was still trying to deal with his surprise.

"This marriage is a sham, J.T. We live apart, we never talk, and even though we share the same house and the same bed, we don't ever make love."

A dull red spread up over J.T.'s face. Anxiety slowly mutated to anger. He forgot that he'd intended to try and patch up things between them. He forgot everything but his humiliation at the knowledge that he wasn't a perfect lover. The muscle in his jaw tightened, and when he spoke, his voice was as frigid as hers. "I thought you didn't like making love with me."

Pauline made an impatient gesture and crossed her arms over her breasts. "Everyone says things when they're angry that they don't really mean."

"Oh," J.T. said, his voice curt, biting. "So now you're saying you didn't really mean it. Well, what the hell did you mean?"

"No! I did mean it," Pauline said, her voice rising the slightest bit. She shook her head in confusion. "All I meant was that there was room for improvement."

J.T. picked up the charred sandwich, now gone soft and soggy. He looked at it pointedly, looked at her and dropped it. "No kidding." He had the grim pleasure of seeing Pauline's face grow red.

As she looked him in the eye, he could almost see the despair and fury warring for the upper hand. She compromised with civility.

"Look, I don't want this to deteriorate into a yelling match, and I don't want to trade insults."

"No?" J.T.'s nostrils flared and his lips thinned. "What if I do?"

Her gaze bounced away from his. "Just let me get this off my chest, and then you can have your turn, okay?"

J.T. pinned her with a penetrating look. "Fine."

A noisy breath rushed from between her lips, and her eyes sparkled with a reckless anger. "When you tried to break up with me last spring, I admit that I would have done anything to keep you, and when you came home from basic training, I had every intention of seducing you."

As if she couldn't face the condemnation in his eyes, Pauline rose from her chair and went to the kitchen window. She addressed herself to the encroaching darkness. "I had this crazy idea that if we . . . went all the way, you'd realize you loved me."

So. He'd been right about her tricking him into marrying her. Where was the satisfaction he should be feeling? Her shoulders slumped, and he fought the urge to go to her and knead the tension from them.

"I dressed for Bubba's party that evening like I was going to see the President, but when I got there and saw you with all those girls around you, I decided I couldn't go through with it. It hurt too much. I was going to leave, but you stopped me." She turned to face him, a look of sorrow and confusion in her eyes. "You should have let me go, J.T."

"I should have."

Looking as if he'd slapped her, Pauline unknotted her fingers and gripped the edge of the countertop behind her, as if she needed the support it offered. Her breasts, fuller since the pregnancy, pressed enticingly against the soft cotton of her blouse. In spite of all the unanswered questions, the unspoken accusations and the undeniable anger throbbing between them, J.T. felt an unexpected urge to touch her.

"Why didn't you?" she asked.

"Because Bubba had told me about the trip to Mexico, and I figured if you were giving it to Matt Jeffries, I might as well have it, too."

Pauline gasped in surprise.

"You wanted honesty," he reminded. She nodded. "So I asked you out, and the rest, as they say, is history."

"If you believed I'd been with Matt, why did you marry me?"

J.T.'s gaze bored relentlessly into hers. "Because I knew the baby could have been mine, and my dad said I should do the honorable thing."

"The honorable thing," she mused. "So you did what the world expected of you, and you've resented every second of it . . . me, the baby . . . losing your precious freedom. All of it."

J.T. didn't deny the accusation. Couldn't.

"Well, it might surprise you to know that I've resented a lot of things, too, J.T. I resented you taking what you wanted and then acting like I didn't exist. I resented your being able to go off and pretend that none of this had happened while I got fat and ugly and had to face the people and the whispers, alone."

J.T. started to say something, but she forbade him with a raised hand. Now that she'd opened up her

Pandora's box of grievances, there was no stopping them.

"But do you know what I've resented the most? The fact that Tyler and I both came close to dying, and you've never said one word about it. I can understand how you can ignore me, but how can you be so cold, so uncaring toward the baby? He didn't ask to be born into the mess we've made of our lives."

"It wasn't that I didn't care," J.T. retorted, when she paused for breath. "I didn't know."

Disbelief shone in her eyes. "You didn't know? Surely your dad told you during that drive from San Antonio."

"I was on pain medicine, remember? I slept most of the way. I just found out today. A few hours ago, actually. I ran into Lettie Mae in town, and she told me."

"Lettie Mae?"

He nodded. "If it will make you feel any better, I've already been to my parents' and chewed them out. It seems they didn't think I could handle the added stress after what I'd been through."

He could see that she was struggling to accept what he said, that she wanted to accept it. She took a step toward him, and then another.

"There's nothing like facing death to put things in perspective," she said in little more than a whisper. "Gaining a few pounds and having people gossip about me was nothing compared to the fact that I could have died—or worse, that Tyler might not have made it." Her eyes filled with tears. "I was so afraid, J.T."

Fear was an emotion he had more than nodding acquaintance with. The sharp blade of a soul-deep remorse twisted inside J.T.'s heart. His steady gaze fastened on Pauline's. "I should have been here."

She stared back at him for long seconds, and something of what he was feeling must have communicated itself to her. She moved a little closer. Until she stood no more than an arm's length away. J.T. moved his good leg and reached out his hand, taking hers in a warm grip and drawing her into the vee of his legs. He put his hands—trembling from excitement and fear—on her waist and started to pull her onto his lap.

The bare flesh of her waist was warm to his touch. The scent of the soap she'd used in her bath whirled around him, as seductive as an expensive French perfume. The ripe fullness of her mouth, devoid of any artifice, was as tempting as forbidden fruit.

Long denied desire flared between them like a match thrown to a field of dried grass. J.T. forgot about not being the perfect lover. Forgot everything but that it had been aeons since he'd made love. A lifetime since he'd made love to Pauline. His wife.

A lusty cry came from across the room, where Tyler lay sleeping in his bassinet, interrupting the passion building between J.T. and Pauline. Pauline froze; the mood binding her and J.T. shattered.

"Tyler." It was a breathless sigh. Disappointed. Relieved.

"Go," J.T. commanded in a husky voice. But miraculously, there was not another sound from the baby.

Keeping her eyes on the bassinet, Pauline eased onto J.T.'s good thigh. His arms slid around her and he crushed her to him. She looped her arms around his neck, and her blue gaze, troubled, questioning, found his.

J.T.'s answer was to slide his hand through her short hair and pull her close for a kiss. Her mouth melted, parted beneath the passionate onslaught of his, accepting the bold thrust of his tongue with a matching hunger.

His hands worked at the knot beneath her breasts, deftly untying it and dispensing with the remaining fasteners with ease. The clasp of her bra succumbed without even a minor skirmish, and he filled his palms with the soft mounds of yielding flesh.

"J.T.," she whispered.

"What?" he breathed, drawing back to look at her.

She shook her head and lowered her mouth to his again. Though he was on fire with wanting, and longed for nothing more than to ease his ache in the warmth of her body, J.T. forced himself to slow the pace.

No more firecrackers.

Somehow, they found themselves in the middle of the kitchen floor, yet neither of them noticed the hardness of the pegged planks. They kissed for long moments, hours maybe, reacquainting themselves with each other's mouths and bodies, working themselves into a frenzy of desire and discarding pieces of clothing along the way.

J.T. did his best to recall every bit of information Alfred Kinsey had written about what it took to satisfy a woman. Only when Pauline cried out and pressed his hand more tightly against her did he feel that maybe...just maybe, this time would be different.

When the delicate ripples ceased, she reached out and touched him with a slow and languid caress. "Now," she commanded in a harsh whisper. "Please."

"Are you sure it's okay?" J.T. said, and thought he would die if she said it wasn't. "I don't want to hurt you."

Pauline opened her sleepy, passion-glazed eyes and looked up at him. "If you don't finish what you've started, J.T. McKinney, *I'm* gonna hurt *you.*"

Giving him a gentle push, she rolled him onto his back. The naughty, tempting smile he loved so well was on her lips, in her eyes. "Hold on, cowboy," she said in a soft drawl. "You're in for a long ride."

CAROLYN ROSE to refill Cynthia's mug. "No more for me," she said, holding up her hand. "I've had enough."

Carolyn looked at the half-full coffee carafe—the second they'd made—put it back on the warmer and turned it off. "Me, too."

Jennifer had just awakened and been changed. She looked up at Cynthia and smiled, showing off the two perfect white teeth that had given her parents so much anguish.

Cynthia imagined how alone Pauline must have felt with no support from her husband and the knowledge that something serious was wrong with her son.

She counted her blessings. There wasn't a night since Jennifer's birth that J.T. hadn't volunteered his help. More often than not, she refused to accept it. She still worried about his health—the thought of him having another heart attack scared her to death—and she hadn't wanted to seem incompetent...especially since everyone remembered so clearly just how competent Pauline was.

More than ever, Cynthia understood how much she and Pauline had in common. They were both hardheaded and softhearted. They both took their family responsibilities seriously. They both wanted to be perfect wives and mothers. In both their universes, J.T. McKinney was the sun.

THE SUN in Cynthia's universe was blazing...with fury. Yes, Cynthia had stopped by to have a few words with Reverend Blake, but he'd been at the hospital. Still was, Lola said. Was anything wrong?

J.T. assured Pauline's old friend that everything was just peachy and bade her goodbye. Back in his truck, he picked up his cellular phone and called home. No one answered.

J.T. gritted his teeth and slammed down the receiver. Where in tarnation could she be? he asked himself for the hundredth time. He was running out of leads, and the afternoon was drawing to a close.

He snapped the phone closed and started the truck's engine. He'd just go home and wait for her, and when she walked through the door, he'd let her have it.

He was outside the town limits when he thought about Carolyn. Maybe Cynthia had confided in her, told her what was wrong. And if she hadn't, maybe he'd confide in Caro himself.

Meanwhile, back at the ranch...

"So," CYNTHIA SAID, wiping cereal from Jennifer's mouth, "I gather the sex between J.T. and Pauline was good this time."

"Wonderful. And that's a quote."

Cynthia thought of J.T.'s skill and tenderness and the unrestrained passion they'd shared in the early days of their marriage. Their sexual encounters since Jennifer's birth had been few and far between. She certainly had no complaints, but she imagined J.T. had a few.

When she thought of the way she'd behaved lately, she was ashamed. She'd been so caught up in nursing her hurt feelings and bruised pride that she hadn't taken advantage of the help around her.

She could let Lettie Mae do more of the cooking, and Virginia could certainly do the laundry. J.T. could do his own book work until Jennifer got over her colic, and she could concentrate on being a better wife and mother. After all, weren't her organizational skills and her ability to delegate two of the things she was noted for? She might even find a little time for herself if she really tried.

Cynthia sighed, and cuddled Jennifer close. "I'm glad they got things worked out. And I'm glad you told me about Pauline and J.T. I think I'll have a little more forbearance when I'm compared with her now."

"Don't grab your car keys yet," Carolyn said. "I'm not quite finished."

Cynthia looked surprised. "What else could possibly happen?"

"Nothing major," Carolyn said with a smile. "But if you remember, J.T. still hadn't told Pauline he loved her. There was something he had to do first."

"What's that?" Cynthia asked with a frown.

"He had to prove to himself that he was still a man."

"You mean proving that he was a skilled lover wasn't enough?"

"Not for J.T., it wasn't," Carolyn said.

CHAPTER ELEVEN

May 1959

WHEN PAULINE WOKE UP the next morning, the sun was shining through the slats in the venetian blinds she'd neglected to close the previous evening. Even half asleep, she felt a curious lethargy and a marvelous sense of well-being. She stretched and realized she was naked beneath the sheets.

A smile as lazy as she felt curved her mouth. Recollections of the night before tiptoed into her memory, tantalizing reminders of why she felt so content, so...happy. Last night had been...wonderful...fabulous...satisfying. She'd finally experienced the culmination of all those feelings that kissing and caressing aroused. J.T. had been eager, yet patient, exciting and communicative—a fantastic lover by anyone's standards. Together they had undertaken a trip of exploration and discovered new and delightful secrets about each other.

Still smiling, she rolled to her side and watched him lying beside her, his broad chest bare, his lean hips barely covered by the sheet that had ridden indecently low. She wanted to reach out and touch him, to see if it was possible to recapture those sensations in the

daylight, but a snuffling sound came from the Jenny
Lind cradle a few feet away.

Tyler was waking up. A quick glance at the clock
brought a surprise. It was an hour past the baby's
usual feeding time. She sighed contentedly. He had
certainly been an angel the night before.

Easing her feet to the floor, Pauline reached for the
robe draped across the padded seat of her vanity table and slipped her arms into the voluminous sleeves.
She picked up the baby, kissed his soft cheek and carried him downstairs to the kitchen, where she gave him
his drops and fixed him a bottle that he devoured
hungrily.

When Tyler was settled, his wind-up mobile turning overhead, she started breakfast—cheese toast fixed
under the broiler—and bacon. The bacon was siz
zling in the skillet when she realized it was Mother's
Day, and she and J.T. were supposed to have lunch
with her mother after the morning church service.
Dinner that evening would be with Emily.

Pauline hadn't been looking forward to spending
time with either set of parents, but now the excursion
showed promise. She wasn't sure what would happen
between her and J.T. now, but she took last night's
actions as a step in the right direction.

She was draining the undercooked bacon—she was
trying hard not to burn it—and humming the popular
"High Hopes" when she heard J.T thumping down
the stairs on his crutches.

She pivoted on the ball of her bare foot, the egg
turner in her hand, a strange alliance of fear and an-

ticipation in her heart and in her eyes. J.T. was dressed
in starched, creased jeans. The seam of one leg had
been ripped out to the upper thigh to accommodate
the bulky cast. He was wearing a white T-shirt with the
sleeves rolled up to reveal his muscular arms. Just
hours ago, those arms had held her closely, posses-
sively. A delicious shudder tripped down her spine,
and her heart began to beat faster.

Her gaze traveled up to his handsome face. He'd
shaved, and a piece of tissue was stuck to his chin to
stop the bleeding of a minor razor nick. She knew that
he would smell wonderful, like a combination of
Mennen after-shave and warm man, a scent all his
own. There was no welcoming smile in his eyes. A
niggling apprehension threatened the happiness she'd
felt since rising.

"Good morning," she said, her voice breathy and
uncertain.

"Morning," J.T. answered.

Was it her imagination, or did the look in his eyes
soften the slightest bit? "Did you sleep well?"

"Once I finally got around to sleeping," he confessed.

The statement triggered a plethora of tantalizing
memories, and Pauline thought she saw a hint of red
creep into J.T.'s lean cheeks. Was he uncomfortable
with what had happened between them? Was he sorry?

After finally getting this far, Pauline was determined not to let him off the hook so easily. She set the
platter of bacon on the table and went to stand in front

of him. If he thought she'd used her wiles before, he hadn't seen anything yet.

When she was so close she could see the almost imperceptible flecks of gold in his dark eyes, Pauline slid her arms around his lean middle and pressed herself against him, breathing in the mingled scent of starch and soap and after-shave.

J.T. drew in a sharp breath, a reaction she found curiously satisfying. She leaned back and looked up at him, everything she felt for him evident in her shining eyes. She opened her mouth to tell him she loved him, but J.T. leaned on one crutch and stopped her with a hard kiss that stole her thoughts and her breath.

"Don't say it, Paulie," he cautioned, his breath warm and sweet against her mouth. "Please."

The joy inside her plummeted, shattering on the rocky shores of disappointment. Tears stung beneath her eyelids. She nodded. While she was trying to figure out how to salvage what was left of her pride, J.T. lifted his head like an animal who senses danger, his startled gaze moving past her.

"Something's burning."

Pauline whirled. Black smoke billowed out of the broiler. "Oh, damn!" she cried, running across the room. "The cheese toast!"

She grabbed a potholder and bent down to rescue their breakfast. Four charred squares of what had once been bread and cheese lay smoking on the cookie sheet. She set the pan on top of the stove to cool off. Tears of dismay tightened her throat. She'd wanted this breakfast to be perfect for J.T., the culmination of a perfect night,

"I'll make some more," she said, raising her chin and turning to face him. "It won't take a minute."

J.T. looked from her face, to the still-smoldering toast, to the half-raw bacon sitting on the table. "You'll never be a cook, Pauline," he said. "Why don't you hire Lettie Mae? I have some savings from show cattle I can use to pay her with."

Pauline gasped. The words were like a knife slicing at what was left of her battered heart. If his reticence and reluctance to talk about what they'd shared the night before were any indication, J.T. still didn't want to make a commitment. And it was obvious that he was still as uncaring about her feelings as he'd ever been. The tears she'd fought so hard to contain spilled over her lashes and trickled down her cheeks. She turned toward the sink and stared out the kitchen window at the rugged hills.

"I didn't—"

J.T. started to say something, but thought better of it. Pauline was so caught up in her misery, she was hardly aware of the sound of his crutches as he crossed the room.

"I'll see you later."

She jumped at the sound of his voice, which came from just behind her. He was leaving! Just like that. Without talking. Without any explanations.

"Fine."

"Paulie..." She felt his hand, heavy on her shoulder. She wanted to reach up and grab it, to hold on

and never let him go, but she just stood there, gripping the edge of the countertop and biting her lip,
trying her best not to make a bigger fool of herself
than she already had.

"I have a lot of things to think about," he said.

"Just go," she managed to choke out.

She heard him sigh, heard him thudding across the
floor, heard the squeaking of the screen door as he
pushed it open. "Oh," he said, and she could picture
him turning to look at her, "I won't be home for
lunch."

Pauline didn't reply. The loud thwack of the door
shutting noisily behind him seemed almost symbolic.
It sounded like the slamming shut of the door to all her
dreams.

J.T. GOT into the pickup and drove away, feeling like
a louse. He'd hurt her again when he'd said that about
hiring Lettie Mae, but he hadn't meant to. He'd been
thinking of Pauline, not trying to hurt her. She'd given
cooking her best shot, and it was pretty obvious that
it was one skill she wasn't going to master, so why
should she concern herself with it when it would be
much simpler to hire someone?

It occurred to him that even the best intentions
could be misconstrued or go awry...like his failure the
night before to make a commitment. He'd wanted to.
Intended to, but even though he'd done his best to
show Pauline how much he cared with his body, he
couldn't say the words he'd known she was about to
say this morning. He wasn't ready yet to hear them, or

say them. He still had things to think through, things to prove to himself before he could commit to Pauline and their marriage... if he ever could.

As he drove down the dusty roads and along the secondary highways that bisected Claro County, memories of the past several months rolled through his mind like West Texas tumbleweed. Memories of leaving home, learning he was going to be a father, getting married. Memories of how he'd rebelled, all because he'd felt as if he was being robbed of his freedom.

J.T. turned the pickup off the highway and onto the dusty road that led to one of his favorite fishing places on the river. Beyond the expanse of water that meandered through the sandy riverbed, a herd of Angus cattle grazed on still-tender shoots of grass.

Farther away, a red and yellow biplane droned through the clear azure heavens, like a giant fly looking for a spot to land. While J.T. watched, the plane dropped through the sky, and his stomach lurched as a sickening fear rushed through him. Then he saw the plane level out low to the ground and noticed the white trail spewing out behind it. Bud Adams, he thought, heaving a shaky sigh of relief. Bud was just out crop dusting. It was a testimony to J.T.'s troubled state of mind that he hadn't realized sooner.

He watched as the little plane shot up into the air, banked for a wide turn, came back and hurtled toward the ground again. He passed a shaky hand over his face.

There was a time he'd loved going up with Bud, a time he'd sneaked out of the house just so he could savor the exhilaration of looking down from such a lofty height. He could barely remember the time he'd loved experiencing the quicksilver descent of the plane, when the bottom dropped out of his stomach and the hair on the back of his neck tickled.

Now J.T.'s heart pounded with remembered fear and his leg began to throb in empathetic pain. Once, but no more. Not since the fire in the T-33. Maybe never.

He wasn't the same kid who'd defied his parents' orders. For several months now he'd suspected that he was growing up, changing. Spending yesterday afternoon with Bubba and the guys had pointed out just how much he'd changed without his realizing it.

The past year had taken its toll. A year ago, he'd cherished his freedom. Freedom to go where he pleased, when he pleased. Freedom to have a good time with the guys, to pursue girls, to live it up.

Well, last night had proved what he already suspected: no girl but Pauline interested him. And after yesterday, he realized that what constituted a good time could change from year to year, month to month, day to day. Flirting—with danger or girls—treading the tricky line between being good enough to qualify as the perfect son and bad enough to be considered an all-around good guy had lost its appeal.

A picture of Pauline standing at the stove, a silky robe tied around her slim waist, an egg turner in her hand and a look of fearful expectation on her face, filled his mind. He realized that a good time was watching his wife decorate Christmas boxes and going with her to pick out furniture for their first home together. A great time was watching her feed Tyler, as he had last night, the baby cradled against her bare breasts while she gave him a bottle, her face aglow with love, her eyes smudged with dark shadows from too little sleep.

It came to him quietly, as it had when he'd looked death in the eye and realized he was going to die: he loved her. In that split second before he ejected, he'd thought that he would change things if he could, but he'd been home all this time and had done nothing to breach the chasm separating them.

How many times had he had the opportunity to tell her that he loved her and he was sorry for behaving like an ass? A dozen? A hundred? Why hadn't he?

I was afraid.

Afraid she didn't care anymore after the way he'd treated her. Afraid that he couldn't be the husband and lover she wanted . . . needed . . . deserved. Afraid to take on the responsibilities that a confession of love would demand, just as Howard Blake had said. Even as he enumerated them, J.T. knew that his excuses weren't good enough.

He remembered what Pauline had said about how the marriage and pregnancy had changed her life. Thought about how she had faced the whispers and death and fear, alone. J.T. was unaware that his eyes were moist with unshed tears.

As he had, Pauline had defied death. Unlike him, she hadn't run, hadn't sought sanctuary in another place, a different life. Unlike him, she'd found the courage to stick it out and face her fear with courage and dignity.

Pauline had been right the day she'd had her hair cut and told him that someone had to face the reality of things not changing. He could see that now. Denying his responsibilities, running from his problems, wouldn't solve anything. Hadn't solved anything. All he'd done was make both their lives miserable.

J.T. brushed at his eyes with his fingertips. He'd been a fool. Would Pauline forgive him? Could she? As before, when guilt had driven him to the brink of an apology, he wondered if mere words would be enough to make things right between them. He didn't know. But he wanted to try.

He turned the key and started the engine. There was something he had to do before he went to Pauline with his heart in his hands and his tail tucked between his legs. By tonight, he and Pauline would be together forever or they'd be a thing of the past, with only a baby to remind them of what they'd almost had, but lost.

J.T. BROUGHT the truck to a stop in front the bright-yellow corrugated metal building that housed a small single-engine plane of gaudy purple and gold. Across the front of the building in vivid red letters at least two feet tall was emblazoned ADAMS'S CROP DUST-

ING SERVICE. Beside the building sat the biplane J.T. had watched earlier. Bud Adams was refueling.

J.T.'s mouth was as dry as the Hill Country in late August, and his heart was pounding so fast and so hard it threatened to jump out of his chest. He shoved the gearshift into park, got out and reached for his crutches.

Bud, tall and lanky, with a head full of salt-and pepper hair and outdated tortoiseshell glasses, spotted J.T. while he was several yards away. He waved.

"How's it goin', crip?" Bud teased as J.T. drew near. His smile settled his weathered face into a road map of lines and wrinkles.

"Fair," J.T. said with an attempted smile.

"I heard about the crash. Too bad."

"Coulda been worse," J.T. said, and this time he did smile. Sickly.

Bud joined him. "No kidding."

They talked a few minutes about the Air Force and J.T.'s pilot training and what planes he'd flown and would be flying. When they'd exhausted that topic, Bud asked, "So what are you doin' out here, fly-boy? Slumming?"

J.T. shook his head. "I thought I'd see if I had any nerve left."

Bud frowned. "What do you mean, kid?"

J.T. squeezed the handgrip of his crutches so hard his knuckles turned white. He met Bud's troubled gaze with a bleak one of his own. "I don't know if I can do it anymore, Bud."

"You've always loved flying, J.T."

"I know."

Bud whipped a red bandanna from his back pocket and began to clean his glasses with careful, thoughtful precision.

"Take me up, Bud," J.T. said, his hoarse voice a dead giveaway to his fear.

Bud looked up from his chore and gave a slow shake of his head. "I got a better idea."

J.T. looked at him, a question in his dark eyes.

"You take me up."

DEBORAH CALLED at twelve-thirty and asked if Pauline and J.T. were coming for Sunday dinner. Pauline hadn't been able to bear the thought of going to church and trying to keep from falling apart, so she'd opted not to go. She'd forgotten about having lunch with her family. When she confessed as much to her mother, Deborah demanded to know what was going on.

Reluctantly, Pauline gave her mother a sketchy account of what had happened between her and J.T. the night before and that morning. Deborah, who never cursed, uttered a mild oath and demanded that Pauline and the baby come anyway.

"It's Mother's Day, and there's no sense in your sitting in that big house all by yourself. Besides, misery loves company," Deborah quoted, in an attempt to lighten the situation.

"Okay, Mama," Pauline said with a sigh. "Give me a little while to get some things together for Tyler, and I'll drive on over."

"I'll hold lunch," Deborah said, "but hurry. You know how your daddy gets when he has to wait to eat."

Pauline promised. She hung up the receiver and went upstairs to change her clothes, wondering, as she fixed her hair and put on her makeup, what else she could have done to make things better between her and J.T.

After he left that morning, she had cried for at least an hour. She'd wanted to believe that their lovemaking was a step in the right direction, that J.T. would realize that he cared for her, but though they had made love far into the night, he hadn't once told her he loved her. She had noticed it then, of course, but had calmed her fears with the old platitude that actions spoke louder than words, and that J.T.'s actions said he did love her. After all, afraid of another rejection, she hadn't said it, either.

She laughed, a rueful sound that echoed throughout the lonely bedroom. How many times had her mother told her that sex had nothing to do with love? A hundred? More? It was a lesson she was having a hard time learning, Pauline thought, donning a straight skirt of pale yellow linen and a sleeveless, white cotton blouse with a boat neck.

She slipped her small feet into white leather sandals and regarded herself in the mirror. She looked a lot better than she felt, which was encouraging. Maybe she could make it through the day without going to pieces. She packed Tyler's diaper bag and took several bottles from the fridge. Picking up the sleeping baby, she went out and started the Chevy. It promptly died.

On the fourth try, just when she was ready to get out and strike a match to it, the engine roared to life, and she backed out of the carport. The car wasn't running well, even though she'd had it in the shop several times. Like her marriage, she'd tried to fix it, and nothing had worked. Maybe there was only one thing to do: let them both go.

IT WAS MIDAFTERNOON, and Pauline was stretched out on her old bed, trying to get some rest while Tyler slept. Her mother, a strong believer in staying married at almost any cost, had been sympathetic to her plight and told her to hang on a little longer, at least until the time for J.T. to report back to Randolph. If things between them weren't settled by then and Pauline decided to leave him, the family would support her decision. The thought didn't give Pauline much comfort.

She was dozing fitfully when she heard a commotion coming from the kitchen. She could hear her dad's angry voice and her mother's conciliatory tones. Her heart sank at the thought of them arguing. Curiosity and the idea that maybe she could say something to avert a major upheaval prompted her to get up. She was getting to her feet when Carolyn poked her head in the door.

"J.T.'s here, and I think Dad's gonna punch him out."

"What!" Pauline screeched, her eyes wide with disbelief.

"You'd better hurry."

Pauline leaped up and looked around the room to see where she'd kicked off her sandals. "Don't ever fall in love, Carolyn," she said as she slid her feet into the shoes. "It isn't worth all the heartache."

"So you keep telling me," Carolyn said with bored disdain.

On her way to the door, Pauline peeked at Tyler, who was still sound asleep.

"I'll watch him if he wakes up," Carolyn said.

Pauline dropped a kiss on her little sister's head. "Thanks, Caro," she said and headed for the kitchen.

Her mother was standing by the sink, wringing her hands and staring toward the back door. J.T. and her father stood there, glaring at each other. Steven turned, and J.T. looked up when Pauline stepped through the doorway. Her dad was livid, but the reckless gleam in J.T.'s eyes said that he didn't give a damn.

"I need to talk to you, Paulie," he said.

He must have made up his mind about their marriage. Well, so had she. As distasteful as the confrontation would no doubt be, she was anxious to get it over.

"If you go with him, you're crazy," Steven barked. "All he's done is give you the most miserable year of your life."

Sorrow flashed in J.T.'s eyes. "That's true, Mr. Randolph." He looked at Pauline. "I'm sorry."

An apology? From J.T.? Pauline noticed that there was a flushed look about him and wondered with a burst of maternal concern if he had a fever.

She looked from her father's face to her mother's. Steven's was contorted with anger; her mother's held a sort of hopeful concern.

"Pauline?" J.T.'s eyes begged; he wouldn't.

She took a step toward him, and his gaze found Deborah's. "Will you watch Tyler while Pauline and I talk?"

"Of course, I will."

Steven swore violently, and without another word, Pauline started toward J.T., who pushed open the screen door for her to precede him. When she was on the porch, he looked back at her parents. "I promise to take good care of her."

Pauline saw the faint smile that curved her mother's lips. "I'm sure you will," Deborah said.

J.T. closed the door and started toward the battered pickup. Ever the gentleman, he hobbled to the passenger side and opened the door. Pauline climbed in, and he slammed the door shut. She watched him round the hood and balance on one leg while he set the crutches between them. Without a word, he climbed in, cranked the engine and headed down the dusty lane.

"Where are we going?" she asked when the house was a speck in the distance.

"I don't know."

Ten minutes later, he was headed toward the spot on the Claro where they had almost broken up on her graduation night. He slammed on the brakes, and the truck slewed to a stop in the loose gravel. He cut the engine and rested both forearms on top of the steering wheel while he stared out at the slow-moving river.

Pauline sat silently, trying to figure out how to say what she knew she had to say. The thought of letting him go was as painful as the thought of cutting out her heart.

"J.T., I—"

"I'm sorry about this mor—"

They spoke simultaneously; they stopped simultaneously.

"You first," she said, still uncertain how to begin.

J.T. looked uncomfortable and finally blurted, "I'm sorry that I made you cry this morning."

Had she heard right? Two apologies in one day? Pauline turned a questioning look on J.T. and found that he was studying her.

"I didn't mean to hurt your feelings when I said that about your cooking and Lettie Mae. Really." He tilted his head back until he was staring up at the dusty, flyspecked headliner.

"I know how hard you've tried to learn to cook, and I know I haven't said it before, but I appreciate your efforts. All I meant was that there's no reason for you to worry yourself with it if you don't want to. You have plenty to do with Tyler. Lettie Mae needs a job. I just thought hiring her would solve two problems."

He sounded sincere. He looked sincere. It made perfect sense. Another thought grabbed her attention. Did the fact that he wanted her to hire a cook mean he didn't want to end their marriage?

"What were you going to say?" he asked.

That if you wanted your freedom, I was willing to let you have it. "It wasn't important."

J.T. nodded. "Oh." He looked out the window again for a moment. "I'm sorry about taking off without any explanation this morning, especially since we were supposed to go to your mom's, but I forgot it was Mother's Day and..."

He had to be sick, Pauline thought, hearing him apologize the third time. He must have some strange fever.... "It's okay."

"It's not okay," he said, "but there was something I had to do before I could say what I need to say to you."

The determination in his eyes was daunting. The fragile sprout of hope growing inside Pauline withered. "And what was that?" she asked, more to stay the inevitable heartache than because she really wanted to know.

"I drove over to Bud Adams's and asked him to take me up in his plane."

"Why?" Even as she asked the question, she recalled what Eva Blake had said about J.T.'s fear and his need to conquer it.

"To see if I was man enough to go back to Randolph and finish my training, because if I wasn't man enough, I was going to have to give up something very important to me."

Flying, she thought. "And?" she asked in a soft voice. "Did Bud take you up?"

"No," J.T. said with a solemn shake of his head. As she watched, a slow smile curved his hard lips. "He made me take him up." The grin widened, and his voice was breathless with excitement and pride. "And I did it, Pauline! I was scared spitless, but Bud just kept talking to me about how much fun we'd always had and how my chances of being in a car accident going home were greater than being in a plane crash."

Pauline felt tears stinging her eyelids. So, she thought. She was going to lose him to the Air Force and his precious freedom again. She was happy for him...really she was, but... "I'm glad for you," she said, hoping she sounded more sincere than she felt.

"So am I," he said, reaching out and fingering the curl that lay against her heat-flushed cheek. He was still smiling. "I'd hate like hell to have to give you up, now that I've finally figured out how much I love you."

For a second, Pauline thought she was hearing things. Hallucinating. After all, her nerves had been strung pretty taut since the baby was born. "What did you say?"

J.T. wove his fingers through her short hair and, cupping the back of her head, drew her close. Their lips met in a soft kiss. For long moments, his mouth nibbled at hers playfully, drank from it as if he'd never get enough, worshiped it with his.

"I'll never get tired of kissing you," he told her, resting his forehead against hers. "Not in a thousand years."

Her smile was shaky. She was still in shock. "Good."

He closed his eyes. "You know, when I was gone to basic, I'd try to be mad at you, but then I'd start thinking about kissing you, and the next thing I knew, I'd be missing you like crazy." His arms closed around her in a tight embrace, and his voice was thick with emotion. "It scares me to death to think that I might have lost you and Tyler."

She felt the wetness of tears against her cheek and knew she was witnessing something precious. "Shh," she whispered. "You didn't."

Pauline held him until the tremors shaking his broad torso stilled. Until the fear faded. When he lifted his head to look at her, there was a devilish smile on his face that was at odds with the lingering sorrow in his eyes.

"So you kneed Matt right in the groin, huh?"

Pauline's eyes widened in surprise. "Who told you?"

"I called the SOB and told him I knew he was lying and that he'd better come clean or he was going to be eating dirt the next time I saw him. He must have believed me, because he told me what really happened." J.T. laughed. "Lord, I can't believe that conversation we had last August. Me talking about you and Matt making it and thinking from what you said that you were admitting to his lie, when all the while you were talking about letting him have it."

Remembering, Pauline smiled. "When you said everyone knew and the whole town was talking about it, I couldn't imagine why he'd tell anyone what I'd done to him. Talk about lack of communication!"

They shared a moment of laughter at their own expense. Pauline was wiping her eyes when J.T. leaned over to get something from under the seat. He pulled out two small boxes, both wrapped in floral paper and tied with lavender satin bows.

"Happy Mother's Day."

Her eyes grew wide with pleasure. "My first Mother's Day." She took the top gift and tore off the paper. The white box was stamped in the corner with Metcalf's, the name of Crystal Creek's jewelry store. With trembling fingers, she lifted the lid and saw a gold charm bracelet nestling on cotton batting.

"It's from Tyler."

"It's beautiful," she said, lifting it from the box.

"He'll be glad you like it."

"Oh, look! There's the charm with his picture they made at the hospital," she said, fingering the tiny memento.

"I'll have it put in a gold charm later, but I wanted it on there for today. There's a book on there—I know you like poetry—and a cheerleader's megaphone, and a little replica of a class ring with '58 on it. You can add other things along the way."

Tears shimmered in Pauline's eyes. "Oh, J.T., I love it."

"I'm glad." He cleared his throat and thrust the other gift at her. "I know you're not my mother, but this is from me."

Pauline laughed. As excited as a kid at Christmas, she ripped open the paper and tossed it to the floor of the pickup. This box, too, bore the jeweler's name.

When Pauline opened it, she saw a gold heart-shaped locket. "Oh..." she said, pressing the catch. It sprang open; inside were small snapshots of her and J.T.

"Where'd you get that picture?" she asked.

"Carolyn. I made her bring me all the photos she could find of you so I could pick the one I liked best. I took the pictures and the charm to Mr. Metcalf's last week so he could get everything fixed up, but I forgot to pick them up until an hour or so ago."

"But it's Sunday. How did you get them?"

"I banged on Mr. Metcalf's door and told him my marriage was going to be over if he didn't open up the shop for me."

"That's so sweet," Pauline said.

"Actually," J.T. said, rubbing his palm along his cheek, "I gave him twenty bucks over cost. Did you see what I had engraved on the back?"

Pauline giggled and shook her head. Then she turned over the small heart and read the inscription: *Yours forever, J.T.* When she looked up at him the tears were back. "I love you," she said, and he smiled.

She unfastened the catch of the delicate gold chain and held it up around her neck. "Will you fasten it for me?" she asked, turning her back to him.

As J.T. took the chain and leaned toward her, intent on his task, a feeling of déjà vu swept through her. She felt his lips against her neck and leaned back against him.

When she looked up over her shoulder and smiled at him, J.T., too, felt that history was repeating itself. Reaching up a slender arm, Pauline drew his head down until their lips were a whisper away.

"Don't ever stop loving me, Pauline," he begged before their lips touched. "Promise."

"I'll always love you," she said. "Promise."

They sealed the promise with a kiss.

"AND SHE ALWAYS DID." There was a fond smile and the hint of moisture in Carolyn's eyes as she finished the tale of J.T.'s first marriage.

Cynthia's eyes swam with tears, too. It was a perfectly beautiful love story. All the hard feelings she'd nurtured against Pauline had vanished . . . as if they'd never existed. How could she harbor ill feelings about someone who had loved so much?

Oh, there was no doubt that Pauline had made her share of mistakes, but what eighteen-year-old hadn't? For that matter, what thirty-five-year-old hadn't? Cynthia thought, recalling how she'd thrown away her birth control pills knowing full well J.T. didn't want another child. She sighed.

Carolyn's story had given her new insight to J.T., too. She understood now why he loved the wide-open spaces so much and why, even though he loved all his children, Tyler held a special place in his heart.

More important, she knew that, like Pauline, she wanted to hold on to J. T. McKinney, whatever the cost. And if it took keeping her mouth shut when he said, "That isn't the way Pauline did it," she'd darn well keep her mouth shut...and do as she pleased whenever he wasn't around.

She would be sweet and even-tempered if it killed her. She'd...

The sound of a truck door slamming broke into her new resolutions. Carolyn went to the kitchen window and looked out.

"It's J.T.," she announced. "And he looks fit to be tied."

CHAPTER TWELVE

J.T.! CYNTHIA'S STOMACH churned in nervous apprehension. Why did she feel so guilty? She hadn't done
anything wrong—at least not since she'd yelled at him
that morning. She'd just spent the day with a friend,
talking about old loves, old times. . . .

The kitchen door crashed open and J.T. strode into
Carolyn's kitchen as if he owned it. The large room
seemed to shrink when he stepped through the door.
Cynthia suspected it had more to do with the strength
of his presence than his physical size. Her wary gaze
traveled down the tall, vital length of him. Darn, but
he was a fine specimen of manhood, she thought with
grudging admiration. Six feet and one inch of pure
male.

His recovery since the heart attack had been nothing short of miraculous, and she'd match him any day
in looks or strength with a man twenty years younger.

"Where in the hell have you been?" he demanded,
placing his callused hands on his lean hips.

The adoration Cynthia felt for her husband vanished before a fury as clear and pure as a mountain
stream. She leaped to her feet, crossed her arms over

her breasts and thrust out her chin. "Just who do you think you're talking to?"

For a heartbeat, J.T. just stood there, a stunned look on his handsome face. So much for her resolve to be sweet and amicable, Cynthia thought with dismay.

"Sweet heaven! What have you done to your hair?" J.T. asked in a voice all the more deadly because of its calm.

Cynthia lifted a hand to her newly shorn head. For a moment, her anger faltered. "I . . . cut it."

J.T. made a noise that sounded suspiciously like a growl.

"Well, it was too long, and I looked like a witch."

"Too long! It was gorgeous."

"It was hot," Cynthia snapped, adding, "and too much trouble."

"Well, that's pretty much my opinion of you, at the moment."

"Excuse me," Carolyn said, picking up the car seat, where Jennifer sat watching and cooing. "Jennifer and I are going to go outside and look at the clouds while you two discuss this like adults."

Neither J.T. nor Cynthia heard.

"Why didn't you tell me you were coming to see Carolyn?" he asked, his voice softer, but no less aggressive.

"Because you weren't at home, and I didn't know I was coming," Cynthia replied in kind. Furious at his high-handed attitude, she reached for her cup and carried it to the sink.

"I've been looking for you all over town."

Cynthia's face flamed along with her temper. She whirled to face him. "You've what?"

"I've been all over town looking for you."

"Oooh!" Cynthia wailed. "What is everyone going to think?"

"Frankly, sweetheart," J.T. misquoted, the edge in his voice growing sharper, "I don't give a damn."

"Well, I do. I didn't know I had to leave my itinerary with you when I left the house," she said with sugary sarcasm. "Did you make Pauline check in with you at regular intervals, too?"

"Dammit! Leave Pauline out of this!" J.T. thundered.

"Believe me, I'd love to!" Cynthia said, thrusting out her chin to a pugnacious angle. "As a matter of fact, that's a great idea. I will if you will."

There! She pursed her lips. The real problem between them was out in the open again. The ball was in J.T.'s court, and Cynthia was eager to see what he did with it.

Still scowling, J.T. said, "Stop pouting and get your things. I'll get Jennifer." He headed for the door.

"J.T." He turned to face her.

"It may have escaped your notice, but I'm an adult. I haven't needed anyone to tell me what to do in a long time."

J.T. looked as if he wanted to say something, but instead, he turned and left her standing there, wondering how her good intentions had gone down the tubes so fast.

CYNTHIA WAS acutely aware of J.T. during the drive back to the Double C. How could she not be, when his teal-colored truck was visible in her rearview mirror?

Jennifer gurgled, drawing Cynthia's attention from J.T. She glanced over at her daughter and smiled. "Hey, punkin', don't ever marry a man as stubborn as your daddy," she said, touching Jennifer's forehead with the backs of her fingertips. The baby seemed to be feeling much better. The antibiotic must be working already.

Cynthia recalled how worried she'd been that morning, knowing something was wrong with Jennifer, knowing things were amiss in her marriage. How had Pauline handled the pressure at such a young age?

"You do what you have to do."

How many times had she heard Lettie Mae say that in the past sixteen months? There was a remarkable amount of truth in the old adage, and Cynthia was convinced that people didn't know what they could do or how much they could handle until the challenge was set before them.

The months since Jennifer's birth had been hard, but she'd survived them. She knew that she'd done things wrong and taken more on herself than was necessary, just to prove a point . . . to prove she was as much a woman as Pauline McKinney.

Talking to Carolyn had put things into perspective. Though Pauline had grown into a wonderful woman, she had been no closer to perfection than Cynthia herself was. And, after hearing the story of Pauline and J.T.'s rocky beginning, Cynthia knew that vying for a dead woman's place in J.T.'s heart was not only futile, it was unnecessary.

She was as sure that J.T. loved her as she was that he had once loved Pauline. There was no need to feel threatened. The corner of his heart reserved for his former wife was a pure and untouched place where he'd tucked his memories of her, and it would be self-ish and cruel to violate those remembrances. Actu-ally, it was comforting to know that J.T. was a man capable of such a deep and abiding love, even if he could be a real pain in the derriere sometimes.

Jennifer was asleep by the time Cynthia pulled the car to a stop beneath the carport. She carried the baby in; J.T. carried the diaper bag. They didn't speak, and as soon as he set the bag inside the kitchen door, he announced in a gruff voice that he had to go over to the vineyards and check on something with Tyler. He'd be back in time for dinner.

"You'd better be," Lettie Mae said, pinning him with a stern look.

"Yes, Lettie," J.T. said in a pseudo-obedient tone.

Cynthia marveled that Lettie Mae could get away with talking to him that way. Of course, she had to remember that Lettie Mae had been employed by J.T. for almost thirty-six years, while she had been mar-ried to him for less than two. There was bound to be a certain amount of familiarity that came with ex-tended relationships of any kind.

"Is the baby all right?" Lettie Mae asked, as Cyn-thia set Jennifer's car seat on the table.

"She's fine, thank you," Cynthia said, regarding the woman who'd been Pauline's longtime friend. "Dr. Purdy said it was just an ear infection. He gave her a shot."

Lettie Mae's smile, as she gazed into Jennifer's sleeping face, was soft, pleased. "That's good."

Lettie Mae is still an attractive woman, Cynthia thought, as the cook turned back to her task at the sink. And a good one. It was a shame she'd never found anyone to take Clark's place. Maybe this Mose Gilchrist she was seeing would be able to touch the heart no one else had been able to penetrate in more than thirty years.

As if sensing her scrutiny, Lettie Mae looked up. She couldn't quite meet Cynthia's eye. Cynthia had the distinct impression the cook wanted to say something, but the brief moment passed.

"Why don't you catch a nap before dinner? I'll keep an eye on Jennifer if she wakes up," Lettie offered.

"Where's Virginia?" Cynthia asked.

"She took sick in the night. Fever and vomitin'. She never did come in today. She sent a friend's daughter over to help me out." Lettie Mae gave a sniff of disdain.

Cynthia smiled. Obviously, the girl's performance wasn't up to Lettie's expectations. "Maybe you can stand her for a couple of days."

"I can stand anything for a couple of days," Lettie Mae said.

"If you're sure it won't be too much trouble, I'll take you up on your offer," Cynthia said. The thought of a nap—however brief—sounded like ecstasy.

"I can handle her. Just put her in the cradle there."

Cynthia laid Jennifer down. She gave a sleepy wail that ceased the instant her mother popped the pacifier in her mouth. The baby gave it a couple of hard sucks, sighed and went right back to sleep. Poor little thing, Cynthia thought. She was probably as tired as her mama.

Heaving a sigh of her own, Cynthia started to leave the room. She paused in the doorway and looked at Lettie Mae's ramrod-straight back.

"Lettie."

"Yes'm?" she said, turning from the sink.

"I spent the day with Carolyn."

"Yes'm?" Lettie said again, obviously uncertain what that had to do with her.

"We talked a lot about Pauline...and J.T." Cynthia looked down at her clasped hands, unsure what to say, unsure whether or not she should say anything, but feeling the need to get her thoughts out in the open.

"I know it's been hard on the family having a stranger come in and upset your lives, and you've all been very patient with me and the mistakes I've made."

Lettie Mae wore a dubious frown.

"It's been hard for me, too...moving from the city to the country, taking on children almost as old as I am, and becoming a mother before I learned how to be a wife.

"I know you've all compared me to Pauline in the past, and that I often come up short in your estimation. I know I don't do things the way Pauline did them." She drew a deep breath. "I've resented you for that. You and Virginia and the kids and even J.T. And I've even resented Pauline for being more of a woman, or a better woman than I'll ever be."

"Miz Cynthia, I—" Lettie began, but Cynthia cut her off.

"No. Let me finish. Please." She smiled a weary smile and moved closer to the cook. "I found out a lot of things about Pauline today, and I found out some things about myself, too. One of those things is that Pauline and I have a lot in common, and the most important thing we have in common is that we both fell in love with J.T."

The same soft smile Lettie Mae had worn when she looked at Jennifer curved her wide mouth. "That woman loved him to distraction. She purely did."

"I know." Cynthia took Lettie Mae's hands in hers. "And I know she loved you, too."

As much as the statement, the unexpected action took Lettie Mae by surprise.

"Carolyn told me about how you and Pauline sort of grew up together, how she sat with you after the accident, and how you helped her get through those tough times with J.T."

"I didn't do nothin' any friend wouldn't do for another," Lettie Mae said, her embarrassment evident.

Cynthia squeezed Lettie Mae's hands. "Well, whatever you did, she loved you for it. And now that I know more about your friendship, I understand your loyalty to her and why it's been so hard for you to accept me." Cynthia smiled. "After hearing Carolyn talk about her, I find myself wishing I'd known her."

The comment brought tears to Lettie Mae's ebony eyes.

"I know that I can never be the kind of mistress of this ranch that Pauline was, because we're two different people. But I hope you can see that I can still be a good and caring person."

"You are."

"I don't want to take Pauline's place, Lettie Mae—not in the house, not in your hearts. I just want to make a place of my own." Cynthia drew a deep breath and gave Lettie Mae a trembling smile. She gave the cook's hands one last squeeze and released them. "I'll see you at dinner."

Lettie Mae nodded.

"If Jennifer wakes up and you need me, I'll be in my room." Without waiting for an answer, Cynthia escaped to her room, wondering if she'd finally crossed an important hurdle.

J.T. NEVER MADE IT to the vineyards. The truth was, he never intended to go. Instead, he drove to the place that had been his favorite haven through the years, the place along the Claro where he and Pauline had once necked for long endless hours. The place he had finally confessed his love.

J.T. turned off the ignition and rolled down the window. As he had countless times in the past, he sat and stared at the fingers of water that were the Claro. There wasn't much left of the river these days. Except in the spring, when the rains necessitated the opening of the floodgates, the Claro was little more than a creek, its power and beauty diminished by the diversion of its energy to another source, the dam at the new power plant.

Like Cynthia's energy.

She was so intent on being the superlative mother that her vitality was being drained bit by bit. She was so focused on Jennifer and just trying to make it through each day that her interest in the people and events going on around her had dwindled to a trickle.

He'd seen it happening and had even talked to Nate Purdy about it. Postpartum depression, Nate said. Most women had it to a degree—a hormonal thing, you know. Some got over it fast. Some didn't. Could last up to a year. Don't worry, he'd said. It'll pass.

Maybe it would, J.T. thought, but their argument that morning was like a red flag of warning. Things between them weren't good, and just as on that afternoon he'd made his confession of love to Pauline, he was afraid. As afraid of losing Cynthia as he had been of losing Pauline.

He thought of Cynthia's beautiful blond hair falling beneath the beautician's shears and remembered the day Pauline had come home from town with her hair snipped to just below her ears. He remembered his anger and what she'd said, about facing reality and trying to simplify her life.

It had taken him months to see that she'd cut her hair for a deeper reason than to simplify her life. She'd cut it in an effort to reassert herself, to keep her life from getting the upper hand, to prove that she was still in control . . . of something. And to make her feel better about herself. A new look would make her feel prettier after the pregnancy. Older. More in control.

He didn't doubt that much of that reasoning was behind Cynthia's new look—with one exception: Cynthia would want to look younger. He smiled to himself. As if she didn't look young and pretty enough. J.T. forced his mind away from his wife's looks and back to the problem at hand.

There were so many similarities between the events of the past few months and the time immediately following Tyler's birth it was uncanny, frightening. And while there were many similarities between Cynthia and Pauline, it had finally hit him this morning that the differences between the two women was the problem; or rather, his insistence on pointing out those differences.

He and Lettie and Virginia only meant to help, not criticize, when they offered advice and comments about how Pauline did things. But Cynthia, who had controlled an office and millions of dollars of other people's money, had taken it as a personal attack. To her, Pauline was the yardstick she used to measure her own worth as a wife and mother, and she had come up short every time.

He vowed to talk to Virginia and Lettie. They had to stop making those comparisons, no matter how innocent they might be.

Innocent.

Even after six years, his thoughts often drifted back to those early, innocent days with Pauline, and this time, more specifically, to the day he had told her to hire Lettie Mae. A bittersweet smile claimed J.T.'s lips. His offer, meant to make her life easier, had only hurt Pauline and made her angry, just as his offer to buy Cynthia a bigger dress had hurt and angered her this morning.

He wondered if all men were so out-of-touch with the way women thought or so clumsy in their speech. Or was he just one of the unlucky ones who'd missed that particular gene at conception? He couldn't imagine the silver-tongued Cal ever making such a faux pas.

The low drone of a small plane intruded on J.T.'s thoughts. He searched the horizon and saw the glint of sunlight on metal. As he watched, the small red biplane neared and made a nosedive toward the ground. It was Rusty Adams, Bud's son, who'd taken over the business when Bud passed away two years ago.

The memory of the day Bud had forced him to go up, some thirty-five years before, crept into J.T.'s mind. That day had been a turning point for him. Bud had made him take out his fears and face them . . . like a man, something he'd been forever grateful for. He missed Bud.

Life goes on.

How many times had he heard Grandpa Hank say those words? People were born. They died. Life went on. Happiness wasn't guaranteed. Change was the only constant. The secret, if there was one, was to make the most of the time you had, to create your own happiness . . . to guard it as best you could so no one and nothing could snatch it away.

His heart attack had been a vivid reminder that he wasn't immortal, that his days, like everyone else's, were numbered. And his argument with Cynthia had made him realize he didn't want to lose the joy in any of those remaining days because of depression or exhaustion or a silly argument. He loved Cynthia. And it was time he packed up his memories and went home and told her just how much.

LETTIE MAE WAS GIVING Jennifer a bottle when J.T. entered the kitchen.

"Dinner's almost ready," she said, not bothering to look up.

"Where's Cynthia?"

"Restin'." Lettie Mae looked up at him over the rim of her glasses. "She's wore out, bless her heart."

J.T. heard the unspoken warning in his cook's voice. *Don't bother her.* "I know," he said. "Can you hold off dinner for awhile?"

Lettie Mae's lips tightened and her jaw firmed. Her eyebrows rose. "You be easy with her, now, you hear?"

"I will." J.T. started down the hall that led to the stairs. Lettie's voice followed him.

"She's a good woman, J.T. McKinney."

"I know that, Lettie Mae," he called over his shoulder.

"Stubborn, but good."

J.T. smiled. Though Lettie Mae and Virginia had accepted Cynthia months ago, something had happened to elevate Cynthia's standing in the cook's eyes.

CYNTHIA WAS ASLEEP when he entered their room. J.T. went to the bed and looked down at her. Why had he gotten so mad over a haircut? It was nothing in the scheme of things, and the new, short style was as cute as all get-out, actually. Love rose inside him on a giant tidal wave of emotion, a feeling so poignant and overwhelming that he felt the sting of tears beneath his eyelids.

He didn't want to lose her. Couldn't. He sat down on the edge of the bed and reached out a trembling hand to touch her cheek. Cynthia stirred and opened her eyes. When she saw the love reflected in his, she lifted a languid hand and curved it around his neck, drawing his head down until their lips met.

Lovemaking had been scarce at best the past few months, and J.T. felt the hungry stirrings of long-denied need and the excitement of good old-fashioned lust building inside him.

He felt Cynthia's fingers working his buttons free and got busy reciprocating. They were naked in a matter of seconds, their bodies pressed together in an effort to get closer, to assuage the growing ache of passion.

Her body was as familiar to him as his own, and he knew where and when to touch and kiss to elicit a maximum response: kisses scattered across her breasts, down her stomach and beyond. They were both whipped into a frenzy of desire in a matter of minutes, and when J.T. slipped into the warm sheath of her body, he felt as if he'd come home after a long absence.

Afterwards, they lay side by side, their legs wound sinuously together, their gazes locked in a silent message of love. "Not bad, Mrs. McKinney, ma'am," he said, when his breathing had eased up enough to make conversation possible.

"You weren't half-bad yourself, cowboy," Cynthia said with a teasing smile.

"We really ought to do that more often. I was beginning to think we forgot how."

Cynthia ran the palm of her hand over his muscular shoulder, as if she couldn't get enough of touching him. "It's like riding a bicycle. You never forget."

"Thank God!" His smile was slow, sexy. His kiss was long and lingering. Knowing it was time to get serious, he disengaged himself from her arms, propped himself on one elbow and said simply, "I'm sorry for being such a fool."

Cynthia placed her fingertip against the fullness of his bottom lip. "Oh, J.T., you haven't been a fool," she said with a shake of her head.

"No?"

"No. A louse and a jerk, maybe," she intoned in a solemn voice, "but not a fool."

"Get serious," he growled in her ear.

"I think I've been way too serious," she said, "but if you insist, then I apologize for being such a witch."

J.T. grinned and kissed her tenderly. "Oh, sweetheart," he breathed against her lips. "You haven't been a witch. A shrew and a bitch maybe, but not a witch."

Cynthia giggled. "Touché."

J.T. took her hand and carried it to his lips, pressing a moist kiss to her palm.

"Carolyn told me about you and Pauline," Cynthia said, out of the blue.

J.T. raised his head and looked at her. "What about me and Pauline?"

"Everything. About her tricking you into making love and her being pregnant with Tyler when you got married. About you not being happy with the situation, and how long it took the two of you to work things out."

J.T.'s dark eyebrows drew together and his nostrils flared in anger. "What was between me and Pauline was private. Carolyn had no business telling you."

Cynthia sat up and drew the sheet up over her bare breasts. "I'm glad she did. And if you love me, you should be, too."

"What are you talking about? What could my marriage to Pauline have to do with my love for you?"

"Maybe it doesn't have anything to do with it," Cynthia said. "Maybe it has to do with my loving you. Oh, J.T., I was so bent out of shape because everyone in Crystal Creek had put Pauline up on a pedestal, but

Carolyn showed me that she was just a woman. A woman who loved and was loved. She showed me that she was just a spoiled kid who grew into a lovely, responsible woman. A woman who made her share of mistakes, just like the rest of us."

"I never meant to imply that she was perfect."

"Well, that's the way it seemed to me."

"I'm sorry."

"I know. And so am I. I know I've been terrible to live with, but adjusting to marriage, and then Jennifer . . ." She shrugged.

"Are you sorry we have her?" J.T. asked.

"Of course not! I adore her, but I've learned that no amount of organization can organize a baby. She may be just five months old, but Jennifer is the boss of this household."

"I beg your pardon," J.T. said in mock offense.

"Think about it. When she cries, we both jump."

"You're right," J.T. admitted.

Cynthia threw up her hands. "I rest my case. But I learned I'm going to have to adjust to the changes in my life. I might even have to ask for help sometimes. At any rate, I want you to know that hearing about you and Pauline was a big help. Actually, I think I have a lot in common with her."

"Yeah, she was as bullheaded and hotheaded as you are."

Cynthia smiled, and twined her fingers in the whorl of dark chest hair that sprawled over his pectorals.

"No. We both fell in love with you and are determined to keep you."

"You both cut your gorgeous hair."

"You don't like it?"

J.T. cocked his head to the side. "Actually, Cindy, I think it's cute as hell."

Cynthia's eyes flashed. "Don't you dare call me Cindy!" she warned.

To her surprise, J.T.'s face broke into a wide grin. He reached out a strong arm and pulled her into a rough embrace, yanking the sheet down and kissing her thoroughly. For the next few minutes neither said a word.

J.T. finally came up for air. "Damn, Cindy," he said, "I love it when you blow up at me like that. Your eyes flash, and you look so sexy."

"Don't call me Cindy!" She gasped when he ducked his head and pressed a kiss to her navel. "Besides, I thought you liked your women malleable and—" she sighed "—complaisant."

J.T. raised his head and looked at her. "I do, but somehow I don't seem to marry that kind."

"Why do you suppose that is?" Cynthia asked, sliding her palm down over his hard stomach.

J.T. caught her hand just short of its objective. "I suspect it's because they're boring," he said. "But no one could ever accuse you of that."

"Thank goodness!" Cynthia said.

J.T. stared down into her beautiful, smiling face, glad that it was the face he'd see when he woke every morning. His own smile faded, and the teasing light left his eyes. "Promise me you'll never stop loving me," he said in a trembling, urgent voice.

Cynthia's eyes were filled with love as she placed her hand on his cheek and gave a slow shake of her head. "I never will," she said solemnly. "I promise."